MURDER UN

Published by Mission Point Press
2554 Chandler Lake Road, Traverse City, MI, 49696
MissionPointPress.com

MISSION POINT PRESS

ISBN: 978-1-943995-20-2
Library of Congress Control Number: 2016917306
Printed in the United States of America.

The author would like to thank Timothy Boursaw and Milton Marentette for providing technical details concerning classic cars and old firearms respectively, as well as the Traverse Area Historical Society for making its resources available.

Murder Undone

STEPHEN LEWIS

sequel to Murder on Old Mission

Mission Point Press

FOR CAROL

CHAPTER ONE

Sam Logan had expected the question would be asked. He knew what he must say if he wanted any chance of success. He also recognized that not only must he answer in a certain way, he must do so with the most credible sincerity. All to indicate that he was a changed man, fit to rejoin the larger society beyond the prison walls.

To do so, he would have to abandon his alibi, and confirm the jury's judgment that he was a murderer.

But there was the sticking point. Murderer. Try as he might, he could not apply that term to the man he knew himself to be. Then and now. That being the case, how could he convince the panel that he was a changed man?

Of course, he could say he regretted that Margaret was dead. And worse, that she was pregnant with their child. But that was not what those three men wanted to hear. Such an expression of regret was, he knew, much too easy. No they wanted him to own both those deaths.

So as he sat before the three members of the parole board, and the man in the middle conducting the examination phrased the question, he gathered himself to answer.

Nathan Lowe looked out of his office window on the fifth floor of the Pullman Building on Michigan Avenue over the top of the Art Institute to the blue waters of Lake Michigan beyond.

"That boy took off right after the trial," he said while still gazing out of the window. "Came down here to stay with his aunt and uncle just long enough to sign on as a hand on a freighter."

"You did the best you could," said Wendell Benson, who was standing a few paces behind Lowe, "the best anyone could have done."

"I'm not used to losing," Lowe said. "You know that. And I

thought with that boy's testimony supporting the alibi, in spite of the community's obvious dislike of Logan, I thought we had a good shot. Until…."

"Yes, until they produced their witness."

Lowe walked over to his desk.

"I want you to find that dark-skinned gentleman. I have reason to believe that I might be able to introduce a revision of his testimony. At the right time. To the right person."

Benson nodded.

"I'll find him. No doubt about that. It might take some time…"

Lowe took his wallet out and counted out a few bills.

"Just find him."

Isaiah Logan adjusted his sailor's gait to the flat surface of the road leading to the church. Everything else was eerily familiar. It had been five years since he walked up this road on the day that began to change his life. But the road itself, inanimate and without memory, just lay insensate beneath his shoes. Somehow he had thought that the dust rising beneath his feet would carry with it echoes of that day, perhaps a word, a sigh forced out between clenched teeth, an image of a face drawn in pain, a tear trickling down a man's unshaven cheek or finding a path along the worn furrows of a woman's face, and above all a pervasive black of mourning.

On this morning to be sure, the shadow of death argued against the bright rays of the sun this late spring day. But this time, death's face wore a bemused grin, a weary acknowledgment that the deceased had simply run his appointed course and it was time for him to be gathered into the ground. In that respect, this occasion could not have been more different than that one five years ago when a person in full bloom had been cut down.

The handle of the church door felt the same as it did that day when he had grasped it with a hand warm and wet from sweat, his lungs gasping for air. And the hinges squeaked just as they did then. On that day, when he pushed the door open ever so slowly to minimize the disturbance of the squeaking hinges, he was confronted by an empty building. He was too late. Through the rear door, he could see the mourners gathered around the freshly dug grave into which the woman he loved would be interred, and standing, ashen faced, among the mourners was his father soon to be convicted of putting her there.

Today, however, the congregants were all in their seats. He stood for a moment at the rear of the church. As in the past, the door had squeaked, and he fully expected heads would turn around to gaze at him. He had tried to prepare himself for that eventuality, but had not come up with a suitable response. Several people did turn in his direction, but then swiveled their heads back toward the front of the building. Perhaps, he figured, they had not recognized him. It had been, after all, some years.

He walked down the familiar central aisle to the front row where he was accustomed to sit with his grandparents, occasionally joined by his father. There he found his grandmother looking up at him and beckoning him to take his seat. Although she was not kin to the bereaved family, she was wearing the same black dress she first put on when her husband of fifty years died two years ago. Isaiah had been on the lake at that time and learned of his grandfather's death too late to make it to the funeral. He could only imagine how packed this old church must have been on that day when old man Logan, once the richest man on the Peninsula, died.

On the bench next to his grandmother there appeared to be a thick envelope. Seeing it in this environment presided over by death itself, he recoiled just a little, imagining as he did, that his grandmother was going to resume the old argument, the one his father had lost but he, to this point, had kept at an arm's distance if not with a firm, irrevocable denial.

He simply did not want what was left of his grandfather's hundreds of acres. The recent panic had diminished but not wiped them out as it had done to so many other farms. His grandfather had been too careful to lose everything, and now he imagined the thick packet in his grandmother's hands contained papers that would make the remaining acres his. No doubt the death about to be commemorated had produced in his grandmother her own sense of her approaching mortality.

He prepared himself to offer an absolute but gentle refusal.

He could not see himself chained to the land that had been so inhospitable to him before. He searched for the right words, and opened his mouth to utter them, when his grandmother's surprisingly firm and warm hand grasped his.

"I could always read you," she said. She placed her free hand on the packet. "This is not what you think it is. I don't know whether when you hear what it is about if you would have preferred to have been right in your assumption."

As he began to mouth his apology for being so presumptuous, she placed her gloved hand on his lips to close them, and gestured first to the pulpit where the minister now stood looking out over his congregation, and then to the woman, also in black, sitting across from them. He had not seen her since that day when she and her husband buried their daughter. Arriving late as he had, he made his way through the empty church to the little cemetery behind the building, there to watch as the coffin was lowered, his eyes catching, as the brown box disappeared into the brown soil, the eyes of his father wearing an expression of pain beyond bearing.

He turned his attention back to the pulpit and tried to concentrate on the minister's eulogy. It was, of course, filled with the usual platitudes, early settler on the Peninsula, successful farmer, devoted husband. He waited for what he knew should come next. After the deceased's role of spouse, the logic of the sequence demanded a comment about him as parent. There had been two children born of the union with his wife, the stern faced woman dressed in black sitting in the pew across the aisle. Everyone in the church knew what happened to the little boy and the young woman. Isaiah held his breath, but then expelled it as the minister moved on from spouse to Cutter as soldier in the great Civil War, and then as a member of the town board.

Still Isaiah listened. At last, the minister turned his head to look at the back of the church beyond which lay those two children born of the deceased and his black clad widow. The minister returned his gaze to the congregation and nodded. So that was it, Isaiah figured, a silent nod to the sad facts of this family's loss of a following generation.

He expelled his breath, realizing that he had been holding it in anticipation against not only the statement that the minister did not utter, but his expectation that it would have reminded everyone hearing it of his role in that dark event. He felt strong pressure on his left hand, and glanced at it. His grandmother's fingers pressed against his flesh with astonishing strength. She held his eyes with the long remembered warmth of her reassurance and he relaxed. It would be alright. He would be able to get through this day. Let tomorrow and thereafter take care of itself.

The minister's words rolled over his head like a fly buzzing in the summer heat. He did not try to separate the sounds into individual words. Instead, he fixed an attentive look on his own face while his mind wandered to more comfortable venues, such as the well tendered garden in front of his Aunt Clarissa's modest house in Chicago, or the smell of gasoline and oil in Uncle Frank's service station. From these, he drifted into somewhat more distant sensation of the deck rolling beneath his feet as the ship rose and fell over the waves of Lake Michigan.

A sharp nudge in his ribs from his grandmother's elbow brought him back, and he realized with a start that a small smile had formed on his face. She nodded toward the front of the church and he understood that she had not seen his expression. Rather, she wanted him to understand that the minister was no longer talking and that the congregants were shifting in their seats in preparation of rising for the sad walk through the rear door behind the coffin, even now being hoisted by the pallbearers.

He and his grandmother took their place on the line. At the door stood the minister and the widow. As Isaiah and his grandmother approached, the widow looked past the individual whose condolences she had just received. She squinted in a near-sighted glance, and then stared hard at Isaiah.

"Not him. Not today. Not ever," she said.

Isaiah stepped aside so that those lined up behind him could pass by and gather around the freshly dug grave in the little cemetery, established fifty years ago, and now beginning to run out of space. But the space for this new grave had been carefully preserved against the pressure of an aging local population. No discussion had ever been held, but there had quickly arisen a tacit understanding that two spots would remain open to accommodate the bodies of the parents whose children already lay beneath the earth.

He felt a soft pressure on his arm.

"I would have thought," he said, turning to face his grand-mother, "that it would have been long enough, even for her."

"Let her be. You've done your duty. Go on..."

He understood.

"I'm looking for a room in town. For now."

"My big house..." she began, but just then shrugged. "I forget. It won't be mine much longer."

"You are moving? It is too big a place for one person."

"No," she replied. "Not for that reasons. Memories fill it up. But the money was more important. For Mr. Lowe. To keep fighting."

"Where?" he asked.

"To my sister. In Chicago. You know her."

"Of course. I'll come by tonight, to say good-bye to the old house."

She smiled.

"Yes, for tonight." She extended the envelope to him. "Please," she said, "for me. Take this. Look at it. I can do no more."

He nodded, took the envelope and watched her walk ahead, pause and exchange words with the widow, and then without looking back at him continue on to join the other mourners gath-ered around the grave.

He stood for a while in the empty building, the envelope feeling warm and threatening in his sweaty palm. The minister's words from the graveside reached him. Turning his back, he walked out the front door.

Waiting there, as if for him, was a white haired man, with a bushy mustache.

"I think if you hurry, you can join them at the grave. In the back," Isaiah said.

"But I was waiting for you."

"I don't know you," Isaiah replied. "Now if you will excuse me." He started to walk around the man, but he felt the stranger's hand on his arm.

"I know you. At least, I observed you at the trial. I was cover-ing it for a Detroit paper."

"I wouldn't have noticed," Isaiah said, and pulled his arm free.

"Name's Drummond," the man said. "Thomas Drummond. I'd like to talk to you."

"Good day," Mr. Drummond," Isaiah said and walked past him. "I assure you I am no longer news."

"We will talk. At some point," Drummond said.

On the street in front of a small frame house near the Boardman River and within sight of the courthouse in Traverse City, Jonathan, a stocky ten year old with blond hair, pointed to the clock tower on top of the building. His mother, her black hair graying, but her figure still pleasantly rounded, followed his gaze. Absently, with a slight smile, Eunice smoothed back his hair from his forehead.

"You know," he said, "I remember when you took me there."

She strained to maintain her smile, but could not stop her lips from turning down into a frown.

"You were too little to remember anything about that."

His jaw set in a way that reminded her with a shiver of an adult man's version of that assertion of stubborn righteousness.

"But I do," he insisted.

She put her small hand on his jaw and with the most gentle pressure turned his head toward the front door of their house where stood a gray haired woman waving her hand.

"Mind grandmother," Eunice said. "And don't be late for school."

"I wish you could walk me there," Jonathan said and tried, unsuccessfully, to turn his naturally beaming expression into a frown.

"You are much too old for that, now, just be good, and when I come home from work maybe I'll have a surprise for you."

She watched as he trotted back to her mother who threw her arms around the boy and took him into the house. As the door closed, she began to wonder, rather absentmindedly, what she could bring him back from the store next to where she worked in the office of the leather goods emporium.

Her walk to work took her along the river where she felt most at ease. Somehow, the slow moving water calmed the thoughts that otherwise disturbed her equanimity. As much as she hated to admit it, even to herself, there was some truth beneath the anger in her ex-husband's complaints about her during their divorce proceedings. Of course, she did not blame herself for his entanglement with the young woman whom he is said to have murdered. It is true that even though they continued to share the marital bed they had not been sleeping together as husband and wife for some months. She knew he was a man of strong physical needs, and yet the anxiety she felt from some unknown sources, and for which she regularly calmed herself with laudanum, made her unresponsive. Still, though, it was a long way from her acknowledged coldness to his forsaking his vows and taking up with a woman, scarcely more than a girl, and less than half his age at that.

Her life now settled into a dull and not entirely pleasant routine. Her mother, who had cautioned her about marrying a man already divorced and carrying a reputation for a careless attitude toward women, could not refrain from reminding her of how she had "ruined" in her mother's words, her life and left them in dire circumstances, her salary as a bookkeeper hardly sufficient to pay their bills, and their standing among the congregation at the Baptist Church down the street from their house, uncomfortable at best. She was sure she detected something behind the welcoming smiles she received each Sunday, something that said she had failed as a wife, for why else would her husband have strayed, and as ridiculous as that idea appeared at first glance a part of her could not dismiss it altogether. And even if that were not the reason for that unstated something in the friendly glances of the congregation, perhaps it was simply that the ex-wife of a convicted murderer brought some of his stain into their midst, and for that they could not entirely forgive her.

Traverse City was still very much a small town even though it was straining to live up to the urban reference of its name. However, among the factories that lined the burgeoning waterfront and the bustling commercial activities of the stores on Front Street its residents retained the small town love of gossip, and the whispered murmurings that reached her ears as she sat behind her desk working with debits and credits in her large ledger book informed her every so often over the years that the convicted murderer's mother had not ceased in her efforts to free her son from a verdict she firmly believed was a miscarriage of justice.

That same rumor mill, perhaps with greater credibility, now was proclaiming the arrival in town of the convicted murderer's older son, the half brother of her own boy.

How, she wondered, should she react to him?

She paused as these thoughts ran through her mind as she approached the leather goods store where she labored over its books. An odd, but troubling, thought formed as a coda to her ruminations. Why, she asked herself, did she always character-ize her ex-husband as the "convicted murderer" rather than the straight forward term without the modifier? Could it be that she, like his mother, harbored some doubt as to his guilt? Or perhaps it was that she could not imagine that the man with whom she had shared the marital bed, albeit so unhappily toward the end of their marriage, could have done what he stood convicted of doing.

She ate her lunch in a back room heavy with the aroma of leather being worked into products by the two skilled craftsmen, one old, the other an apprentice. She enjoyed the solitude, as the two workmen chose to spend their lunch away from their workplace, and the rich scent of the worked leather gave the feeling of a luxury she knew she would never enjoy. As she unpacked the sandwich made of leftovers from last night's supper, Mr. Muel-ler, the owner of the business, stood in the doorway waiting for her to notice him. When she didn't he cleared his throat, and waited for her to turn toward him.

"Excuse me," he said, "I didn't mean to interrupt your lunch."

Her mouth full, she could only nod.

"I've been thinking," he said, "I've got that little apartment over the store, which I was saving for my nephew, who has now made other plans, so I'd like to rent it out."

"Yes," she said.

"To some one respectable."

"Of course, Mr. Mueller, someone respectable."

"I'd like you to handle that for me."

"I'll put a sign in the window. If that's alright."

"Whatever you think is best. I've got an appointment with a fellow who wants me to install new leather seats in his buggy. Just close up at the usual time."

That night, Isaiah lay in the same bed that he had slept in so many times as a child and even into his teens when his father's tempestuous life sent him, after the sudden departure of his mother from his life, like a bobbing cork toward the security of the stability of his stern grandfather and the warmth of his grandmother. There must have been a conversation, one of those held out of the hearing of its object, for a decision was reached the consequence of which was that his stays at his grandparents became restricted to special occasions. What he surmised after a while was that he had been a bargaining chip in the often acrimonious relationship between his father and his grandfather as the old man tried, with limited success to impose his will on his sole heir, to set his reluctant feet on the same path that would lead to a continued success of the Logan fruit empire.

Isaiah did not mind the enforced regularity of living with his father, for in truth he found attractive Sam's willful, somewhat rebellious, nature. In small matters, such as having the opportunity of sharing Sam's passion for baseball, or in somewhat more important activities, such as being taught the intricacies and the necessary care and patience of carpentry, he felt privileged, and finally, it was a relief to find an alternative to his grandfather's monomaniacal focus on the health and well-being of his cherry trees.

That more positive relationship with his father changed when, perhaps hormonally driven, he found himself in competition with him for the affection of Margaret. That was an idea he could not wrap his mind around. He knew Sam could be, and often was, selfish and irresponsible in spite of, or perhaps in conjunction with, his considerable personal charm. But he was not a violent man. Had he not so testified during the divorce proceedings that dissolved Sam's marriage to Eunice? She was the one who pressed a knife against his own throat while Sam restrained her hand from moving and doing perhaps fatal harm.

Then, of course, there was the note he had hidden in the family Bible, knowing Sam seldom opened that volume. After the trial he gave the note to his one friend, Daniel, the tubercular reporter, the note that established beyond any doubt that Sam and Margaret were to meet on that afternoon when she died. With a start, he wondered if that man who had accosted him outside the church, what was his name, Thomas something, with a musical sounding last name, perhaps somehow that man had come into possession of that note, or had heard about it.

He tossed from side to side under the thin wool blanket on his childhood bed. Images from that time began to flash across his mind's screen. For years he had worked so hard to drive those images into a dark closet in the very recesses of his mind, but now that man had opened the door and they came tumbling out. There she was very much alive in his memory. There was the smile that lit up her face although it was by far brightest when aimed at his father rather than himself. He knew that his feelings were purer than his father's, that Sam had carelessly permitted this impressionable young woman to give her heart to him while he could not in good conscience return his to her. There simply were too many complications, mostly emanating from the stern old man whose house Isaiah now found himself in.

Through the long night, his mind insisted on presenting him with the words in that note, "I'll meet you at the usual place tomorrow," she had said, and in her innocence or indifference to his own feelings for her, had given him that piece of paper, trusting that he would not read it, and, more damningly, not caring if he did.

Dawn came and he got up in sweat soaked bed clothes, preparing to tell his grandmother whether he would undertake the mission to free his father. He had been too tired and emotionally drained to open the packet she had given to him. It now sat on the chair next to his bed where he had left it. With an effort to overcome his reluctance, he sat up, extended his hand.

An hour later, he placed the documents back into the envelope, freshened himself up as best he could, and with the envelope tucked under his arm, he walked down the stairs where he found his grandmother waiting for him at the breakfast table. He placed the envelope next to his plate, and watched as she ladled scrambled eggs and bacon onto it. For several moments they both stared at the envelope, not willing to confront the significance rising up from the papers in it like the smoke over smoldering embers.

"I think I know more about the circumstances of that dreadful," she hesitated, "that dreadful day, now years ago."

He restrained the look of surprise that was forcing his face to present. How could she, he thought, but then, as if to chastise him for his foolishness, his memory recalled the innumerable instances that he had intuited that behind her always warm smile was a keen intelligence that had never bowed to her husband's iron will, but rather deflected it away from what she most valued, as the thick leaves of the sheltering tree kept off the pelting rain.

"I see," she said, "your surprise. I do not intend to enlighten you any further. There would be no point. To put the matter simply, I have never doubted your father's innocence any more than I ignore his less than noble impulses that carried him to places he, I am sure, in hindsight regretted, much as he no doubt, in his jail cell, must be spending his hours telling himself that he had permitted, one more time, to tempt fate, not only his, but that unfortunate young woman."

He found himself unable to respond..

"You're not..." she began, "going to refuse."

"No. I'll keep these papers for a while. To see what I can do."

"Mr. Logan, do you not understand my question," the chairman of the parole board asked, his voice a mixture of irritation and bemusement.

Sam took a deep breath.

"I do," he said.

"Understand the question?"

"Of course."

"Your answer, if you please?"

"Yes. I do regret…" he hesitated, " that she, she and our child, are dead. Because of me."

CHAPTER TWO

Sam tried to form his face into the expression of insouciance that had served him so well in the past. Warden Higgins, the little man sitting across the desk from him, seemed to be unimpressed. He barely glanced up from the papers on his desk when Sam was ushered into the office. Now, fixing his spectacles on his nose he held Sam with the most steady gaze Sam had experienced since the last time he had seen his father on the day he left the courthouse, now a convicted murderer, and his father had fixed him with that same kind of steely stare that pierced right through all defenses and buried itself in the heart. Still, Sam forced his face to maintain the look of a man who could not be intimidated. The little man behind the desk that seemed much too large for him gave the papers in front of him one more look, and then lifted his head, his hand once again reaching for his spectacles, and Sam noticed the angry welt where they sat on the man's long, narrow nose.

"The parole board was not convinced, they have turned you down."

"I am not surprised," Sam said. And he wasn't. As soon as he finally answered the question in that halting manner, he knew he had failed.

"I've been looking these over," he said, his hand now on the papers. "Do you know anything about them?"

"No," he said. "I have no idea."

"Why I didn't think you would. Although every one of these papers is all about you, about how innocent you are, how you had been railroaded, and how you're really just a victim of circumstances and a hostile public that wanted only to see you off to jail." He lifted the stack off the desk, and with elaborate care pressed his hands gently on the sides of the papers so that they were precisely lined up, no edges protruding, then laid them down again. "All nonsense, of course," he said.

Sam felt the blood begin to rush to his face and bit down on his lips.

"Is there anything more?" he said in as calm a voice as he could manage.

"Only that we are moving you. The governor has decided that your previous accommodations were too harsh. I can't say...he has some modern ideas..." he began, but then simply shrugged.

His new cell was in a recently completed wing of the expanding prison. The first thing he noticed was that it contained two beds. The second was that it had a barred window through which the afternoon sun now filtered into the cell. He stood for several minutes staring at the shadows of the bars on the floor.

"Been a while, hasn't it, since you saw anything like that?"

Sam turned to face the guard who had led him to his new quarters.

"You don't know how much you miss the little things, even more than the big ones, like your family, your children or your parents, or your wife," he paused, "if you're lucky enough to have one. Do you have one, a wife, I mean?"

"Sure. But I don't know how much I'd miss her."

"Well, I've had two, and..."

"A dead girlfriend."

Sam's fist tightened, but then he shrugged.

"I guess I'd better get used to that kind of thing."

"That, and a lot worse."

Sam glanced at the next bed.

"Your roommate will be joining you soon enough."

"I don't suppose..."

"No, I don't know if he killed anyone. Maybe he just stole some money."

After the guard left, Sam sat on his bunk, trying to figure out the moral hierarchy in this place. Where exactly does a convicted murderer stand? At the top? What about a rapist? A child molester? And did it matter who was killed, and who the killer?

Of course, as he told himself, he was looking to place himself into that hierarchy and to do that he would have to do what he avoided since the jury foreman stood up and with a steady, even withering, gaze at him announced his peers' conclusion that he was guilty, as charged, that he had murdered his pregnant girlfriend. That verdict could not begin to explore the complexity of the situation that landed him where he now sat on a cot in a cell, wondering with whom he would be spending his indefinite future.

In the eternal darkness of his solitary confinement cell, at any moment, like a physical presence she had joined him, sometimes in eerily present evocations of their trysts at the spot they had made their own, the one he had joked was more valuable to him than all the acres of orchards he leased and farmed while at those moments her face, still girlish, would turn into first a frown and then a reassuring smile, Don't be silly, she would say, we will have a proper house on our own land one day, and that day is not far away.

His face felt warm and for a moment he thought it might be some long repressed feeling, if not of guilt, for he could not yet attach that word to himself, but of something akin to guilt, perhaps, he concluded, it was something like shame, but that was not it either, as he remembered how cornered he had been by events, by a young woman's stubborn insistence on how her love for him would smooth out all difficulties, and maybe most those coming from his domineering father.

Then, with a start, he realized that the source of the warmth was external. It was the sun's rays reaching him through the bars of his cell. From long ago habit in the orchards of figuring time by the position of the sun, he recalled that the guard who had led him out of his near perpetual darkness had said the warden was back from some morning engagement, and was now free to see him. If it were now afternoon, that window must be facing west. He stretched back and enjoyed the simple, sensuous pleasure of the sun shining in his face.

But then memory intervened and returned him to that other day when the western sun shone through another window, this time in the courthouse, late afternoon, he sitting at the defendant's table next to the high priced attorney his father had hired more to protect the family name, he believed, than his wayward son. He had turned his gaze away from the foreman about to stand, sweat on his wrinkled face, it was his neighbor Thompson, much more than a peer, but the man he had chatted with so many times about the price of cherries, the weather, the killer frost two years ago that had wiped out the harvest, there was stolid Thompson about to do his civic duty, and Sam swiveled his head to the right, toward that window in the west wall of the room and there the sun's rays formed halos around the heads of the spectators pressed against the glass waiting to see what they could not hear, their eyes fixed on Sam whose demeanor would tell them what words Thompson uttered in response to the judge's question.

He had steeled himself. He would not give them that satisfaction, those good citizens who despised him for the passion, the joy, with which he lived his life, and which had landed him in this very seat. Somehow, though, at the critical moment they understood. He did not know if he had betrayed himself, an expression forming itself on his face against his sternest effort, or as he learned later a chosen individual among those fortunate enough to have a seat inside the room had signaled the verdict. Within the courtroom there was more an explosion of pent up breath being expelled, but through the thin window glass that in the winter admitted the frigid wind came a howl of delight such as he imagined would rise from devils circling around the latest sinner arriving in their fiery domain.

At that moment, as the communal shame showered down upon him, he turned to the back of the courtroom where sat, between his always supportive mother and his domineering father, his son, and he realized then what he had been too indifferent before to understand, that among all the victims of this tragic situation, Isaiah was the most damaged.

Isaiah at this moment as his father's thoughts centered on him was walking along Front Street. He had arrived for the funeral without much thought as to what he would do after it, and now he could either take his grandmother up on her always open invitation, repeated with some insistence this morning over a full breakfast of eggs and bacon, to join her until the end of the month when she would have to vacate the big house especially empty since the death of her husband whose presence had filled all the rooms. But to move in there, even temporarily, would be to invite the unwelcome return of memories still sharp enough to sting after all this time. No, he'd find a place in town better than the boarding house in which he had rented a nondescript room, someplace not home, but a space he could call his own.

With a start he realized how seldom he had enjoyed just such a place.

With the envelope from his grandmother in one hand, and his suitcase containing what could be called his earthly possessions in the other, he walked down Front Street with no particular destination in mind. It was still early enough in the day to find an alternative to the cheap hotel he had been staying in when he arrived in town or his grandmother's house.

Up ahead a man bent in front of his car, turning its crank. The man tried again, but the engine remained silent. As Isaiah got nearer, he could see the man's red face coated in sweat, irritation in his eyes. He put his suitcase down, and carefully placed the envelope next to it.

"Can I help you?" he asked.

The man straightened up, not without some difficulty.

"My driver, he quit this morning, leaving me as you see me. I and this machine do not get along." He eyed Isaiah up and down, much like a horse he might hire to pull his carriage. "Do you know anything about these motors?"

"A bit," Isaiah replied. "If you step aside I'll see what I can do."

"Gladly." He pulled a gold pocket watch out of its pocket in his vest. "I'm late," he added as he stepped away from the vehicle, casting a glance he might have offered a wayward child or disobedient servant.

Isaiah leaned in to the vehicle, found the spark retard switch and pushed it into the off position.

"Are you sure you know what you are doing?" the man said. "I saw my man put that lever where I just had it."

"I do. And you are lucky that I came along when I did. If you had succeeded cranking as you were doing, you might have had a bad accident." He returned to the front of the vehicle and turned the crank slowly feeling for resistance.

"Young man," the man said, "can't you turn it harder than that?"

"Sure I can. But I have to know when the pistons are lined up properly."

He turned the crank again, and stopped when the resistance indicated the four pistons were right. He then stood up, walked to the side of the car and flipped the switch to on.

"Now," he said. "We should be OK."

Again in front of the vehicle, he gave the crank a turn and the engine sputtered into life.

He straightened up .

"You're good to go. Do you think you can drive it now?"

"Sure thing. Once it's running I can manage, though I'd rather be behind a team of horses. My wife wanted us, well you get the idea."

He extended his hand.

"Name's Herman Mueller," he said. His eyes focused on the suitcase and the envelope. "Are you looking for work? "

"More like a place to stay, " Isaiah replied, as he picked up his things.

"I've got an apartment for rent. Above my shop, Mueller's Leather Goods a few blocks up that way," he said pointing down Front Street."

"I might be interested in the apartment," Isaiah said. "But I've got a job."

"Driving cars?"

"No. Personal business."

Isaiah saw the disappointment on Mueller's face.

"But," Isaiah said, "if I take the apartment, you'll know where to find me, when you run into trouble with your motor again."

Eunice sat at her desk at the rear of the display area of the shop. In front of her was her ledger, neat columns of numbers,

debits on one side assets on the other. The clarity of their significance comforted her, providing a solid anchor in the flux of her
life. Ever since she was a child in school, numbers had provided
her a safe harbor. She had never been able to read people very
well, the nuances of language, the subtlety of facial expressions.
In retrospect, she had realized that her difficulty in accurately
perceiving the signals, both verbal and non-verbal, with which
people communicated with each other, that difficulty went a good
distance to explain the failure of her marriage to Sam, for, with
a certainty that gripped her stomach when she thought about it,
she recognized that she had never understood her vibrant husband, his confidence and charm overwhelming but also confusing her. The confusion led first to doubt, then to anxiety, relieved
by more and more frequent doses of laudanum, and finally a
retreat from the marital bed as it became clear that the energy
that drove him finally found another, more pliable, target.

She turned again to the numbers, added a column, entered
new figures in another, and only then looked up from her work to
glance out the front window of the store. Later she would wonder
what caused her to look at just that moment, but for whatever
reason, her eyes fastened on a man moving with an oh so familiar long loping stride causing her for a moment to believe that
he who never left her thoughts for too long was now out of prison
and walking down Front Street.

The man stopped, turned toward the store, and appeared to
be looking through the glass right at her. Yet, his eyes did not
focus on her. Instead they stared intently at the window, and
she realized he was reading the notice advertising the room for
rent above the store. Having finished reading, the man stood as
though undecided whether or not to pursue the notice. It was
only then that his glance landed on her, and when he offered a
shy smile, with a start she recognized him.

On the other side of the glass, Isaiah stared at the woman,
searching his memory to match her face with the images he
could bring up from his past. With a shrug, intended for himself
rather than her, he realized that the faint echo of familiarity in
the features did not trigger a firm recollection of who she might
be. In any event, he had been gone for some years and there

was only one woman's face that was his constant companion, effectively muscling all others into the dark recesses of fading recollection. His immediate concern was to check out the possibility of finding a decent place to live. All other matters could be dealt with at other times. If he was going to seriously consider his grandmother's request to take up the burden of freeing his father, he could do so effectively only once his immediate living situation could be settled down. With all that in mind, he found the door knob, turned it, and pushed open the door. As he entered the store, the woman rose from her seat, walked out from behind her desk wearing an expression on her face that he could not read, something between welcoming and trepidation, although why he should cause either was a puzzle he could not at that moment solve.

She walked toward him, stopping a few feet in front of him. She seemed about to raise her arms but then dropped them at her sides.

"Well, Isaiah, it is clear that I have the advantage of you," she said.

In the second before he felt compelled to reply, Isaiah first matched the image of the face confronting him with the one lodged in a closed closet of his memory, which for a very long time he had been content to keep shut. But now, standing in front of this woman, that door began to swing open. As it did, he was again a little boy looking up at a young woman's pretty face twisted into a mask that shifted between anger and fear, while in her hands clutched so hard in one hand that the knuckles were white was an empty bottle, in the other hand between thumb and forefinger a cork, her mouth moving with a nervous quiver, her voice a plea, *Please Isaiah,* it said, *before your father comes home can you get me more?* He squeezed his eyes shut and when he opened them he saw before him that woman in an entirely new reincarnation, still pretty, though now with the maturity befitting her age and position.

"Well, hello," he began and paused, searching for the proper form of address.

"Mrs. Jameison will do. You never were comfortable calling me Mother. I didn't understand then, I was trying so hard to fulfill that role for you, but now, as I raise my own boy, I do understand. I couldn't," she paused, "well, I just didn't."

"That was a long time ago," he managed to reply.

"Yes. And now, you're back. I guess for the funeral. I read about it in the paper."

He nodded.

"And you just happened to see me, through the window?"

"Not exactly. I met your boss a while ago."

"Stuck with his car?" she asked with a smile. "And you got it going for him."

"He offered me a job. Which I don't need. And somewhere to stay. Which I do need."

"You've come to the right place."

Those simple, welcoming words, caused a panic to grip him. Was he ready for the new status between them, and all the tangled history that involved?

"I'll need to think about that," he said. "It's just that..." he struggled to find the words to express the feeling of unease that blurred his thoughts and thickened his tongue. "The right place...I don't know." Then, after a moment, clarity came. "It's that ever since I went away, I'm most comfortable on the water. I seem to understand it, and it suits me. On land...."

"More confusing?" she asked.

"Yes."

CHAPTER THREE

The guard rattled the bars of Sam's cell with his baton. "Got to take you to where you'll be working from now on. That is if you don't mind my interrupting your rest."

"What'll I be doing?" Sam asked, realizing he didn't care very much, the prospect of actually doing something after all this time was far more important than whatever the specific activity turned out to be.

"You'll see, soon enough," the guard replied. "How long has it been since you were outside?"

"Outside?"

"Yeah, like beneath the blue sky and the sun?"

Sam felt the smile spread over his face.

"Much too long."

With the guard's strong hand grasping his biceps, Sam emerged into the bright sunlight. The guard stopped while Sam's eyes struggled to adjust. After a few moments, with his hands shielding his eyes, he was able to see that before them waited a wagon with benches on either side on which sat other prisoners.

"Maybe not what you're used to," the guard said.

"Oh, but it is," Sam replied.

They walked to the wagon, and the guard released his grip on Sam's arm and motioned for him to climb up where he found one seat remaining on the right side of the wagon, which, as soon as he sat down, lurched forward. The wagon made its slow way through the yard where prisoners were milling about on what appeared to be a makeshift baseball diamond.

"Do they play there?" Sam asked the man sitting next to him, a grizzled individual of uncertain age whose eyes offered the world a look of knowing weariness. He nodded.

"I'll be damned," Sam muttered.

In front of them, the gates in the high prison walls swung open, and for a moment Sam entertained the thought of leaping off the wagon and running through fields of vegetables, corn stalks a foot or two tall, and beyond them some low growing green plants that from this distance he guessed were probably potatoes, and beyond them a stretch of uncultivated grass that gave way to woods, into which, Sam thought, a man might run and then disappear. As though reading his mind, the grizzled man pointed to the guard sitting next to the driver. At that man's side, his hand rested on the stock of a rifle. The grizzled man shook his head.

"Saw one man try it once. He got, maybe twenty feet away."

Sam settled his back against the rough planks of the wagon's sides and closed his eyes, forcing himself to fall into the rhythmic jolting beneath him, listening to the steady clop clop of the horses' hooves, a comforting sound from his long ago past on his own farm. The wagon slowed to a stop that caused Sam's body to continue its forward motion into the arm of the grizzled man.

"We're there," the man said.

Sam opened his eyes and for a moment thought he must have been transported back to that farm, for in front of him were rows of fruit tree saplings and beyond them acres of dirt waiting to be planted with still more trees that he saw lying in neat bundles.

"Apples," he said.

The grizzled man turned to him.

"How you know?"

"Damned if I haven't planted more than my share of fruit trees, enough so I know one from another."

"Well, I wouldn't know nothin' about that," the grizzled man replied, and held out his hand. "Tom Howard from Chicago."

"Chicago?"

"Thinkin' how I got up here, don't Illinois got prisons to hold me? A woman, ain't that how it is? Got involved with one, and one thing led to another, one place to another, and here I am, been here half my life."

Sam looked more closely at the gray stubble on his cheeks, noticed a long scar running behind his ear.

Tom followed Sam's eyes, then brought his hand up to the scar.

"Man that done that is dead."

"And you're here," Sam replied. "Just like me." He paused as he understood that not only were they both here now, but, in all

probability, they both faced the same future behind those imposing walls, supplemented by well armed guards. "Life?" he asked.

Tom nodded.

"I guess we both got a dead body put us here. Who you kill? And
why? That man who came at me with a knife, we both thought
we had the same woman. Maybe we did."

Sam managed a knowing smile.

"Ain't that the way."

"Yeah," Tom replied. "But you ain't answered my question."

For a second, as Sam turned away from the sun, and looked
out into the field, gathering himself for an answer, he saw her
again, this time lying in the tall meadow grass just beyond the
last row of newly planted trees.

"Like you," he said, "a man that thought he had my woman."

"But you was in solitary, and I wasn't, so there is a difference."

Just then the guard with the rifle, hopped down from his seat.

"Time to get down," he said, motioning with his rifle. "There's
trees got to be planted today. All of them."

Sam helped Tom down from the wagon, and they walked at the
end of the line of prisoners toward the waiting trees. As they got
closer, he could see the shovels. The guard stood next to the tree
on the end of the row and pointed to the shovels.

"Pick one up," he said. "Then take one of those saplings." He
took five careful strides, stopped and extended his arm to indicate an imaginary row. "Fifteen steps, like I did, then line up
across from the trees already planted, and dig a hole so the tree
you plant will line up with the one already in the ground. We
want nice straight lines, don't we?"

"Should be pruning those," Sam said pointing to the growing
trees, "not planting new ones now."

"What you should be doing," the guard said, "is digging holes
like I said."

"How deep, how wide?" Sam asked.

"The hole?" the guard responded.

"Yessir," Sam replied.

"Deep and wide enough to hold the tree. Are you some kind of
a wise fellow?"

"No," Sam said. "I just thought these men should know what they're doing."

"Do you?"

"I've planted more than my share of trees ."

"Well, look at that," the guard said. "We've got a farmer here. Well, Mr. Farmer, suppose you instruct us ignorant folks how to plant a tree."

Sam took the shovel on the top of the pile, grabbed a sapling, strode to a position next to the guard, turned with his back to the row of trees, took fifteen steps, all the while aware that the other prisoners were watching his interaction with the guard with considerable interest, wondering if he would cross a line and wind up in one of the punishment cells he had heard about. Having measured the required distance, he turned, laid the sapling down, and drove his shovel into the ground with all his weight. When its downward motion stopped, he placed his right foot on the top of the shovel blade and stepped down as hard as he could. The shovel bit into the soil. He lifted it up, knelt down and scooped up a handful of the dirt, rolling it back and forth between his hands, forming it into a ball, much like he could have made a snowball.

"Clay," he said. "Not so good. You want some sand mixed in, so the water can sink down in it."

The guard's heavy boot pressed down on Sam's back between his shoulder blades. The pressure, at first was gentle, almost like a caress, but then it increased ever so slowly forcing Sam's head toward the hole he had started to dig. He braced himself with one hand and started to turn so as to grab the boot with the other.

"You'd like to, wouldn't you, farmer. Go ahead. We got ways to take the starch out of such as you."

With that, the boot pushed harder until Sam's face was in the hole. He gasped for breath, and in so doing sucked dirt into his nostrils and his mouth. He lay still until the boot released its pressure, and he was able to straighten up out of the hole.

"Less talk and more digging," the guard now said, and walked away.

Back in his cell, he found another man on the second cot. The man's breathing was labored, and he did not look up when the guard clanked the cell door closed. The sleeves of his shirt were rolled up and one arm dangled toward the floor. The flesh of the wrist on that arm had a circle of red around it where something, perhaps a rope, had been. Sam walked to the side of the cot and looked down at the man. His hair was thinning and gray. He slept with his mouth ajar with a little spittle dribbling out of it. Every once in a while he snored, and by the bend in his nose, Sam figured it had been broken, perhaps more than once.

Sam shrugged and lay down on his own cot. He had his own problems. His hands, though once calloused from hard physical work with wood, whether the trunks of trees in the ground or the boards of a newly constructed house, had grown soft from his long solitary confinement where the only things he had touched were the steel bars of his cell or its masonry walls when he paced about in the throes of terminal boredom, digging his nails into his palms, just for the sensation of pain to convince himself that he was still alive, or the thrice a day handling of the crude silverware with which he ate the tasteless gruel that served for his meals, those hands now featured dried blood where the skin had cracked open under the relentless pressure applied to the handle of his shovel. His own nose, though not bent out of shape like that of his new companion, was stuffed with dirt he had been unable to remove, and in his mouth no amount of his saliva could cleanse the mud wedged between his teeth.

He lay back and listed to the other man's labored breathing, trying to match his own to it in the hope that the rhythm might lure him into something like a restful sleep. After a while, his exhausted muscles, long unaccustomed to any kind of serious exertion, lulled him.

Row after row of trees floated, on their branches ripe red tart cherries, above puffy white clouds against a high blue sky. His body ached but in the pleasant way that follows productive labor. He was a little boy struggling to carry the lug of cherries for his father's inspection. He very carefully lowered the lug to the ground, being sure not to let even one precious piece of fruit slide off the top of the heap onto the ground, and thus become worthless. His father, himself coated in sweat gently plucked one cherry from the top of the pile and bit into it, rolled its juice around his tongue, then took the rest of the cherry into his mouth, swallowed its flesh, and, turning his head spat out the pit. Sam watched all of this waiting for the judgment that must follow. But still his father delayed offering his verdict. Instead, he put his work-hardened hand into the lug and ever so gently lifted a bunch of cherries and held it in front of his eyes. He placed the fruit back into the lug, eased his lips into the briefest suggestion of a smile, nodded, and then motioned Sam toward the heap of empty lugs waiting to be filled.

The scene shifted to a corner of the barn where a teen-aged Sam stood before a lathe, his right foot stomping down in a steady rhythm on the pedal that caused the almost completely fashioned baseball bat to spin against the blade that he held at just the right position to shave off just a little more down near the handle. He eased his foot off the pedal, lifted up the bat and ran his hand over its surface, starting at the thick end of the barrel and sliding down toward the knob at the bottom of the handle. The air in the barn was redolent with the aroma of cut wood, and he breathed it in deeply. Taking a few practice swings, he tested weight and balance of the bat with his eyes closed, imagining the day when he would be employing this new bat in the first game of the upcoming season.

Before he opened his eyes, he sensed his father's steady stare. Opening them, he saw his father glaring, more than just looking, at him from the doorway of the barn, and then shaking his head, his features frozen in disapproval.

A loud cough, followed by a muttered curse, broke into Sam's dream. For a moment, he thought he was still asleep and it was his father coughing and muttering. But he opened his eyes, and saw that the man lying on the cot across from him was rousing and looking at him in a way not so very different from the expression of his father in his dream. The man's eyes were red, and one was swollen and ringed by discolored flesh. He squinted, then turned his eyes into a hard stare.

"Who are you?" he asked. "And what are you doing in my house?"

"House?"

"Yeah, that's what I call it." He furrowed his brow in thought. "You must be one of those I been hearing about."

"One of...." Sam began, but then stood up and walked across the cell, extending his hand. "Sam," he said, "Sam Logan."

"They must have let you out while I was being trained, that's what they call it, trained into being a nice obedient little man."

"I've been out of solitary for a couple of days. Had me out planting trees. Like I used to do."

"You a farmer?"

"Was. And a carpenter, built houses. You?"

"Never had much interest in an honest day's work."

"So, it's no surprise."

"Me being here? No."

Sam realized he was still hold his hand out, so he let it drop.

The man held out his own hand, and Sam grasped it. The man's fingers tightened around Sam's.

"Pete," he said. "Pete Morgan. Got caught this time breaking into a house, maybe one you built."

"Whereabouts?"

"Midland."

"Never been there, except maybe on my way here, but I'm not too sure about that." Sam braced himself for the next question, and then decided to answer it before it was asked. "Murder," he said, "that's why I'm here."

"I knew that without you sayin'. Those are the ones who were put in solitary." He stroked the stubble on his chin, and winced. He worked his jaws open and shut. "I suppose you're innocent."

"Not exactly," Sam replied.

Pete opened his eyes wide.

"Not exactly," Sam repeated. "But not exactly guilty either."

Pete waved his hand in front of his face as though to sweep away anything that would alter the simple dichotomy of the prison, there were those in it and those not in it.

"Save it," he said.

Sam retreated to his cot and sat down.

"Training?" he asked.

"To understand that when I am told to work, I will work. It's funny. They want me to work like the honest man I never was. 'Ceptin' for this job where there's no pay. When I pointed that fact out to them, they took me to what they call the 'punishment cell' like I was a kid misbehavin' in school, only here the punishment is a lot more severe than a whack on the hand or behind with a ruler. First they soften you up with their fists, or their wooden batons, then they put you on a chair with ropes around your wrists, and the other end of the rope is tied to the ceiling, and they stretch that rope just far enough so you have to stand on your toes to keep the strain off your arms. After a while, you can't do that any more." He held out his wrists.

"I see," Sam said. "And did you take your instruction to heart?"

"The hell," Pete said.

"What are you going to do now?"

"Play my part for a little while, then talk to some of my pals, about a little something we've been cooking up."

"Which is?"

"I just met you."

"I understand."

"I hope you do," Pete replied. "For your sake."

CHAPTER FOUR

I t was a simple question for most people, but not so for Edward Franklin. The man asking it folded his thick hands on the desk and waited.

"Well?" he asked. "Sure you can tell me your own name."

Edward searched his memory. What had he been reading in that scrap of paper he found on the floor of the boxcar on the train that had brought him here to copper mining country on the Keweenaw Peninsula?

"Of course," Edward said as the name on the paper came into focus in his mind. But the name seemed to float away. He snatched at what he could still see. "Wilbur."

"Well, Wilbur, that is a coincidence."

Edward concentrated. The paper had had a name on it, Wilbur something, he had to find this Wilbur to ask him for a job.

"You..." he began.

The man behind the desk nodded. He opened the desk drawer, pulled out a piece of paper and handed it to Edward. "Now, I expect you saw something very like this, only you couldn't remember my last name, which you can now see is Jablonski."

Edward studied the paper. Of course, it was a crisp and full version of the handbill stained by the dirt encrusted fingers of who knew how many others before he found it tucked into a crack in the plank siding of the boxcar, probably to keep out the draft from the early winter wind. Out of boredom, he read it, and out of lack of any better possibilities, and with the strong possibility that the law was not far behind him after his aborted and clumsy attempt at robbery outside of Traverse City, he decided to travel up here and see if he could become a copper miner.

Jablonski held out his hand for the handbill. Edward glanced at it and gave it back.

"It says on that paper there are jobs for those who are willing to work."

"Indeed it does. What do you know about mining?"

37

The lie began to form on his lips but Jablonski shook his head.

"I've got a strong back," Edward said.

"There are other jobs need doing around here. What do you think of unions?

"Not much."

"Let me be clearer. I'm not asking what you know about unions, but whether they are a good thing."

"I don't have an opinion. But I'll be glad to take yours."

Jablonski smiled.

"I think you'll do just fine. Come around tomorrow morning and we'll see what we can find for you to do. In the meantime," he reached into his pocket and pulled out a few coins, "clean yourself up and get something to eat. There's a rooming house just up the street from here. Tell the woman there I sent you, and she'll give you a room and a tub of hot water."

Edward was a little perplexed. He had not come this far for a few coins for a meal and a hot bath, although both would be welcome. He had learned a few things in his troubled life, and toward the top of that short list was not to agree with something unless he understood what its consequences for himself might be. And so he tried.

"What exactly will I be doing to earn this pay?"

"It won't be good to be too inquisitive. For a law abiding man, as you no doubt are, I can tell you that what we ask you to do will be lawful."

"I don't care..." Edward began, but then suspecting a trap, he nodded.

"Good," Jablonski said. "Clean yourself up and come by tomorrow morning, just like I said."

"I expect you're hungry," the landlady said. "Sit down there." She pointed to the table where there was a plate onto which she ladled a stew.

"Thank you," he muttered through a mouth full of food.

"One time only," she replied. "From now on, you eat when everyone else does. Finish up, and I'll have a bath waiting for you."

The bath felt good. Edward could not remember when last his flesh had been free of dirt and grime. His room was little bigger than a closet, with a narrow bed shoved against one wall. A window faced out onto the street. He dragged the lone chair next to the window and sat gazing out. Before long a muffled sound of voices and feet drifted up to where he sat.

He opened the window, and recoiled for a second against the frigid air that assaulted his freshly scrubbed face. He glanced up at the puffy white clouds in the brilliant blue of the sky, put his head out and turning first to the left and then to the right found the source of the noise. A crowd stretching from one side of the street to the other moved toward him. As it approached, he noticed that along both sides of the marchers were onlookers, mostly women and children but scattered among them single men.

At the head of the marchers was a tall, ungainly woman carrying a large American flag. Walking to her side was another woman carrying a placard with words scrawled in red on it. He strained to see what those letters spelled, but the distance and his limited literacy prevented him from making out the message. But there was no mistaking the mood projected by the color of those letters. Whatever those words were, he concluded, they invited aggression if not violence.

As the marchers came closer, almost abreast of the window out of which Edward was watching, those on the wooden sidewalks moved along with them. And now Edward could see that among the onlookers were rough looking men holding buckets in one hand, and long handled scoops in the other. It did not take him long to figure out the purpose of that combination, and within seconds he saw that he was correct.

The woman at the head of the marchers continued walking with eyes straight ahead, flag held above her as before even while the clumps of dried manure landed at her feet. Only once did she turn toward the men loading up their scoops as though to challenge them to try just a little bit harder to force her to react. The woman with the placard began to wave it toward the manure throwers in a threatening manner, but the large woman seized her arm and stayed her motion. Her actions seemed to

both stiffen the resolve and temper the anger of those following her, and they too continued moving forward, matching their
pace to hers, and their indifference to the refuse pelting down on
them, just as she was doing.

Edward took his eyes off the woman, and those immediately
behind her, long enough to turn his glance again to those on the
sides of the street, and there standing right below his window,
wrapped in an expensive looking overcoat and puffing on a cigar,
was Wilbur Jablonski. And then, as though he felt Edward's eyes
on him, Jablonski turned around, lifted his hat with one hand,
and with the other holding the cigar, waved. They looked at each
other for a few seconds, and then Edward nodded his acceptance
of the unstated confirmation of the role Jablonski was hiring
him to fulfill. It was a job, Edward thought, and he didn't care
much about what he had to do as long he would be paid for doing
it. That was, after all, how he had lived his whole life.

Sitting back in the chair long after the parade had moved
on, he reflected on the last decent job he had had years ago on
that farm in Old Mission, on the peninsula north of Traverse
City. The work was hard but he never minded that. It was the
best position he had ever held, especially coming as it did after
he had narrowly escaped being horse whipped or worse, just
because that girl misunderstood his intentions, how he would
really have married her if her father had only been amenable.
No, instead her old man brandished that whip and gave him one
hour to leave his farm, and no, he wouldn't be paid for the work
he had done. That seemed always to be the way it was for him.
And then, again, at the Old Mission farm there was another girl
who stirred his blood, always the same, like fruit hanging from a
tree there right in front of him, but if he stretched out his hand
to grasp it, somebody would grab his arm and toss him aside as
so much garbage.

He permitted himself a grim smile. At least that time, he
didn't get the girl, as usual, but the one who did was now sitting
in prison, not so high and mighty as once he was. His memory
paused for a moment at first one image, and then another, the
girl, really on the cusp of being a woman, lying dead, so peaceful
looking with her arms clasped over her chest, and her lover sit-

ting at the defense table next to his high priced lawyer paid for by his father, steadfastly refusing to admit that he at the very least was the last person to see her alive. Edward spat into the corner of the room as though at the feet of Sam Logan. I saw you, he muttered to the shadows in the corner, I saw you heading in the opposite direction from where you claimed to be. Right toward where they found her, and me standing in the trees, so what if I tried to sell what I had to say, isn't that what most people in this sorry world do, only when I did it they scorned me. All I wanted was a train ticket out of there to someplace like California where I could get at a new start. They didn't believe me. But they did take the word of that nigger who hadn't seen nothing. And Mr. Sam Logan is in jail where he is going to stay, and I am up here, doing whatever they want me to do, as long as it puts coins in my pocket.

He turned his gaze back down to the street below. Jablonski was now gone, and the marchers had moved on, only a group of ragged children bringing up the rear. Edward studied them. He could not tell which party they belonged to, whether those following the large woman with the sign or those on the side of the street pelting her with manure. He watched until they were out of sight.

Tomorrow he would find out exactly what Jablonski would want him to do. For now, his belly was full, he was clean for the first time in weeks, and a bed awaited him. It might contain bedbugs, but it would be softer than the plank flooring of that boxcar that had brought him here, and for that he was profoundly grateful.

I am a simple man, he said to himself, with simple needs. I just need somebody to tell me what to do.

He slipped into a deep and dreamless sleep. When he woke the next morning, he found two other boarders finishing their breakfast. One was tall and lean with a long scar running down his cheek. The other was the opposite, short and chubby with peach fuzz for stubble, beneath which were the unmistakable scars left from a case of smallpox. As opposed to his companion, he did not look menacing, that is until you studied his eyes. They were hard and unforgiving.

"You'd better hurry," the short one said. "He'll be looking for you."

"Yeah," the tall one added. "He expects you to earn your keep."

"I always do," Edward replied.

"You were watching out your window. I saw you," Jablonski said. "Let me take a closer look at you, now that you've cleaned up."

They were standing on the wooden sidewalk in front of the boarding house. Here and there in the street were lumps of manure, and the air was rich with their smell. Jablonski continued staring at Edward, as though contemplating whether his few coins had been well spent. At his feet was a small satchel.

"Yes," he said, "you'll do. Except for your clothes." He reached into his pocket and took out another couple of coins. "There's a company store up that way," he said, pointing to the direction from which the marchers had come the day before. "Buy yourself some clothes that a miner might wear. Tell them I sent you."

"A miner?"

"Sure. We want you to blend in. For the work we're going to want you to do. And one more thing." He leaned down to open the satchel, then lifted it up and spread it open so its contents could be seen. Then one by one, he took out a piece of lead pipe, a sheathed knife, and finally, a revolver, placing the pipe in Edward's left hand, the knife in his right, and holding the revolver between his palms, gently, as though it were a lost kitten, or a bird that might fly off.

"Which do you prefer?" he asked.

Edward tested the weight of the pipe, then the knife. He turned his eyes to the revolver.

"Do you want to see how this one fits you?" Jablonski asked.

Edward nodded, and knelt so that he could place the knife and pipe back into the satchel. Jablonski opened his palms and Edward reached for the revolver.

"Have you handled a weapon like this before?"

Edward began to nod his head in the lie. He had never before seen a revolver up close, let alone held or fired one. He shook his head slowly, reluctantly.

"Well, we don't have time right now to teach you. Pick one of the other."

An image of the knife slashing Sam Logan's throat gave way to the more satisfying feeling of the pipe crushing that arrogant bastard's skull.

"I'll take the pipe," he said, and held out his hand.

"Not quite so fast," Jablonski said, as he slid the knife and pipe back into the satchel. "I needed to get a sense of your, let's say, capabilities. But seeing as I only met you yesterday, and that you come to me with, not to put too fine a point on it, without much of a verifiable background, I'm going to start you out with some activities that do not require any of these implements."

"That's ok with me," Edward said, holding out his well worn fists. "These have always done what needed to be done."

"I don't doubt it," Jablonski replied. "The question is who was on the other end of them, and for what occasion they were necessary."

Edward shrugged.

"Those that needed it," he said.

"That'll do," Jalonski replied. "For now."

"What do you want me to do?"

"There's a saloon in the building they call the Italian Hall where the strikers like to hang out. Go there. Drink. But not so much that your ears get clogged."

"And if I hear something I don't like."

"Remember it, so you can tell me. But nothing more than that. Got it?"

"I do."

Hundreds of miles to the south in Lansing, Governor Frank Woodhouse read over and over a telegram on his desk, while his assistant Fred McGinnis waited for him to reveal its contents.

"They want the national guard up there," the governor said, as he slid the telegram across his desk to McGinnis. "What do you think Fred?"

"Past time," Fred replied.

"Winter's coming on," the governor replied. "It gets pretty tough up there doesn't it."

"You think the unions will fold?"

"Don't know. If they had any sense...."

"What do they want, expect to get, when this is all over?"

The governor permitted himself a quick smile.

"Maybe a living wage."

"Well, they won't get it this way. What they'll get is no job, no money, no place to live."

"Could be you're right. But what about us? Calling out the guard to ...."

"To preserve order," McGinnis said with the conviction the governor had come to both depend upon while at the same time tamping down his intuitive sense that the black and white world of his assistant did not coincide with the reality he himself believed to be the case. And, he reminded himself, knowing full well that McGinnis would not let him forget, the next election was not very far away, and the striking unions had little support in the rest of the state. This time, though, the governor decided to push back, just a little, against his assistant's assurance. It would be like building a sand fort to face the onrushing tide, he knew, but maybe he would sleep just a little bit better.

"It's not all that simple," he said, and even as the words left his mouth knew that they sounded more than a little trite. Of course, things were not simple. But sometimes, as in this case, politics could be. Morality, he had learned years ago, was calculus while politics was arithmetic. He acknowledged this difference, but could never fully reconcile himself to it. McGinnis seemed ready to continue the discussion. The governor had enough for the day.

"I'll send in the troops. But then I'm going to want daily reports. From you. Get up there. And give me the facts of what's happening on the ground. And..." he paused, "leave your politics at home."

"Yessir," McGinnis replied.

"The troops will be there only to protect property. Is that clear?"

"Yes."

"One more thing. I'm hearing about this woman up there."

"Big Annie."

"So you've heard about her."

"Hard not to. A real troublemaker."

"See what you can find out about her. She is, as you say, a troublemaker, but primarily because of her sex, and because of her sex we have to be careful not to stir things up in a bad way. Like what happened in New York with those garment workers."

"All of them, they should go back to the kitchen. And then to the bedroom."

"Be that as it may, or maybe, be that as it used to be. Times are changing, and we've got to take notice."

McGinnis shook his head, clearly unconvinced, and the governor realized that his assistant would need more persuading. But now was not the time.

"Take the morning train," he said. "Say a nice good-bye to your wife. I expect you will be gone a while."

After he left, the governor sat at his desk, his eyes closed. Before long, he thought, I will have to see what I can do myself.

Edward walked the now nearly deserted street feeling vaguely uncomfortable in his stiff new clothes, compliments of the mining company run store to which Jablonski had directed him. The heavy cotton of his pants chaffed the skin of his thighs, and his feet felt cramped in the stiff leather of the new boots, a size too small, but that was all they had, they would have to do, the clerk had said, if he had a problem, he could talk to Mr. Jablonski.

Stray dogs sniffed the bits of feces that hours before had been hurled at the marchers. At least the unbending fabric of his fresh shirt, though it irritated his neck where it rubbed against his skin, still provided some warmth. He placed his hand in his pocket and the cool hard surface of his remaining coins strengthened his resolved to find the saloon in the Italian Hall Jablonski had mentioned. He struggled to remember the name, then gave up the effort. He had never been very good at remembering names, but he could surely recognize a saloon when he saw it. The thought of the saloon raised his thirst and he quickened his pace. Up ahead he saw the two story building Jablonski had described. The saloon would be on the first floor. He shaded his eyes and scanned up the building's wooden walls. He could see a fire escape on one side leading to a door on the second story. Jablonski had not told him what kind of business occupied that second floor, and for now he did not much care what it was. His mind was on the cold taste of the beer he would soon be enjoying.

Two hours and several beers later, he was feeling very good although the stool on which he sat seemed to be spinning ever so slowly. When he first sat down, he remembered his instructions. He should listen carefully and not enter into a conversation unless pressed to do so. After a while, perhaps, he could begin to socialize. He had arrived in the late afternoon when only a few men sat at the bar, spaced apart as though each one sought to commune only with himself. In the corner of the room sat a pool table, its green felt dimmed by a layer of dust and its heavy wooden legs festooned with the delicate strands of spider webs. He took a sip and held his thumb on the line of beer now only an inch or so from the bottom of the glass. He thought about raising his hand to the barkeep who was leaning on the counter looking at him as though he, too, realized that another glass would soon be needed. Edward started to raise his hand to signal his interest in a refill, but first he reached into his pocket, where he found only a couple of coins. He pulled his hand out of his pocket, laid it palm down on the counter, looked toward the barkeep and shook his head. The barkeep nodded and picked up a cloth with which he began to wipe up a wet spot with desultory motions. The whole scene lacked any energy or sense of purpose, as though those who found their way into this room did so precisely because they had nothing better to do, no place to go.

But that ennui began to give way a little later as Edward drained the last of his beer. Several men came in and took up their places nearby. As they arrived, they continued the conversation they must have been having in the street, their voices energetic, their eyes bright with the conviction that informed their words.

Edward strained to listen to the fragments of conversation that seemed to be coming at him from all directions. He realized that Jablonski had directed him to this tavern for precisely this opportunity to hear what these men were talking about.

He glanced about him and thought he recognized one or two faces as belonging to marchers he had witnessed from his window perch earlier in the day. Keeping his eyes fixed on the patina of foam across the rim of his glass, he strained to open his ears while erasing any other thoughts or stimuli from his mind. After a few moments, several phrases seem to recur in the whirl of conversation. Among them was the word "Christmas," and then "our kids" and finally in the form of a question "with what money?" He also soon became aware that just as he was looking around and listening, some of the men now began to pay attention to him, and not in a very friendly manner. He reached into his pocket took out a couple of his remaining coins, placed them on the counter and motioned to the barkeep, who strolled to him, picked up his glass, and held it under the tap. Edward watched how the barkeep held the glass at just the right angle to obtain a good head on the beer, not too much, not too little. As a man who had spent his life at jobs that demanded more brute force than fine discrimination, Edward was pleased at this exercise of skill at a given task.

The barkeep slid the glass, with foam flecked on its rim, in front of Edward and reached with his other hand to scoop up the two coins Edward had placed in front of him. Edward sensed someone coming up behind him, and then a large, dirt encrusted hand swooped down and landed on the coins.

"I've got this one, Jim," a deep voice said. "We don't want to take this fellow's last dime do we?"

Edward balled his fist. A lifetime of insult and abuse had schooled him in suspicion of any seemingly kind gesture aimed in his direction.

"Easy, now," the deep voice said. "Maybe you're the kind who likes to pay his own way."

Edward relaxed his fist half way. He was a little confused. Maybe this stranger did not mean him harm.

"I do," he managed to say, "that is, pay my own way."

"I guess so," the voice said. The man who owned that voice lifted his hand off Edward's coins, disappeared for a moment, but then reappeared on the counter where it dropped several more coins.

"Why don't I just buy a beer for myself, if you don't mind, and I'll sit down next and enjoy it in your company. Will that be alright?"

Emboldened by his victory, Edward felt he could hold his own with this stranger, perhaps even find an advantage.

"I don't own that, so help yourself."

Edward sensed the movement of the man as he slid onto the seat next to him. He kept his eyes fastened on his drink as though so doing erected a protective shell around him. He felt the man's shoulders rub against his. Still he looked at his glass, and then lifted it to his lips and took a deep drink from it.

"Name's Forsch, Willie Forsch. From Pennsylvania."

"You're a long way from home," Edward replied.

"And you?"

Edward hesitated before he answered. Maybe this fellow was a detective who had tracked him all the way up from Traverse City. Unlikely, but still possible. He had to say something, and as had been the case when he fumbled the question of his name while talking to Jablonski, he could not come up with a plausible location from which he had come. His mind blanked on any other state not name Pennsylvania.

"From downstate," he managed to say.

"Well, and your name."

"Edward, just call me Edward."

"Well, Edward, that's all I need to know for now," Willie said, his deep voice now layered with menace, "that and those new duds you just bought at the company store with those coins from Jablonski, you're sitting here just trying to blend in, ain't you?"

"Just looking for work," Edward said, his fist again balled.

"Sure you are," Willie said. "And we know just the kind of work you have been hired to do."

Edward felt a hard nudge in his ribs, once, twice, and then again, followed by a splash of cold water on his face. He started up, his fists again ready, his eyes blinking in the slanting rays of the late afternoon sun.

"Easy," Jablonski said. "You need some looking after."

He extended his hand, and Edward grasped it.

"Not sure what happened," he mumbled. As he did, his tongue tasted the blood in his mouth and pushed against his loosened front teeth. "I was just doing what you asked me to do." He looked around. "Where am I?"

"In the yard behind the tavern, a few feet from the outhouse, where they dumped you after beating you up pretty good. I imagine you met Willie."

"Yeah, I think so, guy told me that was his name. But I didn't get much of a look at him."

"No you wouldn't have. But you sure as hell felt him, and probably several of his friends. But tell me, did you hear anything worth remembering?"

Edward struggled to his feet, closed his eyes in concentration, yes there had been some talk, but he couldn't quite bring it up. Then the words began to come back to him.

"Something about Christmas, I think."

Jablonski hauled him to his feet and looked at him hard.

"That's all, that's what my money bought and what you paid for with the beating you took? If so, maybe you'd better get back on the next train taking you back from where you came. I'd ask for your new clothes back, except that they are spotted with your blood."

"No, wait, there's more, I just got to clear my head so I can remember."

"Go ahead."

"Christmas, yeah that word kept popping up, but there were others, something about kids, and then, like a question, where was the money going to come from."

Jablonski's face relaxed into a smile.

"So that's it, I see what they were talking about."

"Can I stay?" Edward asked, convinced he had blown this opportunity.

"Oh, yes," Jablonski replied, "I think we'll be able to use you after all. First those fists, which didn't do you much good against Willie and his pals, but that's to be expected, there will be other opportunities for them to do some good, but later, there's a little something I'm thinking about that you would be just perfect for."

"Thank you, Mr. Jablonski."

Jablonski's smile turned knowing, and just a little nasty.

"Oh, you don't need to thank me. Wait until you hear what I'm going to want you to do."

"Whatever it is..." Edward began.

"Just wait," Jablonski said, the smile back full again. He clapped Edward hard on the shoulder. "All in good time. But before that, in the next couple of days we'll give you an opportunity to show us what you can do with those hard fists of yours."

I saiah sat on the bed in his room above the leather shop. His negotiations with Eunice had been easy enough although he had to force himself to see her, as she was now, and not the stepmother whose fights with his father had placed him, just a little boy at the time, to pick sides. Of course, he had taken his father's side. He was much too young to begin to comprehend the complexity of the struggles between the two adults. He had already been abandoned by one woman, his birth mother, and saw that her replacement did not have the ability, or perhaps the inclination, to mother him. During their conversation this afternoon, he had wanted to ask a question that had long been driven into a corner of his mind, but now he could no longer avoid it. And so he, once the details of his rent and employment had been settled, laid this question in front of them.

"What ever happened..." he began, and then realized that this introduction pointed in an unintended direction.

She had placed her warm hand on his shoulder, a gesture so kind hearted that it almost erased the ill feelings from so long ago.

"You are asking about your brother, aren't you?"

The term struck him mute, and so he just nodded.

"I remember now," she said, "those were such troubled times, for me, for all of us I suppose."

"I left after the trial."

"People say you went to sea."

"I did."

She glanced at the grandfather clock ticking in the corner of the shop.

"He's in school now. He's old enough to walk home to our house. Where my mother will take care of him until I get home."

"His name?" Isaiah asked.

"Jonathan."

The name touched a sleeping memory cell in Isaiah's brain.

"I think I did see him once."

51

"I do believe you did."

Now, as Isaiah readied himself for the day, he rehearsed that part of their conversation, and matched it to the memory that had flashed as though on a screen in his mind, taking him back to that most traumatic time in his young life when he was called upon to testify at his father's trial. There was Eunice sitting at the back of the packed courtroom, her eyes fixed on him with an expression somewhere between beseeching and hostility, as he stiffened his spine, looking at his father's defense attorney who exerted every ounce of persuasive energy to get him to answer a simple factual question, to wit, did that woman, and he pointed to Eunice, of her own free will get down out of the buggy in which the three of them were riding to town, Eunice's belly big with the child soon to be born. He recalled how in order to give himself time to frame an answer, he had turned his gaze away from Eunice to land on the small boy next to her, realizing with a start that he was looking at that baby, his brother, now a tow headed toddler of three or four, whose hair matched that of his father, while Isaiah's was dark brown like that of his birth mother. The boy seemed to return Isaiah's glance, though surely he was too young to understand what was going on, why his mother decided after all to bring him to the courtroom to watch while his father's life was in the hands of his brother.

He shook his head with some vigor, as though to free it from these memories so that he could turn his attention more closely to the contents of the envelope that his grandmother had given him. Lifting out the pile of papers, he placed them in front of him, and picked up the first, which was the newspaper account of Margaret's body having been found. Following it in chronological order were the newspaper accounts of his father's arrest, trial, and conviction. Each account was glued onto a separate sheet of paper on which in the margins he read his grandmother's neat hand picking out points to be pursued. He flipped to the last news story to see how the coverage coincided with the memory burned into his brain, images of faces pressed against the window of the courthouse belonging to those not aggressive enough, or early enough, to find a seat inside the building, the hushed silence as the jury foreman stood to declare the verdict, the palpable sense emanating from these good citizens that only the declaration of his father's guilt would satisfy them, and it was all there accurately presented in the flat, objective prose of the newspaper story that contrasted so sharply with the intensity of the recollection of the scene that even now still troubled his sleep from time to time.

Behind the clippings were pages on which she had written her analysis of the weaknesses in the prosecutor's case. Not surprisingly the first flaw she noted was Isaiah's own testimony as contrasted with that of the prosecution's witnesses, one a clearly perjured individual, the other a former slave who no doubt, she suggested, had been either bribed or coerced to offer his testimony. Isaiah took a deep breath. Somehow his grandmother had hit upon the nerve that he had been trying to sedate all these years, his testimony, which he, and only he at this point, knew to have walked a very carefully drawn line between absolute truth and falsehood.

That line crept into his dreams, sometimes appearing thick black clearly separating fact from fiction, and in his dream he would place one foot ever so carefully on the line, then the other foot, striving all the while to keep his balance, for on one side he would tumble into the truth that would send his father into grave danger while falling the other way would place himself in conflict with himself. At other times, the line would blur into an indistinct gray, narrowing as it did until it seemed to disappear, and he could then not walk another step but stop where he was, afraid to move.

In short, in spite of his grandmother's emphasis on the relative value of his testimony versus that of the other side's witnesses, he knew that pursuing that line of inquiry in an attempt to make a case that would succeed in freeing his father would cost him dearly.

Yet, he also knew that he had to do it.

It was Saturday afternoon, and after a half day of laboring in the orchard Sam trudged with the others through the yard that led to the dining hall. Ahead of him, prisoners from the other work stations snaked toward the entrance to the hall. He glanced to his left and saw the mound and the bases of the crude baseball diamond.

"Hey boss," he said to a guard walking a few feet ahead of him. "When do we get to play?"

"You interested?"

"Sure thing. I used to pitch."

"I know why you're here. Thought you liked to play other games."

Sam stiffened.

"I played baseball," he said.

The guard shrugged and pulled his arms across his chest against a chill wind.

"Won't be too many more opportunities," he said.

Sam picked up his tray, which held a bowl of ambiguous, steaming soup and two pieces of bread between which was some kind of indeterminate meat. Although they marched in like soldiers on parade, the prisoners were free to sit where they liked. Sam surveyed the hall. He was still unaccustomed, after his long time in solitary, to feeling comfortable in the mass social situation that meal time confronted him with. The guard's comment reminded him that the notoriety his conviction brought him most likely had spread among the other prisoners, and as hardened as they might well be from their own misdeeds, he was uncertain how they would react to the opportunity to be breaking their miserable bread with a man convicted of murdering a pregnant woman, and of course her unborn baby, especially when that man came from a privileged background that by itself would set him apart from the general run of inmates.

With all this in mind, he sought a place at a table that if not entirely empty was at least not mostly filled so he would not be forced into the position of placing himself next to someone who would not be happy sharing space with him. Each table offered eight places, four on each side, and he spotted one toward the rear of the hall at which sat only two other men, apparently buddies because they appeared to be in animated conversation with each other. On the wall behind the table was a door, which he had never seen opened. He did not know what it gave to, but figured it would surely be locked. He weighed the possibility that those at that distant table would be so involved in their own conversation that they would pay little, if any, attention to him against the other possibility that they would not welcome his intrusion.

His body still ached from the unaccustomed labor, his stomach demanded to be satisfied, and his patience, never his strong point, was threatening to snap him into a mood that could only bring him grief, so he made his way through the hall, trying to not pay any attention to the stares he sensed of those he passed, ignoring the buzz of conversation, which in his overwrought imagination he perceived to stop and redirect toward him, picking up his pace as his level of discomfort increased, arriving finally at that sparsely populated table with his hands gripping the tray so hard that its edges cut into his flesh, and with his forehead beaded with perspiration.

He sat keeping his eyes focused on the food on his tray as though afraid that it might somehow escape from him if he didn't keep looking at it. For a few seconds, the low pitched conversation he had heard as he neared the table continued, and then it stopped. He waited for the assault.

It didn't come.

Instead a vaguely familiar, but clearly friendly voice, greeted him.

"So you came all this way to join us? Or were you looking to be alone?"

His mind raced trying to identify the voice, which he knew he had heard before and recently at that. He looked up from his food and forced himself to look across the table. There he found Pete sitting next to a man whose bald head seemed to catch rather than reflect the light coming in through a window next to the door.

"Just looking for a place to sit down," he replied.

"Well, glad you found us. I've been thinking about how I need to let you in on that idea I mentioned before, you being in my cell, you're going to feel the heat no matter how it works out."

"What idea is that?" Sam asked.

"All in due time," Pete replied. "This here is Ralph. Almost as famous as you, seeing as he is here dining with us at the pleasure of the state for assaulting a deputy whose wife, well that's a long story that maybe Ralph will fill you in on some time, but I don't think so, he's not all that talkative."

"Suits me," Sam said.

Ralph, who had not yet looked in his direction, now did so, and nodded with an exaggeratedly slow motion.

"I left him worse than he left me," Ralph said. As he spoke the absence of his two front teeth became apparent. "That's all I can say about that."

Pete picked up his spoon and dipped it into his bowl of soup. Ralph took a bite of his sandwich. After a few seconds Pete looked across the table at Sam and pointed toward the untouched food on Sam's tray.

Sam tried the soup. It was slightly salty, but otherwise offered no clue as to its ingredients. After a couple of spoonfuls he switched to the sandwich. The bread was slightly stale, its crust hard, and the meat it contained tasteless.

"I expect you've eaten this miserable excuse for food before," Pete said through a mouthful of sandwich.

"I have," Sam replied."

"Yes, well," Pete said, "dining with friends serves to enhance the experience, don't you think? So much so that maybe you might begin to think that something ought to be done about this rot." He pushed his tray away from him. "If I had my old dog here, I don't think I'd feed him this. He'd turn his nose up at it."

"We gotta eat," Sam said.

"We do."

Pete stood up, and Sam realized that slowly the hall became mostly quiet although scattered conversations continued for a while, until they, too, ceased. Pete raised his left hand, and with his right lifted his tray. With one motion he hurled it into the air. Sam's eyes followed its flight until it started to dip toward a table some forty or fifty feet away. Before it could land, however, another tray launched from a nearby table crashed into it, and then both fell to the floor. At the same time, first one, then another, and another of the inmates began a loud chant, raucous sounds more than actual words, although he thought he could make out a word here and there in the general uproar that seemed to threaten to shake the exposed beams that ran from one side of the hall to the other beneath the sloping ceiling.

"What are you waiting for?" Pete growled. "I told you something was in the works and now you're in it just like the rest of us."

Sam did a quick calculation, remembering the shape Pete was in when he returned from the punishment cell, but at the same time he felt Ralph's hard glare burning into his flesh.

He picked up his tray and aimed for the table far across the hall. As long as he was going to be in it, he decided, he might see if he could make an impact. He watched as his tray sailed toward his target. Before it could land, an inmate stood up and using his tray as though it were a bat, swung and hit Sam's tray. A cheer went up in the room, and others joined in, some pitching, some batting, the sound of tin trays crashing against each other reaching a high pitched crescendo, beneath which rumbled the various voices of the men throughout the vocal range from a deep bass here to a baritone there, and reaching through alto to tenor with at the top a falsetto soprano. When there were no more trays to throw, those who had retained their silverware began tapping rhythms of their own making on the table tops.

Sam watched and listened, waiting, as he knew they must, for the guards to put a stop to this ruckus. Apparently, they were in no hurry. After a little while, the different rhythms began to coalesce into one pulsating beat, and some of the men began to move as though dancing to the music of the pounding forks and spoons.

Out of the corner of his eyes, Sam saw the imposing figure of a giant sized guard, swinging his baton in front of him as he walked into the hall, followed by a line of his fellows, all of them brandishing their batons. The lead guard reached the first table and brought his baton down on the back of the head of a prisoner. Others at that table charged at the guard, but he swatted them away as though they were so many buzzing flies.

A silence fell through the hall. The inmates' eyes were now on the guards, and for a moment Sam thought they might charge. But the huge guard pulled out his revolver and fired a shot into the ceiling. The other guards drew their weapons.

No words were spoken.

But the men began to sit back down at their tables. As Sam reached behind him to grab his seat back, he heard a loud click and then felt a whoosh of outside air. He turned just in time to see two guards enter. One seized Pete, the other Ralph. Neither struggled nor objected.

"Took you long enough to get here," Pete muttered.

"We weren't in any particular hurry," the guard holding Pete replied. "Hey, you," he continued, looking toward Sam. "We know who you are and we'll be back to get you later. The warden wants these two first."

"It didn't take you long to find trouble," the warden said.

"I wasn't looking for any," Sam said.

"You were sitting with Pete Morgan."

"That was an accident. I was looking to be alone."

"Alone? Is that a joke? In a dining room with hundreds of other inmates?"

"I didn't say what I wanted was possible. Just that I wasn't looking for company. Pete happened to be at a table with one other. That's what I saw from across the hall when I came in, two guys, so I headed that way. When I got close I saw who it was. But you did put me together with him in my cell."

"Hmm. An empty bed. We gave you an empty bed. At the time, Morgan was otherwise occupied."

"So I noticed."

"If you did, you would have realized he was trouble." The warden leaned over his desk toward Sam. "I suppose you're going to tell me you didn't know the other fellow at the table."

"Right."

"Ralph, let me see," the warden looked down at a paper on his desk, "yes, Ralph Flowers. Name doesn't fit him, no, not at all."

"Fellow sitting next to Pete was introduced to me as Ralph. No last name."

"I heard he doesn't like to be called by it."

"Look," Sam said, "what is this all about?"

"Whether to charge you with inciting a riot," the warden replied.

"And if I was to be charged, what would that mean? Increase my life sentence?"

The warden pointed to a large pile of papers being held in place by an ornate weight in the shape of a black bear.

"It would influence how I think about what's in those papers from your last parole hearing. What you don't know is that even though you were turned down, at least one person thought you should be given another shot next year, seems he thought that even though you were not very convincing about your remorse, your case might be," he fingered through the papers and pulled one out, "yes here it is, might be more complicated. Whatever that means. Now, I can recommend another hearing, even sooner than a year, or I can stash this report, with that suggestion in the deepest corner of a special storage issue I've got for dead issues."

A sense of sheer exhaustion pressed down on Sam as though a physical force were pushing on his shoulders causing his legs, usually so sturdy, to feel as though they would not support him a moment longer. It was as if the burden of all he had been through, the tangled web of his affair, the none too subtle efforts of his father to end it, the girl's insistence that they be married, his son's competition, the pregnancy, the laudanum, his coming to next to the dead body, then the trial, the community's clear and apparent hostility leading to his conviction, the months of solitary with nothing but the dank walls of his cell for company, and now this just as life had seemed a little bit brighter, some time out in the sun, some exercise of his attenuated muscles, even the sight of the crude baseball diamond in the yard, all of this culminating in a riot that he had no part in starting but into which he had joined, he supposed, as the result of an explosion of his frustration.

"What is it you would have me do?" he asked, his voice now lacking any semblance of his usual jaunty self-confidence. "You put me in with this fellow. Why not just move him, or me?"

"Oh, no, that is not the point at all. You are now useful to me. And if you prove your worth," he pointed again to the papers, "I might be encouraged to look at those with, let's say, a different, more friendly perspective, might even pass along a recommendation to the governor." He leaned back in his chair. "Simple carrot and the stick," he said with a chilling smile. "You choose."

"Put me back in with him, then. He's nothing to me."

"As far as that goes, neither of you are really anything to me. What is important to me is that this prison runs smoothly. Now, for you to be credible, you will need to be punished, visibly punished so that when you again share space with him, you will both see the other as co-conspirators, both victims of this prison's harsh punishment."

Through the fog of his emotional exhaustion, Sam understood. "I see," he said.

"I thought you would."

"But there is one more thing."

"How will you let us know if you hear something being planned? Right?"

"Exactly. I felt eyes on me when I was brought here to talk to you. These guys, well you know what I'm talking about."

"I do. That is why we're going to send you back with some evidence that you were uncooperative. Don't worry," the warden said with a smile, "we won't hurt you too bad."

"Thanks. But you haven't answered my question."

"We'll figure something out. Or you will. Now, we're done."

The beating was not too bad, Sam thought, as he lay once again on his cot in the cell, no worse than some he had experienced after a drunken disagreement, or a game in which some of his pitches had come suspiciously close to hitting the best hitter on the opposing team. He ran his fingers over the area over his right eye, and felt the swelling. He had no mirror to check himself out, but he was sure that if he had one, the skin he was now touching would be a deep purple. He tried to suck in the air and his ribs complained. He wouldn't have to fake having difficulty moving around, or even breathing. He was also reasonably certain that the next time he relieved himself his urine might well be tinged with his blood. All in all he felt he would pass inspection.

"You say it was a riot? In the dining room?" The governor's voice carried a mixture equal parts, surprise, anger, but most, weary irritation.

"Yes," Larry Morgan replied in as neutral tone as he could manage as he tried to read both the governor's voice and facial expression. This was Larry's second day working directly for the governor, and he did not want to misstep.

"Is that all you can tell me?" the governor insisted, and Larry felt the displeasure in Woodhouse's tone. "What about? Who started it? Come on man. I was told you were ready to step into McGinnis's shoes for a week or so. Should I call him back from Calumet? Or get somebody else to tell me what is going on at the prison?"

"No, sir," Larry held his voice firm. A recent law school graduate, he was accustomed to being browbeaten by his professors. "What we know is that the riot started in the dining hall without any obviously particular spark. More like a planned demonstration. If it was about anything particular it would be about the quality, or lack thereof, of the food. Been complaints about that before." He paused, wondering whether he should move into speculation. "But it seems to me that was just an excuse."

"Excuse?"

"To foment trouble. As to who started it. They've been identified...."

"And?"

"Taken care of, with appropriate measures, according to the warden, so as to make sure it doesn't happen again."

"Appropriate measures, I'm sure. I have a good mind what those were, so don't bother giving me any details, if you have any." He took off his glasses and rubbed his eyes very slowly. When he replaced his glasses, his blue eyes were steely.

"It's no wonder," is all he said.

And Larry, now in tune with his boss, was sure he understood.

"No, sir. You can't wonder why they might rise up."

Larry waited for his boss to respond, but the governor sat staring out of his window at the bare branches of an old maple tree. After a few seconds, with his eyes still on the tree, he waved his hand in a motion that carried the full extent of his weariness. Larry nodded, turned, and walked out of the office, closing the door gently behind him.

At his desk the governor drummed his fingers onto its polished surface. An interesting question for an ethics professor, he thought, seeking the proper path between the contending forces of admittedly flawed men now incarcerated for their crimes, major and minor, and the state's brutal dehumanizing of them. Where, he wondered, was the common humanity they surely must share, and how was he to help them find it?

A knock at his closed door interrupted his thoughts, and he remembered that he had made an appointment for this afternoon.

"Come on in," he called out.

Drummond pushed the door open and strolled in.

"Thomas," the governor said. "Back from up north?"

"Yes."

"Any luck?"

"Not much. The young man, which I can understand, did not want to talk to me. I caught him coming out of the church after the service for the dead girl's father."

"Certainly unfortunate timing," Woodhouse said.

"Don't think it would matter where I met him. You know I covered the trial, and he was put in an impossible position, and then to see his father convicted."

"I want you to continue seeing what you can find out. His grandmother has been importunate. And I'd like to be sure we've done due diligence in this matter."

"Due diligence? Is that all?"

"Of course, there's always something else," the governor said. "We've got the riot in the prison, the strike in Calumet, none of it is good. It doesn't seem like I can do much about those, I've already intervened in the prison procedures as far as I can, and as for the strike, I am contending with seemingly intractable issues. But Mr. Logan..."

"Is one man," Drummond said.

"Who might deserve a second look."

"I'll see what I can do." Drummond stroked his mustache. "But some do say, you are too soft on those miscreants locked up for good reason in Jackson."

"Those miscreants happen to still be human beings."

Pete prepared to relieve himself in the bucket he and Sam shared. But first he leaned over and placed his nose right above the bucket. He stood up and nodded.

"I see a little red in there."

Sam shrugged .

"I've had worse times in a bar. Or in the bedroom of a woman whose man took exception to my being there."

Pete's urine splashed into the bucket. He turned to face Sam.

"Ralph was wondering about the talk you had with the warden. You see, me and him didn't have a chat, we were just taken to the punishment cell."

"No beating?"

"Back on that damned chair, like I told you before, and I tell you I'd rather feel their fists like you did, and so I see Ralph afterwards, and he asks after you, and I say I don't know nothing about what happened to you, then I come back here and see they touched you up a bit, so, yeah, I imagine you've had worse in your life."

"I don't know why I got the beating, and you and Ralph got worse, maybe because you and he have come to his attention before. Anyway, he wanted to know what I knew about why the riot got started and I said I didn't really know, I just got swept up in the moment, but if I had to guess, I'd say it had something to do with the quality of the slop you expect us to live on, and if you really want to know what I'm talking about, come join us for a meal."

Sam studied Pete's as he listened to this account. Pete's expression did not change. It did not communicate acceptance or skepticism. Oh, you are good, Sam thought, I might just as well be talking to that wall behind you as far as knowing whether you are buying any of this.

Pete placed his hands on Sam's upper arms and squeezed.

"Well, buddy," he said, "that all may be what happened. I have no reason to doubt it. But I don't have much reason to believe you either. What you should know is that if you struck any kind of deal with the boss man about keeping him informed about any plans you might hear, well, what happens to someone in that position is not a pretty picture. Got me? You're, how should I say, kind of on trial, with me and Ralph judge and jury."

"Got you," Sam said rising from his cot and pushing against Pete's hold on his shoulders.

"And what you should know," he said, "is that I don't take kindly to threats. From you, Ralph, or anybody else."

"Easy boy," Pete said.

"Then easy it is," Sam replied.

CHAPTER FIVE

"This is private property," the man said, sweeping his hand around them as though to indicate a circle at whose center they were standing. Then he pointed to a narrow road, more a footpath, that entered this imagined circle, crossed it, and then exited on the other side. "You understand my point?"

Edward nodded. He knew about boundaries, remembering the fence he was installing on the line between her farm and his that fateful day years ago. That fence was a physical barrier that delineated a geographical border not only between the two farms but one that defined the limits of freedom to move while she could travel into the neighboring property with impunity, there to meet him, her lover.

She could do that, but all he could do was lie on the plank floor of his bedroom, the floor that was also the ceiling of her room, the floor whose ill-fitting planks offered him an occasional glimpse of her, and up through which floated the soft sound of her breathing. As close as she was to him every night, he could not approach her unless she asked.

In a larger sense, his whole life transpired in a circumscribed existence based on his place in the social hierarchy. He was a farm worker. He owned no more than two sets of clothes, one to be worn, the other to be put on when the first needed laundering. On his day off, he spent what little pay he earned on beer or even an occasional woman when he had sufficient discipline to save for that extravagance, and then he would return to work as poor as when he started the previous week. Although he had enough schooling to enable him to read, he owned no books, nor did he care to purchase a newspaper, or pay the few cents to experience the new moving pictures being offered in town. Without any stimulation from sources outside himself, he was limited to his own thoughts, and those thoughts led him to a gnawing feeling of the emptiness of his life, one that divided unevenly between work and the small pleasures of his limited leisure time. Left to live within the world created in his mind, he fell into unhealthy obsessions such as the double-edged one that feature the young woman on the one hand and on the other her privileged lover who could have her as easily as he could buy a glass of beer.

In his darker moments, he even found himself envious of other workers whose position in life was not materially better than his. Even in his last place of employment, the one so prominent in his present memory, he looked with some degree of envy at Jim, never mind that Jim's black skin, bore the scars on his back from more than one undeserved whipping, and yet from Edward's jaundiced perspective, one fully informed by a kind of self-loathing, Jim enjoyed a moment in the sun that Edward could never imagine experiencing himself. At the trial, he was made to look the fool as he attempted to use his potential as a witness to his advantage. Why not, he had thought at the time, make himself available to the highest bidder and tailor his testimony to fit yet another boss's expectations. But that strategy crashed when that smart mouthed lawyer had him on the witness stand, and he was not quick witted enough to talk his way out of the confusion of his statements that fully discredited any testimony he might seek to offer. It would have been better if Sam's crusty old father had shelled out the money that would have enabled him to seek a better life somewhere far away. But no, the old man apparently saw that investing in Edward would be too risky, and Edward, privately, had to agree that the old man was correct.

Then with his own testimony savaged, and he left on the sidelines as the trial edged toward its climax, who but Jim, the black ex-slave takes the spotlight and nails the prosecutor's case against Sam. Never mind that in his own self-interest Jim had fled before Sam was even apprehended. Edward had to admit that the nigger was smarter than you would have expected. So, Jim was the hero of this story, while Edward had to skulk away in disgrace, only to botch an attempted train robbery in which his accomplice, the supposed master mind, but just another man telling Edward what to do, had been caught and was now in the same prison that housed Sam. For that, at least, Edward was grateful.

Since he was born, his life had been dominated by men telling him what to do, first his alcoholic father, then his grandfather when his father disappeared, and after that a seeming endless succession of men in positions of power, at the end of which line came Jablonski, who had now sent him to one more boss, the foreman of this copper mine.

And so as he stood outside the copper mine listening to the foreman, he waited patiently to hear what it was he was to do now.

"You do understand, don't you?" the foreman repeated.

"You're showing me that the mining company owns this whole area. Right?"

"Yes. And that path?" he pointed to the ribbon of dirt.

Edward nodded.

"You understand, then, the path is crossing private property, our property, and whoever walks on that path across our property without our permission, why that person is trespassing."

"Sure I know about trespassing. In my last job I was digging fence posts on a property line."

"Well, we don't have fence posts, but we do have these." He reached into the pockets of his coat, one hand in on each side and slowly withdrew them. In his hands were two snub nosed revolvers. "These will do just as well as a fence. To keep trespassers out. Mr. Jablonski sent you to me to help me do just that. And he wanted me to give you one of these. Said you had earned the chance to learn how to use one."

He handed one of the guns to Edward.

"You going to show me?"

"Sure." He broke the revolver and spun the cylinders slowly. "See the bullets, one in each place."

"I see," Edward replied.

"Six bullets." He snapped the gun closed. "Now to fire, you pull back the hammer until it is cocked, meaning it won't move if you release it. Then you aim, and pull the trigger." He handed the gun to Edward. "You take it and try cocking the hammer."

Edward took the gun, but the foreman shoved it to the side.

"You were aiming that thing at me. You gotta be more careful. Now point it away from me or anybody or thing you don't want to hit and pull the hammer back."

Edward started to push the hammer back, but the foreman's hand stopped him.

"Get your finger off the trigger until the hammer is cocked and you're aiming at somebody or something you might want to shoot."

Just then another man hurried up to the foreman's side and whispered in his ear. The foreman nodded.

"I've got a problem inside I've got to deal with. Some damned fool's got himself trapped under a cart." Put that gun in your pocket until I get back. In the meantime, keep your eyes on that path, and if you see anyone coming, you get me." He pointed to the mine entrance. "Someone just inside will find me."

It was a cloudy evening, the sun just beginning to drop behind the hill that rose above the mine opening. Edward slid the gun into his pocket and sat down on a large boulder on a rise, giving him a clear view of the path. He kept his hand on the gun, enjoying its hardness, wondering when he would get a chance to use it. After a while, he felt the need to stretch, so he got up off the boulder and walked a few steps in one direction and then another, never taking his eyes off the path for more than a few seconds. A long life of taking orders had taught him the importance of obedience, even when the orders were difficult, wearisome, insulting, or meaningless. In this case, he understood the principle, namely that this was the private property of the mining company and the foreman seemed to want to make sure nobody crossed it without permission. That made sense, just like all the fences he had helped install. In fact, one of his fondest wishes was to own a piece of property, however small, around which he could place a fence to announce to the world that he was an individual of some substance.

Even though a slight evening breeze carried cooling air, his hand around the gun sweated against the metal of the weapon as though it was generating its own heat. He took his hand out of his pocket and wiped the perspiration off against his pants leg, and then shoved his hand back into his pocket, desiring again to feel the comfort of its hardness. Just as he sat back down on the boulder, he thought he saw movement coming toward him on the path. He strained his eyes. For a few seconds, he saw nothing. Then, more distinctly, something dark emerged out of the shadowy dusk darkness. Whatever it was appeared to stop. Then it took off into low brush on the side of the path. Edward took a breath and relaxed. Some damned animal, he thought, maybe a deer or even a wolf or bear, he had heard that such creatures prowled throughout this area. But now with his gun in his pocket, he was unafraid.

He searched his pockets with his free hand for his last ciga-rette, brought it to his lips, and then found a wooden match. Still using just the one hand not occupied holding the gun, he flicked the head of the match with his nail, got it to light, and brought it to the tip of his cigarette. He inhaled and held the smoke in his lungs. He felt almost content. He was being given a measure of freedom of responsibility he had rarely experienced.

As his cigarette burned down, he again saw something approaching on the path. This time, the clouds that had been blocking the declining sun moved on and the path was now sufficiently illuminated to enable him to clearly see that the something approaching was a couple of men. His hand on the gun tightened just a little, and he rose from the boulder. For a moment, his indecision froze him. His impulse was to draw the gun and confront these trespassers on the mine's property. Although he could not so express it, he felt as though the prop-erty he had been charged with protecting was his own, and anger welled up in him at the presumption of anyone to disregard the boundary within which he stood guard. But his ingrained train-ing of always doing what he was told to do, so as to stay in the good graces of the man whose favor was necessary for preserving his well-being, counteracted that first impulse. His hand on the butt of the revolver relaxed, and with one more glance at the approaching men he trotted toward the mine entrance.

A few feet inside the entrance, he encountered the foreman as he emerged from the depths of the mine.

"Men," Edward said just a little breathlessly. "Two of them. Coming along the path. I come to tell you like you said I should."

The foreman nodded, and waved his arm, summoning forth another man from the shadows. He was thin and his gray hair seemed to shine in the dying sunlight.

"Let's at'em," the foreman said, "this is what we've been waiting for, to teach them a lesson they will remember and take back to their pals."

Edward took a step forward, but then his natural inclination to be led paused him. The foreman glanced at him, shrugged, and then strode down the slight decline leading to the path. The second man fell in behind the foreman, and Edward, now comfortable in his usual position, followed, his hand beginning to sweat around the gun in his hand.

The two men continued toward them. When they were close enough to make out the features of the foreman, one of them stepped forward. The two groups advanced toward each other until they were no more than ten feet apart.

"Hi, there, Jack," the one of the two who had taken the lead called out. "Pleasant night."

The foreman held out his hands, palms out, as though he would by the force of his will shove the two men back.

"Jack, is it," he said. "When you're up there," he pointed toward the mine entrance, "It's 'boss' Jack, ain't it Billy?"

"But we ain't in the mine," Billy said, "as you very well know."

"The more your problem," Jack replied. "Because you're trespassing on the mine company's property. So just turn around."

The second man now stepped up to stand beside his companion.

"You know everyone uses this path, have been doing so for years. We're just heading home, like we always do."

"Today ain't like it used to be, Ben Jenkins, when you two were working."

"We still got to get home," Ben said, and took a step forward.

Edward had experienced enough instances of men pawing the ground like two bulls about to lock horns to know where this interaction was heading. He tensed, waiting for the signal to jump in. He studied the two walkers. The one called Billy was short and squat with a barrel chest and broad shoulders. He would be a tough one in a fight. And the other, the one called Ben, was taller, but just as wide. On the other hand, Jack was thin, maybe wiry, but not much of match for either of the miners and the gray haired man, well, he looked as old as his hair suggested. Still, Edward was ready, as usual, to depend on his hard fists. They had rarely failed him. And now in his pocket he had an equalizer.

"You're gonna have to find another way home," Jack said.

Later, Edward could only shake his head at how fast the verbal back and forth exploded into action. In a blur of movement, Billy hurled himself into Jack, knocking the foreman back and onto the ground. Ben shouldered the old man aside as though he were no more an impediment than a leaf before a gust of wind. With both Jack and the old man on the ground, Edward stood before the two miners.

"This isn't your fight," Ben said. "Just step aside."

For answer, Edward, foregoing the revolver in his pocket, removed his hand, and swung hard at Ben's face. Ben had just enough reaction time to lift his shoulder so that Edward's fist glanced off it and landed high on the side of the head.

Billy stepped forward and before Edward could gather himself again, Billy hit him hard in the belly. Edward bent over, and Billy brought his knee up into Edward's jaw, sending him sprawling on the ground right next to Jack and the gray haired man.

"Told you," Ben said, while he straddled Edward. "This is none of your concern. Just stay down."

Edward started to rise, but Jack's hand grabbed his arm.

"Wait," Jack said in a low voice. "Our turn will come soon enough."

Ben and Billy glanced at each other, turned and headed onto the path at a comfortable pace. When they were a hundred yards away, Jack released his grip on Edward's arm.

"Now, get up. Still have that gun?"

Edward reached into his pocket, felt the hard steel, and nodded.

"Good," Jack said. "You'll get a chance to see if you know how to use it."

Jack got up, reached down for old man to grab his hand and helped him back on his feet.

"This here is Mike, Mike Norris. Don't let his gray hair fool you. He's a tough old bird."

The three of them started in the same direction as the two miners, but not fast enough to overtake them. Every once in a while, one or the other of the miners looked back over his shoulder, but they did not move any faster. It was like a silent movie playing out toward an unknown conclusion.

"I know where they're going, to that boarding house in See-berville. We'll take them there. So the others there can see what we're doing."

It was just at sunset when the boarding house on the edge of the town loomed in the dying light.

"Now," Jack said, "let's catch up to them."

They increased their pace and then broke into a trot. As they entered the street where the boardinghouse stood on the corner, they found the two miners standing in front of the building. A boy of about six or seven was playing with a hoop a little way up the street. A woman came out of a doorway where she had been talking to someone inside a small house, surveyed the unfolding scene, and hurried to scoop up the boy and pull him away. The boy, whose attention had turned in the direction where his mother was looking, dug in his heels. She snatched his hoop with her free hand, and with the other around his thin arm, dragged him away into the shadows.

Jack walked up to the two miners.

"You boys need to come with us," he said.

"I don't think so," Ben said, and Billy nodded. "If you want to try the case again, we can give you more of what we did back in front of the mine."

Jack reached out to grab Ben's arm, and the two men strained against each other. Ben pulled himself free, and started to walk toward the entrance to the boarding house. Another man opened the front door.

"Trouble?" he called out.

"Not much," Billy said, "only a misunderstanding."

Jack pulled out his gun.

"Only thing you two don't understand is that you've got to come with us to answer for trespassing on the mining company's property."

"On whose authority?" the man at the front door asked.

"Why, I guess I forgot to tell you back there on the path," Jack answered, "I've been deputized by the sheriff." He pointed to Edward and Mike. "These two answer to me and I've made them deputies as well."

Billy and Ben began to walk toward the entrance.

"Halt!" Jack yelled. "Boys," he said to Edward and Mike, "take out your guns."

Edward pulled his gun out of his pocket. He tried to remember what he was supposed to do to fire, but his mind blanked. Another man appeared in the doorway and stepped out of the house. As he did his arm swung in a hurling motion. In the half light, Edward was not sure what object was coming at him, but whatever it was, he threw his arm up over his head and ducked. He felt something whiz by his shoulder and then heard it thud into the ground.

"What the..." Jack began. Edward straightened up and turned around in time to see Jack pick the object up. "A bowling pin, I'll be damned," Jack said. He tossed it in a gentle arc back toward the house. It landed between the feet of the Ben and Billy. They stared at it as though it were some sort of alien creature, then trotted through the front door. The man who tossed the pin had also disappeared into the house. The one who had been standing in front of the door was still there.

Edward heard a shot ring out from his side where Jack stood with his revolver pointed at that man. A wisp of smoke rose from the muzzle of the gun. The man clutched at his belly and crumbled to the ground. Hands reached out from inside the house and pulled him into it. The door slammed. More shots rang out from Jack and Mike's guns. The slugs thumped into the closed door raising a small cloud of splintered wood. Light shone through several windows. Jack seized Edward's shoulder.

"What do you think I gave you that gun for? They're going to try to kill us. They no doubt have their own guns in the house. Shoot at those windows where the lights are on."

Edward raised his gun, aimed it at one of the windows, pulled the trigger. Nothing happened. For a moment, he stood there perplexed as Jack and Mike shot at the windows, hitting a couple but most of their bullets landing on the siding of the house. Edward remembered. He cocked the hammer, aimed, and pulled the trigger. As the hammer came down on the cylinder, his hand jerked, and his shot went skyward.

The lights in the house now went out. Edward crouched, unsure whether he should try to shoot again, and if so, at what target. Jack and Mike had stopped firing, and were pulling the shells out of the cylinders of their gun. The shells plunked with a soft whisper onto the ground at their feet. That sound was followed by the metallic click of new rounds being shoved in, and then the louder snap of the cylinders being snapped back into place.

Still crouching and listening, Edward tried to remember if any shots had been fired at them from the house. He was not sure. He could remember the bowling pin hurtling toward them, but in all the sounds of gunfire, especially his own, which still resounded in his ears, he had no recollection of returned fire. But as was his wont, he was sure that Jack, the man in charge, knew what he was talking about. Then like an unwelcome guest, the image of the man at the doorway collapsing onto the ground cycled into his mind, the man standing, the sound of the shot, the man clutching his belly, the man falling. He felt Jack's strong hand again on his shoulder.

"We're going in," he said. "Come along. With your gun."

"Me?" Edward said again.

"The governor sent the guard up here precisely to avoid this kind of thing," Fred McGinnis said.

Across from him, his face wearing an expression of settled confidence, Sheriff Henry Cooper shrugged. He was a large man gone to beef, and even this non-confrontational movement of his shoulders seemed to carry an implicit threat that behind that expression was someone well used to getting things done his way.

"No offense to the governor," Cooper said, "but he's hundreds of miles away and I am here with a situation on my hands, getting more and more dangerous every day."

"So that's the reason for deputizing all those men?

"Sure. The guard has not been doing much, probably because there isn't much they can do unless a full riot were to break out. But the situation here is a bit more subtle, but no less explosive for all that."

"And arming these deputies? Was that necessary as well?"

"Rumors were that the strikers were arming themselves. Many of them already have guns, use them to hunt."

"Rumors," McGinnis said. "Guns in the hands of your deputies. One man shot dead. A little girl who was sleeping in her bed, now with a bullet in her head. The whole boarding house shot up to hell. And for what?"

"Those men resisted," Cooper replied.

"Their offense?"

"Trespassing on mine company property."

"On their way home."

"Trespassing," Cooper repeated. "And disobeying lawful authority.'"

"Lawful," McGinnis said with a shake of his head. Just how, he wondered, would he present this latest development to the governor.

As if reading his mind, Cooper reached his large hand to McGinnis's shoulder and gave it what was meant to be a comforting squeeze.

"No problems here we can't manage. I hear we already have a man set up to take the heat, whatever heat there is. Just tell the governor everything is under control."

McGinnis shook his shoulder free.

"He's not going to be happy," he said. "He wants this thing settled before the next election. Settled without any more dead bodies."

"No more dead bodies," Cooper echoed. "But," he muttered

under his breath, "not saying anything about bruises or broken bones."

"What?" McGinnis demanded.

"Just saying to remind myself, seeing as I can be forgetful, saying it plants it in my head, 'No more dead bodies,' just like you said.'"

As Edward prepared for bed, he wondered where he should put his gun. He thought he might sleep with it in his pocket, but then it occurred to him that he might roll over on top of it and shoot himself. But if he left it out where it could be seen by somebody coming into his room, that would raise questions, for which he had no answers. He realized that word of the shooting at the boardinghouse no doubt had spread. What would he say if he were asked what he thought about that? Especially if they saw he had a gun?

He lay on his back under the thin cotton blanket, his right hand holding the gun pointed toward the wall on the side of his bed. He had thought about unloading it, but he had forgotten how to break open the cylinder. He knew that if he looked at it for a while he would remember but he was afraid to keep the gun visible for any length of time. At any moment, one of the other boarders, or the landlady, or her daughter who did the cleaning, might come through the door, and then what would he say? From outside the closed door to his room, the voices of the other boarders filtered in, along with the sound of door knobs clicking open and shut. No, it was better to keep the gun safely out of sight until he figured what he would do with it, and when it would be safe to do it.

Now, lying in bed, still fully dressed, the hard metal of the gun still felt good in his hand, still gave him a sense of empowerment, still permitted him to think of himself as somebody with a degree of status. All this, the gun gave him. But along with those positive feelings came the memory of both his botched attempt to shoot, and even more powerfully, the recalled image of the man at the front of the building crumbling with a fatal bullet in his belly, and then, inside the boardinghouse as under Jack's instructions they searched for weapons they never found, recalling what they did find, a woman cradling her daughter's head in her lap, blood oozing from the wound above her left ear, in her hands a raggedy cloth doll, also stained with her blood. Never a sentimental man, too self-centered ever to feel much empathy for another human being, this scene hit him in the gut with unanticipated force. Perhaps it was the memory of his own sister dying in their mother's arms from pleurisy, the pain etched in the very fabric of his mother's face beneath the tightly repressed bun of her hair, a woman who years of abuse from her alcoholic husband had encased her emotions beneath a steely stoicism which now had tears running down her cheeks, her thin, hard lips quivering from a grief beyond expression. It must have been some such intrusion from his long ago past that now caused Edward to squirm on his thin mattress while his hand remained clasped tightly around the gun.

In the morning, before he was fully awake, there was a loud knock on the door. He got up, tucked the gun into his belt, and pulled his shirt out to cover it. When he opened the door, he found himself confronting the large body of Sheriff Cooper. With a smile, Cooper reached his hand to the bulge under Edward's shirt and pulled out the gun.

"We'll need to take a look at this, and then we'll want to talk to you."

CHAPTER SIX

"I don't think we've ever met," the burly man sitting across from Isaiah in the dining room of the Park Hotel said. He extended his hand across the table. "Benson," the man said, "Wendell Benson. I work with...."

"My father's attorney, Mr. Lowe," Isaiah said. "My grandmother gave me Mr. Lowe's address in Chicago."

Benson nodded.

"Yes, your grandmother got in touch with my boss after your grandfather died."

"My grandfather refused to spend any more money," Isaiah said, allowing just a trace of disappointment, if not bitterness, find its way into his voice. "He wasn't going to send good money after bad, so he said, I wasn't sure whether he was talking about the money or his son. Or both. Then it took some time for my grandmother to get access to money he had tied up. He wanted me to take over the farm. I wasn't interested."

"Well, your grandmother sent Mr. Lowe a retainer then, and regular payments since, and now he has sent me to you to see what we can do."

"To get my father out of jail."

"That won't be easy, but not impossible."

Isaiah pointed to the package on the table in front of him. Just then the waitress approached. Benson held up his hand.

"What'll you have young Mr. Logan? I hear the steak here is good."

"I wouldn't know."

Benson held up two fingers.

"Make mine rare, with a little blood," he said.

"The same," Isaiah said, "but without the blood."

Benson looked hard at Isaiah with the glance of a detective who has spent his life measuring the men that life cast into his path. Maybe the young man had just revealed something of importance, something that Benson would want to use later for some advantage.

"I see," he said. "But to business. Your grandmother has bought some of my time, but we should try to spend your resources prudently."

"Then let's begin with the fellow whose testimony contradicted mine."

Isaiah had prepared for this question, and was pleased that he answered it without any hesitation, without revealing the hours tossing and turning in his bed, wrestling with the conflict between this most logical starting point in the effort to overturn his father's conviction and the hard physical fact of the note written by Margaret strongly suggesting that the support Isaiah offered for his father's alibi was more than a little suspect.

"With this nigger, what's his name, oh, yeah, Jim."

"Yes," Isaiah said. Instead of feeling relief that a weight had been lifted off of his shoulders, that weight now seemed to press down even harder. Still, he had opened this door, and he must see what the room behind it contained.

"Can you find him?" he asked.

Benson nodded.

"I'm a step ahead of you. Got a pretty good idea where he is."

"And when you do?"

"See if we can, let's see, ask him to consider a revision of his testimony, recognizing the pressure he must have been under at that time. A man like him, with suspicion going to fall on him because of the color of his skin, unfair as that it is, that's the way of our world, wouldn't he have been happy to say something, anything, that would take the suspicion off of him..."

"And place it on someone the whole town had already convicted," Isaiah completed the thought, which made perfectly good sense to him now, but one that had never occurred to him before.

On a potato field on the eastern end of Long Island in the state of New York, Jim straightened up and felt the heft of the burlap bag containing the spuds he had picked. He joined the line of his fellow workers approaching a table behind which sat a lean man with narrow shoulders stroking his beard with one hand, a pencil in the other suspended over a ledger book. To the side of the table was a mule drawn wagon on which sat a pile of potatoes. When a worker reached the table, the man reached across it to take the bag of potatoes from him. He stretched his arm out to test the heft of the bag. Sometimes he would enter a figure in the ledger, reach into a tin box to withdraw a few bills, extend them toward the worker with one hand, and give the bag back with the other and nod toward the wagon. The worker then dumped his potatoes on top of the heap, pocketed the bills and walked off with more spring in his step than when he approached the table. Occasionally, though, after holding the bag for what seemed an interminable period while the worker shuffled his feet, he would shake his head, and give the bag back and point toward the field of unharvested fruit. The worker trudged off to pick some more potatoes, his pay and his freedom not yet in his grasp.

Jim had seen this process now for several days, and as was usual with him he made sure his bag would qualify. Years of experience taught him the importance of not calling attention to himself one way or another. So, he did not want to be sent back to the field, nor did he want to create too positive impression by submitting a bag stuffed too full of product. Doing so would cause his fellow workers to look upon him as setting the bar too high for them, thus opening himself up to various subtle and not so subtle forms of retribution. He well knew that the color of his skin made him particularly vulnerable to such treatment. On the other hand, he did not want to have the boss man think that he was currying favor in a way that might lead to unwanted attention. No, he could not change his black skin to white, but otherwise he would, as best he could, blend in to the crowd of workers, all sweat stained, smelly, and hands caked with dirt from digging out the spuds beneath the hot sun.

He had been traveling from place to place, from menial job to menial job, sometimes in a field such as this, or an orchard, other times in one of the factories springing up as the country accelerated into its industrial age, once talking himself into a position as a house servant, but always in the back of his mind was the conviction that it would not be safe for him to stay in any one place for any length of time. Sooner or later, he figured, his past would come roaring up behind him, or perhaps not roaring, but slithering at him from behind a rock and wrap itself around him, hauling him back to that time years ago when his testimony sent a white man to prison. Should that happen, the secret behind that testimony would inevitably be revealed to his utter destruction. He had violated the maxim passed on to him by his mother so long ago that he should never put himself in the position to hurt a white man, even by telling the truth, for retribution would surely follow.

He sensed an unusual quiet on the line, the chatter of men getting paid and looking forward to a night of beer and women to erase the stiffness in their fingers, remove metaphorically the dirt beneath their fingers, the re-establishment of themselves as flesh and blood beings fully invested with feelings and desires rather than the humanoid harvesting machine they were for six days of the week, all of that transformation waiting for their wages to be paid.

Jim glanced around, saw eyes upon him, returned his gaze to the man behind the table, pencil still resting on the ledger, his other hand extended holding crumpled bills and some silver, a week's pay.

"You are Jim, ain't you?" the boss asked.

"Yessir."

"And you do want to get paid?"

"Yessir. I guess my mind was somewhere else."

"No doubt thinking what you're gonna do with your pay, find yourself some sweet black meat."

"Yessir, that must be what I was thinking."

Jim pocketed his money, offered a shrug to the men still waiting on the line, and walked off to return to his rented room near the railroad station where he would rest for a while, and think about where next he should go and when he should leave. He was beginning to feel, for reasons he could not explain, that the net always following him like a shadow was about to catch up at last and ensnare him.

Benson continued to work on his lunch while Isaiah pecked at his steak, leaving a good half of it on his plate.

"Not hungry?" Benson asked.

Isaiah shook his head.

The waitress ambled over and began to pick Isaiah's plate up. Benson motioned for her to slide it over to his side of the table.

"I'll have another beer," he said. "And a little later, pay attention now, when my plate and that other one, when both are empty, bring me a fat piece of apple pie, along with a steaming hot cup of black coffee."

"Will there be anything else?" the waitress asked.

She was in her twenties, a little plump. She made sure to let her leg brush against Benson's as she leaned across the table to reach Isaiah's plate. She slid the plate slowly to a position next to Benson's, leaning so that her breast pushed against his shoulder. He looked up and smiled.

"Just the pie and coffee," he said. "You?" he asked Isaiah.

"Just the coffee," Isaiah replied.

Benson finished his meal and what was left of Isaiah's, and the waitress returned with coffee for both and a slice of apple pie for Benson. The desk clerk, a short, fat man in his forties with a waddling walk like a penguin making its way across an ice floe hurried toward the table. For a moment, he and the waitress stood facing each other in the narrow space between two tables.

"Please," said the desk clerk in a high pitched voice. "Move aside."

The waitress shrugged, turned, and with an exaggerated motion of her chest held in her breath as the clerk passed by.

"This telegram just came in," the clerk said holding out a folded piece of paper as he reached Benson.

Benson laid the paper on the table.

"Will there be a reply?" the clerk asked.

Benson unfolded the paper, scanned its content.

"Yes," he said.

The clerk took out a pencil and a pad.

"You won't need to write it down. Just wire back and say I'm on my way. Just those four words. Got it?"

With seeming reluctance, the clerk nodded and put the pencil and pad back into his pocket. He waited, and Benson reached into his pocket and handed him a coin.

Benson watched the back of the clerk as he headed to his post, then turned to Isaiah.

"From one of our operatives. Looks like I'll be heading to New York."

"Do you ever..." Isaiah began to ask.

Benson permitted himself a frown that after a few seconds turned into a half-hearted smile, then phrased the question.

"Think about the man I am being paid to hunt?"

"Yes," Isaiah said. "To consider whether what you're doing..." he paused again, unwilling to give full expression to the question.

"Whether I should leave him in peace?"

"Yes."

"No," Benson said, "I don't."

Isaiah took his time walking back to Front Street. It was a pleasant, sunny day and nobody on the streets seemed in a hurry to get to a destination. He decided to take a more circuitous route that would bring him within sight of the Boardman River as it made its way toward the bay. The sight of moving water, whether in a river, or the currents in the lake, always lifted his spirits. He recalled how right after his father's trial he had answered the pull of water by signing on as a hand on a steamer very much like the one he knew Benson would be taking to Chicago. In the back of his mind was the thought that when this business of attempting to free his father, which had brought him back to the land was finished, one way or another, he would once again seek a post on some kind of boat, it didn't much matter what kind, as long as it was one that would carry him away from the land that seemed to be the root of all the misery and disappointment in his life.

For now, though the land on which he trod seemed somewhat less hostile and menacing. Perhaps it was because he was in town rather than among the orchards where he grew up on the Peninsula, and where he had fallen so deeply in love with a young woman who was so much a part of that environment. He stopped on the bridge over the river, leaning his back to the rail and watching the passersby. A young woman, probably returning to a shop from her lunch hour break, approached. By her pace, she, too, seemed not to be in much of a hurry to be back indoors. He did not want to stare at her, that would be offensive, but he could not help but notice how attractive she was, with abundant auburn hair framing a pretty face from which bright blue eyes looked back at him, acknowledging his presence. He raised his hand to his bare head and lifted his pretend hat to her as she passed, and she offered a smile in return, a smile that could be read as an invitation to introduce himself. In spite of his limited experience with women, he understood the message.

"Nice day," he said.

"Very," she replied, pausing before him.

She waited for him to continue.

"Well, I must be on my way," she said when he did not.

"Isaiah," he said to her retreating back, "my name is Isaiah."

She waved but did not stop or turn around. He watched her continue walking until she reached a corner where she turned onto a cross street. He realized that he had fallen in to his old habit of not providing his last name, a habit that began as a way of avoiding the notoriety of his father's conviction. With a start, he wondered how his half brother, Jonathan, dealt with the same issue, or more precisely how Eunice did. Was she able to shield not only herself, but her son, from the rapt attention of a small town community, the inevitable gossip, speculations, concerning how the failed marriage of this woman to the convicted murderer might have led to his downfall. A woman was supposed to provide a happy home for her hard working man. Had she not? Isaiah realized he had never seriously considered this question from her point of view.

He shut his eyes hard in an effort to cleanse his mind of these troublesome thoughts, and if he could not rid himself of them, at the least he could manage to shove them into a corner. They would out again, no doubt, but for now he again amused himself people gazing, and as he did, he permitted himself a smile at the aborted flirtation he had just had with the attractive young woman. There would be time for that, and he would be more than ready and less tongue tied when that time arrived.

He found Eunice, as usual, at her desk at the rear of the shop. "He didn't need me today," he said.

"I'm not surprised. It's the idea of that car more than actually using it, that he likes."

"Yes, well, I guess I'm sort of on a retainer, on a call when needed basis."

"He's paying you, isn't he?"

"Yes, probably more than he should."

"I wouldn't worry about that."

Isaiah turned around at the sound of the door to the shop opening. Through it with a big smile on his face walked a little boy followed by a short, stout older woman. The boy was carrying what appeared to be a school book in one hand, and a lollipop in the other.

"Jonathan, come here, there's somebody I want you to meet."

"Do you think he should?" the older woman said in a sharp tone while taking hold of the boy's arm.

"Yes," Eunice replied. "It's time Jonathan met his brother."

"Never a right time for that, if truth be told," the woman said. She released Jonathan's arm. "Go to your fool mother, never could tell her a thing, that's why...."

"Why nothing," Eunice said. "Nothing at all."

The boy looked up at his grandmother, then toward his mother, and finally with an expression of intense curiosity, at Isaiah. He took a step forward, looked back at his grandmother, and then continued.

"Jonathan, this is Isaiah," Eunice said as the boy reached her. The boy looked up, put the lollipop in his mouth, and extended his hand.

Later, that image of his little brother's hand extended, sticky from the candy, the lollipop in his mouth, lingered in Isaiah's mind as he lay in his bed above the shop, the late afternoon sun shining through his westward facing window. He had to admit to himself that he had never taken seriously the idea that he had a brother, that there was another human being through whose veins ran blood from the same source as his own. Now that he had been confronted with the incarnation that had been, at best, an abstract idea, he tried to sort out his rather confused feelings. Growing up in the household with his father and his stepmother, then later embroiled in what he now could see as the absurd competition with his father for the love of the same young woman, and then dealing with her death and his father's conviction, he recognized that he just had no space in his emotional or cognitive capacity for Jonathan. Why, in fact, Jonathan was *in utero* when the final dissolution of his father's marriage to Eunice occurred on that wagon ride into town when she ordered the wagon to be stopped so that she could continue on by herself, not only to the doctor's visit to which they had been heading, but to the rest of her life.

Now that day, and all the complicated feelings encumbering it, had been thrust before him in the form of a shyly smiling face of a boy, lollipop in his mouth, schoolbook in one hand, and the other, sticky from the sugary candy, extended in greeting to him, he felt compelled to accept the reification of the idea of there being somewhere a brother. So vivid was this initial encounter, that, try as he might, he could not recall much of what transpired afterwards, only that the grandmother had beat a huffy retreat out of the shop and that Eunice had to separate his hand from Jonathan's as each looked hard into the eyes of the other, as each dealt with their new reality. And then he had excused himself, saying he felt a little unwell so that he could make his way up to his room, where now he lay staring out the window at the dying rays of the falling sun as though they might, somehow, provide him enlightenment.

Eunice witnessed the awkward coming together of the two brothers, a meeting so long delayed, and prompted by a combination of circumstances, the death of the father of the murdered girl, which brought back to town the wandering older brother, who, she realized without being told was staying on to continue the long delayed effort to free his father. Perhaps if old Mrs. Logan had predeceased old man Cutter, that effort would have died with her, and there would have been no reason for Isaiah to come back to Traverse City, and her little Jonathan would have grown to manhood without ever having met his brother, who would have remained just the faintest sketch in his memory of some long forgotten relative, one who was not spoken of much, and if at all, in hushed tones as though the embodiment of some hideous secret that should not be exposed in polite conversation.

In spite of Isaiah's disappearance after the trial, she had heard like everyone else in this small town, that he had made his way down to Chicago where he stayed with Sam's sister and her family, and later still had gone to work as a sailor on the lakes, in spite of all that information, which seemed to indicate he was gone from her life, she had prepared for the unlikely eventuality that one day she would have to deal with the possibility of Jonathan and Isaiah brushing shoulders, should Isaiah find reason to return. In anticipation of that remote possibility, and given Jonathan's still tender years, not to mention her mother's intense antipathy to anything Logan, she had mentioned in the lightest and most age appropriate terms that Jonathan did have a sibling who for unspecified reasons had long ago left and whose life path might never cross his own. Jonathan had showed a little curiosity but it did not last long, being easily displaced by more immediate stimuli and concerns, such as whether his grandmother would permit him to have an ice cream treat after school and before supper.

That part of Eunice's preparation had really been the easiest. Far more complicated, as she now fully understood, was dealing with her own emotions. During the troubled times right before the dissolution of her marriage to Sam, at the point when it had become clear that she could no longer deal with his impetuosity, his passions that were not confined to their marital bed, when the affair she knew he was having and had tried to dismiss as just a folly that, with some effort, she could forgive, when she had found herself more and more resorting to the comforts of her bottle of laudanum when he would come home his body fresh from the young woman's and still want the privilege of the marital bed, in the middle of all that, she was still charged with helping rear his son from his previously failed marriage.

At first, she had taken on that challenge, brought to her bosom the shaken child that Isaiah was, so fragile from the sudden exit from his life of the mother he so clearly and desperately missed. And Isaiah had responded, after a while, accepting her warm acceptance of him, made easier by the fact that his own mother showed little interest in continuing any relationship with him. Eunice considered that dereliction as unforgivable. How could a mother so abandon her child even when she had felt it so necessary to move away from that child's father? But after a while, as her own marriage deteriorated, and her feelings of grudging acceptance of her husband's wandering turned into active hostility, she began to understand why a woman might choose to distance herself from any reminder of a situation that had become so distressful.

With that understanding, inevitably, her feelings toward Isaiah cooled in a regression sliding down from the initial warmth to neutrality to coolness, and finally, and regrettably, to antipathy. Only many years later did she, in retrospect , perhaps influenced by her experience raising her own son, come to understand that Isaiah was the constant in their relationship. His behavior did not change, while his attitude toward her moved more into confusion and withdrawal than a hostility to match hers toward him.

That hostility culminated in that incident, dug up by Sam's defense attorney and confirmed at trial by Isaiah, occurring in a fit of irrational passion, precipitated not by anything Isaiah had done, but rather by a noxious combination of circumstances. One day with supreme indifference to her feelings, Sam came home late and did not even make the effort to come up with the concealing lie, which they both recognized as such, but through tacit agreement, would have accepted at face value. This time, though, when she inquired as to what had delayed him so that his supper lay cold on the table, he had just shrugged, and said he was not hungry, and that if she was upset with him, she could curl up with her bottle of laudanum, in which she seemed to find more comfort than in his company. He turned his back to walk out of the room. Isaiah still sat at the table witnessing a scene that was different from countless others only in its intensity.

She picked up the knife lying next to Sam's plate and placed it against Isaiah's throat. That much, as recorded in their divorce papers and revisited in court, was true. That she really intended any harm to the boy she knew was just not the case. Her action was stupid, mindless, out of a deep well of frustration, disappointment and anger that should have been directed at her husband but instead found in his son a nearer target.

During these troubled times Sam still insisted on her fulfilling her conjugal obligations, to which she acceded, not knowing how she could refuse, and even, in spite of herself, sometimes taking some pleasure in these moments. On the morning of this knife incident, she discovered she was again pregnant, and this news distressed her as she knew that she could not much longer remain married to Sam.

When she unexpectedly saw Isaiah standing outside of the leather shop, she felt she must seize the moment, and as best she could make up for the undeserved hostility she long ago had directed at him. After their initial conversation, she decided that the best thing she could do was to bring Isaiah and his brother, her son, together. In her mind, there was a symbolic rightness to that act that seemed irrefutable.

Now, though, having acted on that impulse, she wondered if she had been hasty. Perhaps she should have waited, kept her son sheltered in ignorance of his brother. These thoughts filled her mind as she walked home from the shop. She knew what she was going to encounter as soon as she opened the door.

She was not disappointed.

"Well," her mother said, "now you've gone and done it. I hope you're happy."

"Will that be a return ticket on the *City of Chicago?*" the ticket agent asked Benson the next morning.

"No," Benson replied. "Don't know when, or if, I'll be passing this way."

On the face of the agent, a young man, no more than twenty, was an expression of wonder.

"I've never...." he began.

"I expect you haven't," Benson said. "It's not as wonderful as you think it is, bouncing from place to place."

"Still," the young man replied, "I'd like a little taste. To see for myself."

For a moment, Benson remembered his own excitement as a young man when he first joined the Pinkertons, and found himself traveling to places whose names he had never heard. But then the fatigue from a poor sleep in yet another night in a hotel began to sit on his shoulders. He took the ticket, slid it into his coat pocket, picked up his valise, and walked up the ramp of the steamer that would take him to Chicago, and another night in another hotel before boarding a train the next morning for his cross country journey.

Sitting on a deck chair, some thirty or forty feet above the rippling waters of Lake Michigan, Benson permitted himself to relax. After all, there was nothing he could do at this point except be transported first by boat, then by train, then by God knows what. However, as much as he wanted to not think about anything more than the view of the water and the distant shoreline off of Grand Traverse Bay to the west, the question Isaiah had started to ask, the one he had peremptorily and curtly answered, demanded that he once again, for perhaps the hundredth or thousandth time, answer for himself well enough to enable him to go about his business as he had so many times before.

For the truth of the matter was that, of course, the question of the guilt of the individual he was being paid to track down and retrieve sometimes forced itself into his consciousness. As a lifelong lawman, he had a dark view of human nature, believing that, given the right motivation or circumstances, most people were capable of just about anything. Still, he retained a kernel of belief that those same people never had reason or opportunity to act on that capability, therefore, leading lives more or less comfortably on the good side of the law. But his experience also exposed him to the vagaries of the criminal justice system, where money and connections usually outweighed the evidence in determining whether an individual was convicted or walked out of the courtroom free.

That last consideration seemed to loom as large as the bulky shape of the lighthouse, now visible as the steamer began the slow circle around the Leelanau Peninsula that would take it into the majestic lake southward toward Chicago. Just as that lighthouse provided a fixed point of certainty, he thought, the rule of money and influence should have established an unwavering pointer toward Sam Logan now being a free man rather than facing a lifetime of incarceration.

Usually, he did not follow the cases he was involved in once he had delivered what he like to think of as his "package." That word helped him avoid the very speculations and considerations that now forced themselves into his mind against his strong desire to immerse himself into the quiet, subtle rhythms of the lake's waves over which the steamer glided. But in Sam's case, he had to admit to himself, something about it drew him into its details. Perhaps it was the mournful fact of the smitten and pregnant girl found lying dead among the trees, or maybe it was the palpable hostility of the whole community toward the accused, so much so that he had recognized before the trial began that its outcome was virtually guaranteed. Or finally, and perhaps most significantly, his interest was aroused by the plight of the young man with whom he had just dined, who was, in fact, now his employer, as the old woman, his grandmother, had turned the investigation over to the very individual whose testimony had been insufficient to counter that of the "package" he now sought to retrieve. And how to trust that individual's word? The color of his skin made him vulnerable to all kinds of pressures that he, as a white man, and a privileged one at that, could only guess at.

He took out a cigar, and reached into his coat pocket for his matches.

"Permit me, please."

He looked up into the face of an elderly man whose face boasted a bushy white mustache. The man struck his own match and extended it toward Benson's cigar. Benson cupped his hands around his cigar's tip, leaned forward, and took a couple of puffs. The man snuffed his match between his thumb and forefinger.

"Thank you," Benson said.

"I trust you are having a pleasant journey," the man said.

"A business trip," Benson replied.

"To Chicago?"

"New York."

"I see," the man replied. "Must be important business to take you so far."

"No, not so much," Benson replied. "Just have to pick up a package."

"But..." the man began.

"I can anticipate your question, why could the package not be sent. Am I right?"

The man nodded.

"This one requires my personal attention."

"Oh, I think I see."

Benson puffed on his cigar.

"Do you?"

"I am, have been my whole adult life, a reporter," the man said with a smile.

"Seen a lot?"

"Too much."

Benson took another puff.

"Well, thanks for the light."

Benson closed his eyes and let his body relax against the slight vibration of the ship caused by its huge steam engines.

"Just one more package," he murmured, more to himself. "Perhaps my last, at least for a while."

He ground his cigar out on the deck, leaned back and started to drift toward sleep, rocking with the ship's motion. But as he did, his mind refused to stop working. An image from years ago floated, a man with that kind of very full mustache, and something in the expression of his face, his gentle but probing way of speaking, why, yes, he had seen that man before. But where?

"Yessir," the wireless operator said, "we are pleased to offer this service to busy men such as yourself."

Drummond lifted his head from the paper on which he was writing.

"Yes, quite a convenience," he said.

He lowered his glance to the paper and wrote, "Frank, I've got him. He's going after someone. Will follow." He slid the paper across to the operator.

"Is that all?" the operator seemed disappointed. He looked at the addressee. "Oh, I see. Official business, is it?"

"Just send it. Now," Drummond said with the same friendly smile on his face, but in a tone that brooked no further delay. As he walked away, he heard the clatter of the operator's key.

Some time later, Benson approached the operator. In his hand were several bills. He placed one on the counter.

"How can I help you?" the operator said. "Would you like to write your message?"

Benson shook his head.

"There was a gentleman with a full, white mustache here a while ago, I believe."

"Was he an acquaintance?" the operator asked.

Benson put another bill on top of the first.

"Not exactly. More a competitor. I would very much like to know what he sent."

"I couldn't..." the operator said, but his eyes fell onto the bills.

"Yes, you can," Benson said as he laid another bill on the counter.

In Lansing, Larry Morgan sat at McGinnis's desk, the telegram spread out in front of him. It was from someone named Drummond, whoever that was, but whoever this fellow was he was on terms intimate enough to address the governor by his first name. And the message was just as cryptic as the name. Who, exactly, did Drummond have? Was this something the governor should be told about right away. After all he was in a meeting with party wise men discussing his prospects in the upcoming election, and from the faces of these gentlemen as they arrived, those prospects were not very bright. He heard a shuffling of feet, muted words coming from the governor's meeting room across the hall, and then clearer snatches of conversation as the door opened. He waited until he was sure the governor was back in his own office.

"This just came in," he said and handed the wire to the governor.

Woodhouse, his face lined with worry, glanced at the paper. His expression seemed to brighten as he apparently saw the name of the sender. He read the brief message.

"Thank you, Larry," he said. "Send a reply."

Larry took out a pad and pencil and waited.

"Just three words. Say 'follow and report'."

"Follow and report," Larry repeated.

CHAPTER SEVEN

A mong the few belongings Isaiah toted around with him during his travels, one item had been with him the longest. He viewed the grass and dirt stained leather covered baseball, with its seams coming loose in several places, as a kind of talisman that could against all opposing circumstances and memories transport him back to the days of his early childhood when first he began living alone with his father. That was a period of relative peace when both he and Sam crawled away from the debris of a failed marriage.

One day not long after his mother had packed her bags and with tears in her eyes bid him farewell in such a way that he, as young as he was then, realized the finality of this departure, on that very afternoon Sam hoisted him onto his shoulders and walked carrying him to the field that had been flattened and marked off for baseball. Taking him down from his shoulders, Sam set him with his back against a tree where he would have a good view of the game. After Sam stroked the winning hit, he carried the ball much as though it were a precious gem and handed it to Isaiah, saying when he was sad he should remember this afternoon.

And Isaiah did just that, not only when he was sad, but rather as part of his routine both at bedtime and in the morning to run his hands over the ball and thus to feel, no matter how strained their relationship became later on, a kind of mystical bond with his father.

"I just don't know," Eunice said. She was sitting at her desk at the rear of the leather shop showroom on Saturday morning. "Maybe it's just too soon. I don't know if he's ready."

"Well," Isaiah answered, "it's just a baseball game. Just," he hesitated, recalling the words that he wrestled out of his conflicted mind all through a sleepless night, "just two brothers enjoying an afternoon watching a game."

The thought had come unbidden into his mind as he lay in his bed after, as usual, he had communed with the ancient ball. The idea didn't begin in the present, but perhaps when he saw the announcement of the upcoming game in a store window down the block from the leather shop, a door to his memory had swung open, and he was, himself again a little boy no bigger than Jonathan, sitting beneath a tree on the third base line of a field carved out of what had been a meadow, watching his father play.

Sam was clearly the leader of that ragtag team made up of farm boys, farm hands, a couple of young men from town looking for an opportunity to develop their skills and move on to a more professional situation, and among that group one college student who played on his university's team, he, Sam had said in a confidential whisper to Isaiah, was somebody worth watching. He had natural ability, but it was not only as a baseball player that Sam pointed him out to his son, but as an example of possibilities that existed beyond the narrow scope of the Peninsula where the thousands of trees in the orchards seemed to create a wall that blocked the view of the wider world waiting beyond. Isaiah did not realize then, but now as he lay in bed replaying these scenes and the snippets of conversation lodged in the deep recesses of his memories, when he brought those ancient words out into the light, he thought he could draw from them the feeling of his father's loss of opportunity, his regret that he had never broken through that metaphorical world but had become a not very successful small time farmer and home builder.

Try as he might, Isaiah had not been able to shove these thoughts aside so as to drift into sleep. Over and over again, the image of Sam pitching, Sam hitting, Sam cheer-leading his teammates roared back into his consciousness.

Until.

Until with a suddenness so unsettling that it caused Isaiah to sit bolt upright in bed, all those bucolic images were gone, and in their place, another far more disturbing. He was sitting between his father and Eunice, his stepmother, concentrating on the sounds the wagon made over the rutted road and the soft thudding of the horse's hooves, trying without much success to block out the heated words passing over his head back and forth between the adults. Then the jolt as the wagon came to an abrupt halt as Eunice's voice strained into a high pitch demanding "Stop, stop, I am getting off. Right here. Right now." And she did clamber down, pausing just for a moment to lay her hand, ever so gently on his shoulder, a pained smile on her face for a brief moment before it turned once again into a stone hard mask of hostility, his father staring at the horse's back as though it would provide some explanation as to what was going on, a woman leaving him, rather than he her, a novel and deeply upsetting experience.

Unable to find sleep after this scene replayed in his mind, Isaiah lay back and tried to make sense out of these contrasting images, approaching them as though they were pieces of a jigsaw puzzle that he could, if only he tried hard enough, fit together into a picture that would make some kind of sense.

And then he found in the most unexpected place the key to the solution of the puzzle. It was Jonathan, he who had been *in utero* on that fateful trip in town, he, whom until recently he had never met, and he to whom his mind had rarely if ever turned. Somehow, these disparate memories coalesced around the fact of his brother, at the same age as he had been when he first watched Sam play baseball, and with the force of ineluctable logic the idea came to him that he must take Jonathan to a baseball game. As compelling as that conclusion was, he could not explain it to himself, just that somehow introducing Jonathan to baseball, as his father had done for him, would somehow square the circle, make sense of the impossible muddle that had been his life.

"Just you two...."

"Yes."

"To the game. And that is all you have in mind." She looked as though she was going to continue this line of questioning, when she began to slowly nod her head up and down. "Oh, I remember now, before me, and I mean before your father and I, he used to like to play baseball, I heard people talking once we got together, people saying don't expect to go to church with him on Sunday during baseball season, because that's where he will be, on the baseball field. And you must...."

"Yes, from the time I was Jonathan's age, I would go to watch," Isaiah said to complete the thought, but he was going to stop it there, no point bringing that narrative up to the time when he was older, his father still playing baseball, but also spending what little leisure time he had with Margaret.

She seemed to read his thoughts.

"I know. It was not just baseball."

"No, it wasn't."

"I'll tell Jonathan."

"Thanks. It's the last game of the season."

Eunice looked out the window that offered a view of an old maple trees whose leaves had already turned.

"I imagine so," she said. "There'll be snow on the ground before too much longer."

"I think it's some kind of championship game, that is why Jonathan is so eager to go, and there won't be another opportunity until the spring, and by then...."

"Don't say it. We're just getting reacquainted."

"I know, but I've got something I have to do."

"Yes, I figured you did."

Waiting his turn to bat, Sam stood off to one side of home plate in the makeshift baseball field in the exercise yard. It felt very good to have a bat in his hands again. He ran his right palm up and down the bat, feeling for imperfections, just as he had done years ago on the bat he had turned on his own lathe in the back of his father's barn. In those days he had harbored the dream of leaving his father's cherry orchards behind and building with wood. He had, in fact, become something of a carpenter, good enough to put up a couple of houses in town, but not devoted enough to that craft to leave farming altogether. He supposed the lure of the wealth represented by all those trees he grew up gazing at through his boyhood's bedroom window was stronger than he had anticipated. In short, he became neither a full time farmer nor a full time carpenter, but did enough of both to almost free himself from his father's heavy thumb. Of courses, that "almost" was a significant contributor to the chain of circumstances that had him standing here behind those high gray walls about, in the most incongruous way, to engage in playing a game that represented the antithesis of his actual condition, for afterwards, instead of enjoying a beer with his fellow players, he would be penned up again with his fellow inmates.

Not escaping his father's controlling hand made it impossible for him to do what he otherwise might have done. In truth, and in retrospect, he could not from this vantage point say with certainty that he would have acceded to that poor girl's desire to be married. The fact was he enjoyed being married. After all he had tried twice to make a success of that institution. Would he have opted for a third try? With a bat in his hand the baseball metaphor seemed apt. Perhaps he would have struck out, and in so doing, foreclosed any opportunities for yet another attempt. His father understood the situation perfectly well. And stubborn old man that he was he would continue to try to force his wayward son back onto the path that would lead to his taking over the empire the old man had built. So, one afternoon his father laid out the case with stunning clarity. "Look out the window," the old man had said, pointing toward the acres and acres of fruit trees. "That is yours if you will close your hands around it." Then, as if playing the magician, he pulled the thick curtains across the window. As the image of trees disappeared, his father punctuated the idea. "What you now see is your inheritance disappearing, and in its place, you can have the affections of a star struck girl who sees in you, Lord knows what, but whatever it is, it will not last, as it did not before with wives numbers one and two. You've given this girl a child, but you do not have to give her your life. Something can always be arranged with money, and I am willing to pay to get you out of this mess. Otherwise…" he shrugged and left the next sentence unsaid.

As much as this theatrical display of power enraged him, he had had to admit there was more than a small kernel of truth in it. Having grown up in privilege, he did not, in all honesty, happily embrace the idea of living in constrained circumstances. That day when she showed up for their tryst with the advertisement for the modestly priced baby carriage along with her egg money to pay for it to show him how they could manage had melted his heart toward her. She was so much in love with him that he could almost forget how naïve and romantic her ideas were. No doubt she would be brave in dealing with their limited resources, making every penny go as far as possible while continuing to bathe him in her all-encompassing love, so like a warm caress, so difficult to resist, such a powerful temptation that argued powerfully against his father's materialistic priorities. Yet he knew, as his father most certainly did, that even her vibrant love would begin to wither against the assault of day to day living, that he would sooner rather than later begin to chafe against having to deal with bills to pay outweighing income.

These remembrances flitted through his mind while his hands continued to work up and down the bat. He did not at first notice that as one and then another of these memories struck him how his hands squeezed hard around the wood, so hard that the flesh of his palms hurt. The crack of crude leather ball against bat brought him back to the immediate moment. The ball spun up and back well behind the catcher, who just turned and watched it land at the feet of one of the guards positioned around the perimeter of the field. The guard picked the ball up and tossed it toward the catcher who waited for the ball to roll to him. He picked it up and threw it with some zip back to the pitcher.

Sam studied the motion of the pitcher. Before throwing again, the pitcher rubbed up the ball with especial care, then shoved his hand into his pocket before grasping the ball again. The pitcher stood gazing in at the catcher, rolling the ball in his hand.

I know what you've done, and what you're doing, Sam thought. You've roughed up that ball with something, maybe a little piece of emery, and now you're looking to get your finger on it just the right way. The pitcher wound up and threw. The batter swung where he thought the ball would be, but it wasn't there. At the last second it had dipped sharply down. He dropped his bat, stared at the pitcher.

"Next time," he yelled.

"Sure," the pitcher replied. "Next time."

Sam heard another voice, this one from one of his teammates. "Hey Logan, you dreamin'? You're up."

Sam turned and saw that the voice belonged to Pete.

"I've been hearing you say how you used to be a baseball player, so here's your chance to show us what you can do, us, who never had the chance to play like you did, seeing how we didn't grow up on our daddy's farm."

Sam took a few practice swings, feeling as he did, the muscles in his shoulders complain.

"It's been a while," he said.

"No excuses, farm boy, show us," Pete said.

Sam took his place at the plate, realizing as he did that his mind had been so absorbed in traveling back over his life that he was unaware of the game situation. He seemed to remember that his team was behind by a couple of runs. He scanned the bases and saw that there was a runner on first base. Well, let's see what I can do, he thought, settling into a stance that old muscle memory dictated, his left foot forward, his hands held high. He took a deep breath, waved his bat once or twice over the plate, saw the pitcher leaning forward to get the sign from the catcher. A trustee was positioned behind the pitcher to serve as umpire, calling balls and strikes.

As the pitcher began his windup, Sam tried to sneak a peek to see where the catcher was setting up and saw that he was leaning outside. The pitcher came set, looked at the runner on first, and then twisted into his motion, left leg up in the air, right arm going back behind his head, weight shifting forward onto his left foot, arm coming forward in a three quarters delivery, the ball suddenly visible out of his hand.

Sam began his swing, read the spin of the stitches on the ball as it headed right toward the middle of the plate, thigh high. He checked his swing and watched the ball dive into the dirt over the outside corner of the plate.

"Maybe you have played this game before," the catcher said.

"A little," Sam replied.

The pitcher again twisted into his motion and released the ball. His arm speed said fastball, and Sam began his swing only to realize he had been fooled by a change-up. Too late to hold up he flicked his bat and managed to make contact, hitting the ball weakly into foul territory down the third base line.

"Let's see what else you got," he called out to the pitcher, who nodded in response.

The next pitch was a fast ball aimed at Sam's head. He threw himself back and the ball whizzed by his face, not more than an inch or two from a collision with his skull. He heard the ball thud into the catcher's glove.

"Ball!" the umpire called out.

Sam righted himself in the batter's box.

"Are you sure?" he called out to the umpire, summoning some bravado from a well he thought had dried up. The pitcher grinned.

"Just my way of saying hello," he called out.

"A little more than that," the catcher said. "Just a warning. Pete says he thinks you're ok, but he ain't sure, and if he ain't, neither are we."

"Understood," Sam said, surprised at how steady his nerves were. "Let's just play the game."

Sitting at an open window in his office overlooking the exercise yard, the warden leaned his head forward, his elbows on the stone sill. He pulled his head back in and turned to answer a knock at the door. His assistant entered and joined his boss at the window.

"Watching the game?" the assistant asked. "This is a new idea, isn't it, to give them some exercise, a chance to get rid of some of their troublesome energy."

"Yes," the warden replied, "another of our governor's ideas. Maybe he's right, but right now I'm studying the game within the game. You see that fellow at bat?"

"That's Logan, isn't it?"

"It is. He just picked himself up after ducking away from a very meaningful pitch aimed at his head."

"Who's pitching?"

"I'm not sure. I want you to find out. And the catcher as well.

That pitch wasn't an accident. We need Logan to stay in one piece."

Just then the loud crack of bat against ball wafted up to the warden's office.

"Well, look at that. Logan's going to take care of himself." He turned to his assistant. "Just find out those names and give them to me. They'll be behind anything bad that happens to Logan."

"If we call them in..." the assistant began.

"Of course, we won't . Unless we have to after we find Logan with a blade in his back."

"You've got spunk, I'll say that for you," Pete said hours later in their cell.

"Well, what was I going to do?"

"Don't know, but I didn't expect you to get back up, and smack the next pitch so hard."

"I was aiming at the pitcher, but I missed."

"Yeah, you missed, and the ball went over everybody's head."

Pete's tone changed.

"I said you got spunk, and we're all impressed. But how you use that spunk is what we're worried about. And you'll have the opportunity to hear things, because I intend to keep you close. Got it?"

"Like I said before. Understood."

Lying in his bed that night, Sam pondered what he, in fact, now understood.

Let's start from this very moment, he thought, I am on a paper thin mattress on a steel framed cot in an eight by ten space with a barred window on one wall, and on the opposite is a door made of bars, and across from me is another cot on which lies my snoring cell mate, that is a good one, he is no mate of mine, he is as likely to shove a blade between my ribs, or have one of his pals arrange for me to have an accident, as it is for him to wish me a good morning.

My cell is one of a row, maybe thirty or forty on this level, and then another above me, and one beneath me. Outside this building is that exercise yard, with its baseball field, and beyond the walls enclosing us on all sides, but beyond that, beyond those walls, there are other buildings in which, I understand, some prisoners are made to work manufacturing chairs and rope, and I don't know what else, because my work station is among those damned trees, which even here I cannot escape.

But the thing to focus on for the moment is not only where I am but in what circumstance I find myself, and that is between a rock and a hard place, for in his wisdom the warden has housed me with a man who is nothing but trouble, for himself, and anybody in his vicinity, including me, so that now I have to play the role of a spy for the authorities, something I never in all my life could have imagined myself doing because if I don't, any chance I have to ever get out of here will, as was made clear to me, be gone, I have to play the hand that was dealt to me, and why should it be different in here than it was outside where I was caught up in another situation that landed me here.

He rolled toward the wall and pulled his thin pillow over his head to drown out his cellmate's snoring, which was increasing, a rattling, snorting sound that made clear thinking impossible. Never a reflective man, but rather one more guided by his appetites and impulses, his time in solitary confinement had taught him the value of reflection, so now, the one thing he needed to do, the one thing he had learned to do all those months and years with no-one but himself to commune with, was to discipline his mind to stay clear, to grasp, without excuse or self-pity, the facts, for only with those facts firmly in his grasp could he have any hope of retaining his sanity, of enabling him to withstand the overwhelming impulse to pound his head against the hard wall of his cell until he lost consciousness, and if he was lucky, his very life.

So, now, as he had done so many times in that darkened hole that was his solitary cell, he rehearsed the events of the one day of his life that he wished with every fiber of his being to be able to revisit and revise, that day, when at the appointed time, he had met her, when common sense should have demanded that he be anywhere else, let her fret in her youthful impatience, she would sooner or later realize the impracticality of her dreams of a happy life as his wife, it simply was not going to happen.

But if he were in the habit of listening to the dim voice of common sense, that seemed to reach him, if at all, from a distant mountain, floating as best it could, through the thick atmosphere of his various passions, for sex perhaps on the top of the list, but followed in no particular order by baseball, the feel of a piece of wood being worked on his lathe or joined in his vice, the companionship of other men of his free spirited persuasion, or even just the simple joy of cutting into a well prepared steak, all of those in a constant swirl and in tense opposition to the demands of his father, not to mention the constant economic pressures his generally unproductive life style layered on him. Thus, the voice of common sense was never better than a faint whisper, soon drowned out by the cacophony of his other inclinations.

So, no common sense did not speak up and intervene, did not offer any resistance to his thoughtless agreement to meet her once again on that day, and meet her he did. Reaching that point in his rehearsal of the day, Sam paused, stretched his body still aching from the unaccustomed stress of the baseball game, as though his mental effort was being mimicked by his body. To proceed, as he well knew from so many past explorations of this day, required an emotional effort that was also physically exhausting.

So, he lay back on the cot staring at the ceiling just visible as the dying light of the late summer sunset filtered through the bars leaving fuzzy black and gray stripes on the plaster. After some minutes, he took a deep breath and forced his memory to bring up the images he kept stored away, to be retrieved only when he had the courage to face them.

There he was walking with some haste eastward leaving behind him his work on the unfinished new road toward the west bay. And now, as that image flashed across his mental screen, the ghost of that aching tooth seemed to assert itself as though that inflamed molar was again in his mouth. He stopped his review of the day at that point to ponder that fact. Such a small, non-consequential thing in the larger scheme, was, when examined in retrospect, of monumental importance. He was no logician, and his schooling had ended after high school at which he had been at best an indifferent scholar. But when he applied himself, even without the terms and processes of formal logic, he could think his way clearly through a problem as well as many much more fully educated individuals. If he had had the technical vocabulary of the logician, perhaps he would have decided that his aching tooth was a condition necessary to the result, that had his tooth not ached so terribly that day, he most likely would not be lying on this cot in this prison cell across from his snoring cell-mate, dangling metaphorically between the menace of that man and the warden, neither of whom would hesitate to use him to his own advantage one way or another.

For this is what he now understood with more clarity than previous attempts at figuring out the sequence of events that led to his waking up from a drug induced stupor to find his lover lying dead beside him. Because his toothache was so intense, and because for her own reasons she had brought that bottle of laudanum, he had drunk of that drug seeking relief. He was familiar with laudanum's calming effects, having witnessed it time and again when Eunice sought its solace as an escape from their increasingly troubled marriage. All he had wanted on that fateful day was for his damned tooth to stop hurting so he could attend to the difficult business of convincing her that her plan of wedded bliss with him was simply not going to be realized. He did not want to hurt her. Not that he loved her, that would be putting the matter too strongly. But he did feel a genuine affection for her, only, and he shuddered for a moment at the characterization that jumped unbidden into his consciousness, but he could be strong enough now to say it, what did it matter if he did with her dead, he here, and the world if it thought of him, did so by thinking of him as that convicted murderer, so now he could say to himself that perhaps part of his warm feelings for her went beyond his usual physical appetites, and that he felt toward her as he might toward a daughter who found herself in this most impossible situation, in love with the thoughtless lover he knew himself to be.

That was his mission that day, as he now confirmed for himself, to disabuse her as best he could of her dream. And to do so he needed his full faculties, which were not available to him so long as the pain of that tooth raged. She offered him the laudanum. He drank. His stretched nerves relaxed. The pain did not exactly disappear. Rather it receded behind a feeling of disconnect as though he were now floating above his body leaving the aching tooth anchored to the ground on which he lay next to her. But of course he was still very much in his body, enough for his face to break into a silly smile, more like that of a contented infant than a grown man. He might have laughed or dribbled drool from his half opened mouth. About any of that he could only speculate for memory could not bring back those moments. He could recall being aware that she was gazing at him with rapt attention, then smiling most likely in imitation of that grin on his own face, then her hand caressed his cheek where he had indicated his hurt was, and as though by magic, but of course it was the laudanum influencing his perception, nonetheless it seemed as though her soft hand lifted the remnants of pain. And then he thinks he might have laughed in giddy relief.

And then.

Then, he paused, gathered himself, then she took the bottle still grasped in his right hand, he was sure it was his strong right hand that could have resisted her taking the bottle from him, had he the will to do so. But he didn't. He was helpless, trapped in the drug induced euphoria, floating in, or better, above the moment. Helpless, he let her lift the bottle from him and bring it to her mouth. She said something then but the words did not reach that part of his brain that would have been able to attach meaning to them. All he could now recall is that she seemed to have a beatific smile on her pretty face, a halo glowed around her head as she sipped from the bottle.

At the last, he realized the danger. He saw that she was preparing to drink all the liquid that remained. Somehow, and of this he was now very sure, somehow the fog lifted for a moment from his mind and he realized that he must stop her. But the muscles of his arm that always served him so well, whether it was squaring a piece of wood for the frame of a window, or hurling a baseball, or embracing a lover, that obedient limb now quite simply refused to move, choosing instead, as though in act of conscious rebellion, to hang limp against his side.

That was as far as he could go, in fact, as far as he needed to, in explaining to himself what happened. Of course, there was the coda, every bit as damning as the main story. He woke, saw her lying still, unsure whether she was asleep or had drawn her last breath. Now his muscles obeyed and he shook her. Roughly. He would force her to breathe again. Maybe he put his hands around her neck in order to lift her head off the ground. Maybe he squeezed harder than he should, what matter if she were already gone. But of course it did matter, for at trial that fool coroner insisted that he had strangled her.

When it became clear that she was dead, and here he wanted to stop thinking because what came next was something so shameful that it took all the courage he could screw up to face it, but face it he must.

Relief.

That is what he must confess to himself is what he then felt. If she were gone, so was his problem, her demand that he marry her, his father's threat to disinherit him, the foolish competition with his own son, all of it would be gone. All he had to do was make clear what had happened. She had in an excess of joy killed herself. But those who would find her, knowing of her distress at their situation, would come to the opposite conclusion that she had drunk that fatal dose out of despair. A perfectly reasonable conclusion to draw.

All he needed to secure his freedom from the snare was to establish that he was elsewhere at the time of her demise. Yes, that was it, he almost said aloud, stopping himself as he realized that the snoring from the bed across the cell had ceased. Had he been verbalizing all this? He panicked. But a moment later the snoring resumed, and through gritted teeth he permitted himself to mutter, what else should I have done? No, the only thing to do was to save myself. She was beyond anybody's help. I would live. And I would learn to forgive myself and to grieve her untimely death, the poor young thing.

The rest unfolded easily. Now fully removed from the drug induced fog his ensuing actions were etched in his memory, his rapid progress back to where he and Isaiah had been working, his alibi established.

A thought crept into his mind, one that he had experienced before but had never been able to pin down. Had not someone called to him as he hurried to their assignation? Oh, yes, that damned nigger who testified at his trial. But Isaiah had contradicted him. And yet.

And yet, he was convicted. By his friends and neighbors. Who took the word of that nigger over that of his son.

"Did you boys enjoy the game?" Eunice asked, and her face immediately reddened as she felt the awkwardness of so addressing her son and once upon a time stepson.

Isaiah, his arm around Jonathan's shoulders, hesitated for a moment as he dealt with the verbal pairing of himself and the boy beneath his hand.

"Yes, I think Jonathan really enjoyed his first game."

Jonathan shook himself free and turned to face Isaiah with a big smile on his face.

"We won, our team won, and Isaiah told me what to watch for."

"There's been no man," Eunice said, "and I don't know much about the game, I never, well you can imagine why."

"Yes," Isaiah said. "You don't need to explain."

Eunice gathered herself from unpleasant memories.

"And you?"

"I have my own memories, too, different from yours."

"I'm sure you do."

Jonathan sensing that the conversation had turned from him and the game to adult concerns well beyond his understanding tugged on his mother's hand.

"What's for dinner?"

"Your favorite…" she began and then aware of the awkward door she had opened looked toward Isaiah.

"I've got plans," Isaiah said.

He ate alone as he usually did, nursing a beer along with his meal, not wanting to return to his lonely room, there to confront the demons he was sure would await him.

"Anything else?" the waitress asked, the same one who had served him and Benson, and that coincidence reinforced the memories that taking Jonathan to the game had caused to rise into the front of his consciousness. He looked around and noted that he was the lone diner left.

"No, thank you," he said.

In bed a little later among all the images of the past replaying in his mind one stood out as the keystone of all the others. This one image was almost tactile in its intensity. He could feel again the folded piece of paper on which she had written that brief note that he now wished from the depths of his soul that he had left unread. But the simple fact is he had read it. And instead of delivering it to his father, he had kept his hand on it in his pocket, and had spoken the message contained in the note out loud. That act was spontaneous, born out of his frustration, his pained recognition that he had lost the uneven competition with his father for her affections, and so he wanted to put his defeat out into the open, watch his father's face as he delivered the simple message, she would meet him at the usual place and usual time, and those were the words he spoke to his father. As expected, Sam did not take the bait, dismissing the idea as foolishness while they both knew that he had every intention of meeting her. At the usual time. At the usual place.

At first he hid the damning piece of evidence, but then in an act of bravado, as though to test his ability to walk that line he decided he must, he fingered it in his pocket as he testified, mouthing words the note contradicted. After the trial, after his father's conviction, after the tangible expression of satisfaction from the townspeople, who no doubt would have accepted no other verdict, after his grandfather had made it clear to Mr. Lowe, his father's attorney, that his services would no longer be needed, after all of that, that piece of paper had felt like a hot coal ready to burn its way through the fabric of his pocket, and as a line he remembered hearing from somewhere, probably in a classroom, that line that declared that murder will out, which he but dimly understood then but now fully grasped its meaning, and so he seeing Daniel, his one friend through the last act of this sad drama, he had reached into his pocket with two fingers as though he literally thought his flesh might be scalded by the innocent piece of paper on which were words formed by her very own hand that he had done his best to hide from the prosecution, lord only knew whether he had been at all successful, but still he could no longer countenance keeping that wretched piece of paper on his person or anyplace where he might be tempted to take hold of it, and with it publish its contents to the world, the consequence be damned if he could only free himself, once and for all, from the terrible burden it had placed on him, with that thought in mind, he laid his terrible secret into the hand of Daniel with the instruction that he not read it until after he was gone. Gone to where? Daniel had asked. Away, he had replied. From this place, from this land, and onto the broad back of the great lake. He had trusted Daniel to honor his request, and no doubt he had. And furthermore, he had entrusted to his friend the responsibility of what he should do once he had read the contents of the note. Day after day, then week after week, month after month, and finally year after year, he waited to read that damning sentence, Meet me tomorrow at the usual place and time, broadcast in some newspaper somewhere, Daniel no longer feeling duty bound to keep his secret and seeing, who could blame him, certainly not Isaiah, if he gave in to the temptation to give his career one final boost before he succumbed, as succumb he most certainly would before very long, to the disease savaging his lungs. But no such announcement ever appeared. Perhaps Daniel had taken the secret to his much too premature grave.

But then maybe he was wrong, maybe Daniel had not honored his promise, an idea he could not credit, but it was possible that somehow because of his increasing disability perhaps the note had slipped through Daniel's dying fingers into the hands of someone less caring.

Someone like that stranger who had accosted him outside of the church.

Will you never stop plaguing me, he mumbled half out loud, as he twisted in his bed, and leave me to live my life with some degree of peace?

He woke up with a start. A thought had forced itself into his consciousness while he slept, and now it demanded to be acted upon. If he wanted peace, he would have to earn it. And to earn it, he would have to confront the devil that was at the source of his discontent.

He smiled. He was pleased at the symmetry. If one piece of paper haunted him into near madness, he would exorcise it with another piece of paper. In the desk of his rented room he remembered seeing a sheet of decent looking stationery. He pulled open the drawer, found it, along with a sharpened pencil as if the gods agreed with his intention.

So he sat down and began to write. With each stroke of the pencil, he felt just a little bit of weight lifting off of his shoulders.

He signed his name with a flourish.

CHAPTER EIGHT

T he train whistle wakened Jim. He sat up. The feeling of someone or something approaching him was almost palpable in his darkened room. He recalled that other time when he was also living near a railroad yard when they had come to get him. They wanted his testimony. More than that, they wanted testimony that conformed to the case they were building. It did not matter that he was not absolutely sure of what he saw that day, or if he had, he had tried to erase the image of that man hurrying through the woods. It was none of his business, he thought then, and at the moment they approached him, white man's business was never his affair. But they were insistent. What was he to do?

He went with them, said what they wanted him to say, suffered indignities on the witness stand when they were surprised that this black man could read and write, that he could convince those twelve white men that his story was more credible than the one told by the white man's son. What they didn't know is that he did not give a damn about the truth, not in the white man's world where the truth is always the white man's truth, didn't he have the scars on his back to testify to that simple fact, it did not matter what actually happened that time some white man thought he was looking the wrong way at a white girl and brought the whip down on his back, saying all the time he was lucky it wasn't a rope around his neck, hanging from a tree branch, that he had always been a good nigger so they would let him live just so long as he now knew how he should live with his head bowed in the presence of their white majesties, and never, never dare lift his eyes to look at a white woman.

But now like a bad dream that cannot be kept buried, the events leading up to that white man's trial and his coerced testimony insisted on forcing its way into his thoughts. As soon as he learned that his boss's daughter had been found dead his survival instincts kicked in and without a word, certainly not to his co-worker who, he knew, had his eyes on that same girl, no, without a word to anyone, who would he have told anyway? he had no family, no friends in that rural community where he was the only one with black skin, so like a thief skulking away in the night he left, taking with him the few belongings he had, at least he did not have to worry about leaving something precious behind, for he had no such thing. He put as much distance between himself and trouble as he could, but it was not far enough.

While working on the Cutter farm, he surely saw the misguided romance developing between the girl and Sam Logan, a man he actually had some respect for simply because he seemed to be someone who lived the way he wanted without worrying about what others might think, of course, his white skin and his daddy's money enabling him to be cavalier. It was with some amusement he witnessed Sam's lovesick son enter into an uneven competition with his father. It was truly a white man's circus, the older lover, the young girl, the son of the lover, the drooling interest of Edward, all playing out as a comedy that suddenly turned tragic.

He did not know if Sam Logan killed Margaret Cutter. He did not know if the man he saw from a distance was Sam, but who else could it have been? Possibly that damned fool Edward. But as he told himself a thousand times what he saw or didn't see did not matter. The whole community wanted Sam Logan convicted, and there surely was no profit for him to try to slow down that tide of hostility by expressing any doubt, so he didn't. All he wanted was to be left alone so again he could move on.

Now, though, he was sure that once again he would have to disappear.

That other time, when they found him miles away and hauled him back to testify, that time he was living in a railroad yard where freight trains came in and out. That is how he had arrived there, riding in an empty boxcar. This time, though, the train whistle he heard belonged to a passenger line a quarter of a mile from his rented room above a dry goods store. If he wanted to flee by train this time, he would have to buy a ticket and risk being exposed among the other passengers. He reached into his pocket, felt the coins from his pay, and knew he had enough for the ticket and a new start somewhere else.

"Yessir," Edward said. "I was there,and that gun is the one I had with me." Edward had learned long ago that his mind was not agile enough to come up with a convincing lie on the spot, so when finding himself in a tight spot, he tried to answer questions directly with as little detail as possible, in the hopes that the damning detail would not be raised by his interlocutor.

"You were there," Sheriff Cooper said, "and so was this gun. The question is what did you and this gun do on that occasion?"

"They wanted me to shoot. But I didn't really know how."

"But we know this gun was fired. And you admit it was yours."

"Yes. I did pull the trigger once. But I didn't hit nothing."

"People died."

"Not from me."

"We have evidence to the contrary," the sheriff said.

"What..." Edward began, but then his old reflex kicked in and he simply hung his head. It never did do any good to argue with authority no matter how much he might want to dispute the facts. Reality, he knew now, as always, resided within the grasp of men like the sheriff.

"What," he now continued, "do you want me to do about that?"

The sheriff clapped his big hand on Edward's shoulders hard enough to just about knock him off his chair.

"Nothing, for now. Just want you to know where you and I stand."

He took out his pocket watch and dangled it on its chain in front of Edward's eyes.

"Do you see how this instrument hangs on the chain, and how the chain is in my hands?"

"Yes."

"Know that from now on you are the watch, and I hold the chain, and you will do whatever I tell you to do whenever I tell you to do it. If you object, I will wind you up like this instrument until like it you will snap. And do you want to know how I will cause that to happen to you?"

Edward nodded, then continued to let his chin rest on his chest, his eyes in abject subjugation staring at his feet still shod in the new shoes he had bought with the money given to him by Jablonski. Why was this man telling me what I already know he thought, but knew the answer to that question, which was simply because that was what such men did.

"Well," the sheriff continued, "I'll just keep this weapon in a secure place until that time when I might need to introduce it into a legal proceeding about that shooting. If you've been good, boyo, I'll say there is no evidence that, as you said, you hit anybody. Or...well you get the idea, do you not, boyo?"

"Yessir," Edward said, relieved that the threat, which he fully expected, had been delivered, and that all he had to do in his own self-interest was to do precisely what was in the best interest of the man in whose hands his fate was held. "Just tell me what to do, and I'll do it."

"I know you will. I thought you would. But now I know."

"What'll it be?"

"We'll let you know. "

Edward eyed the gun.

"No, I don't think so," the sheriff said. "Least not now. Maybe later."

"Can I go?" Edward asked, half expecting to be directed to the nearest jail cell as had happened more than once before.

"Sure. We'll be in touch." The sheriff lowered his gaze to some papers on his desk. Edward started to get up. The sheriff, his eyes still on the papers, held up his hand, and Edward sat back down again.

"One more thing," the sheriff said without lifting his eyes, "try to make yourself useful. Any way you can."

"Yessir," Edward said.

He walked out of the sheriff's office into the December afternoon, happy to still be free, happy to not have to think for himself, which always seemed to get him into trouble, and most happy because the sheriff had said he might get the gun back, 'least not now,' he had said, which meant maybe later he would again feel the power of that steel in his hand, his finger on the trigger, which all he had to do was squeeze, and the ensuing blast would be the equalizer against anyone threatening him.

In the meantime, he would try to, as the sheriff said, make himself useful.

Benson got off the Long Island Railroad train at the Ronkonkoma station and stopped at the ticket agent's window.

"Do you know the McCutcheon's potato farm?" he asked.

"Yessir. It's not far from here."

"Can I walk there?"

"It's about a mile and a half. If you like, I can get you a ride."

"In a buggy?"

"No sir. A fine automobile. You are in Ronkonkoma. Mr. Vanderbilt's playground, why you know he built a private road right out to here so he could race his cars without interference."

"It's a nice day," Benson replied, "and I think I'd like to stretch my legs. Be so kind to point the way for me to walk."

"Yessir. I can draw you a little map. It's really quite easy."

"One more thing," Benson said. "I was supposed to meet a man who is going to work for me. I'll tell you what he looks like, and what to do if you see him." He slipped a bill across the agent's counter.

"Yessir," the agent said.

With the agent's hand drawn map in hand, Benson started walking away from the station. Out of the corner of his eyes, he saw a young black boy sweeping the platform. His eyes registered the boy's color but also noted his age, and so he walked on. A few moments later, Jim emerged from behind a large trash bin, approached the ticket agent.

"One way ticket to the city," he said.

The agent nodded and took the coins Jim put on the counter.

"Next train will leave in an hour," he said.

Jim sat down on the bench. He did not notice the agent picking up his telephone.

This time, mindful of his mission to be useful, Edward gazed at the name of the saloon on the wooden sign over the front door. Kaisers, he would try very hard to remember, Kaisers he muttered as he entered the saloon and found a seat at the bar.

Sitting with several women and one man at a table in the rear of the room was a large woman. Propped on the wall behind her was a huge American flag. The combination of the flag and the woman clicked in Edward's mind, and he remembered looking out of the boarding house window at the marching strikers and seeing at the very front of them this same woman holding a large flag just like the one now leaning on the wall. He noticed the man staring back at him, so he turned his glance away and took a couple of sips of his beer. The barkeep stopped in front of him and ran his cloth over a wet spot on the counter.

"You interested in them?" he asked.

Edward shrugged.

"I'm new here, but I thought I saw that woman before."

"No doubt you have if you've been paying attention. That's Big Annie. Her husband is a striking miner, and he's in jail. Ask me, which nobody does, she should be home with her kids instead of looking to join her husband in his cell. A troublemaker she is, if you ask me, which..."

"Nobody does," Edward completed the thought.

The barkeep kept swiping the spot on the counter although it was now thoroughly dry.

"I wouldn't get too close to that group..." he paused, "but say haven't I seen you here before."

"Sure, I been here before," Edward admitted, deciding as he did that he would say no more.

"Yeah, now I remember," the barkeep said. "And Willie sat down next to you."

"Don't know no Willie," Edward said.

"I'm sure he left an impression," the barkeep said, and then walked down to the other end of the counter.

Edward nodded.

"He did."

"You just keep sipping your beer. I'll run my rag over that end of the bar. They don't pay no attention to me unless they want something."

As Edward lifted his beer mug to his lips, he held his head at just a bit of an angle so that he could see that table out of the corner of his eye. The barkeep worked his way slowly toward that end of the counter. When he got there, he turned to fix the bottles lined up behind the counter. The man at the table got up and walked toward the front of the tavern. Edward studied the foam on the lip of his mug. The man's heavy tread stopped behind him. Edward balled his fist. The tread resumed and then the door opened and closed.

Big Annie watched the man leave, then turned her attention to the other women. Two of the them, one a washed out blonde, the other a brunette, were in their twenties and both had once been pretty but now their faces wore the look of hard times. The third woman was much older, perhaps in her sixties, and whether or not she ever was attractive would be hard to say given the lines that now crossed her cheeks and forehead, her tight lips, and yellowed teeth.

In front of Annie was a shot glass still half filled. Her large hand picked up the glass and drained it in one big gulp. She then put it down with enough force to shake the table. The barkeep kept running his cloth over the a wet spot on the counter. Edward saw the women's mouths moving. They were talking but he was too far away to hear anything. He thought about moving closer, but the barkeep, as if reading his mind, held his hand toward Edward palm outward.

After the women left, Edward pulled out the last few coins from his pocket and laid them on the counter. The barkeep pushed them back. He looked around the room. One man rested his head on his arms and slept, his lips quivering with each breath. Still the barkeep leaned forward and spoke just above a whisper.

"On me," he said. "I know you don't want to talk about it, but I saw what Willie did to you. I also seen you talking to Jablonski.

You don't have to worry about me. I don't take sides, and I don't talk to either one."

"Then why are you talking to me?" Edward asked.

"You look like you could use a friend.

"I never did have one," Edward said.

"Let me tell you what they were talking about," the barkeep said. "I'm sure Jablonski will be very interested. Didn't get it all. They lowered their voices. But just tell Jablonski the little bit I got."

"I will," Edward said, but he did not understand the significance of the fragment the barkeep now whispered into his ear. He did for a moment wonder at the precaution of the whisper. But as usually was the case with him, when anything did not make sense to him, he shrugged it off as of no significance. He preferred to keep his world simple. Just do what was good for Edward, and listen to those in the position to help or hinder his attaining that basic goal.

Benson turned off the paved road onto a dirt track that led to the potato fields. As he approached, he saw that the nearer rows had been dug up. Farther back, several men on their knees worked the remaining rows. Off to one side of the beginning of the field were a makeshift desk made from two barrels holding up a wide plank of wood and beyond it a horse drawn wagon over the sides of which, just barely visible, was the top of a heap of what appeared to be freshly picked potatoes, clumps of dirt still sticking to them. Behind the desk sat a man holding a pencil over a ledger. Benson made his way toward him. The man held him in a steady gaze.

I don't know, Benson thought, how helpful this fellow is going to be. He looks like the type I've seen many times before who keeps his mouth tight and his cards close.

"Howdy," Benson said as he reached the desk. "I take it you are Mr. McCutcheon."

The man nodded.

"Have you come to buy potatoes?"

"No sir."

"Then I don't know how I can be of assistance to you."

"It's not your crop I'm interested in. But one of your workers."

"They're not for sale."

"I take your meaning," Benson replied. "But I do have business with one of them."

The man looked out at the field, turned back, and nodded.

"If you're after that nigger, you're too late."

"Too late?"

"Got paid a few days ago, and took off. Just like I thought he would once he had a few coins in his pocket."

"I don't suppose..." Benson began.

"No, I don't have any idea." He looked down at the book in front of him. "But I can tell you that while he was here he worked hard. I had some hope for him. But..."

"He's gone."

"Right."

As he made his way toward the ticket office at the railroad station, Benson saw the man with the white mustache sitting on a nearby bench.

"Why am I not surprised to find you here?" he said.

The man rose and held out his hand.

"Thomas Drummond," he said. "We met on the steamer, but I don't think we introduced ourselves."

Benson grasped the other's hand in a strong grip.

"Wendell, Wendell Benson," he said. "I knew you were following me, but I confess I do not know to what purpose."

Drummond began to free his hand, but Benson held on to it. "I know I've seen you before, and now I remember. It was at that trial some years ago in Traverse City. Am I right?"

"You are," Drummond replied.

Benson released his grip, and Drummond withdrew his hand.

"As to the purpose," Drummond said, "now that you have recalled our previous shared experience, you can no doubt surmise that we are again engaged in the same business."

"Yes," Benson replied. "But are we pursing it from the same direction?"

"Indeed we are," Drummond said. "To this point you have done our work for us by finding, shall I say, the package you were seeking, as are we."

"Ah, yes," Benson said, "but as you can see I do not have it."

"You have resources to find it?"

"Perhaps," Benson replied.

"I am now in the service of one who very much wants to talk to this individual, toward the same end that you are seeking him."

"For justice?" Benson said with a wry smile."

"As for that, somebody always has a thumb on the scale, so no, not so much for justice. Rather as a card to play if circumstances demand, as they might."

"I have heard that the governor leaves politics to others."

"He does indeed," Drummond replied.

"So, I see."

Drummond looked back over the road leading to the field.

"Any idea where we can find this, what'd you call him, package?"

"No. But he came here by train, and that's how he's going to leave."

Jim found a room above a tavern in that section of Manhattan being populated by thousands of individuals with whom he shared not only a skin color but similar rural backgrounds coming up from the South hoping to find a place where they could begin to live lives of the freedom promised nearly half a century earlier but having found instead legal subjugation being replaced by the burning cross in front of their hovels or a rope thrown around a tree branch sturdy enough to hold their weight as they dangled off the ground before cheering crowds come to witness their demise much as they would attend a visiting circus, complete with souvenir postcards for sale.

He saw his brethren, for such he considered them to be, the scars on his back cementing his connection to them, witnessed their struggle to find a place in this great urban center. In the mornings, he joined them seeking employment as the small cache of money in his pocket slowly leaked out. Like them, having spent his entire working life, starting as a slave child picking cotton to a freed adult in the North picking cherries and apples, to his recent employment digging potatoes, he had few skills to offer appropriate to a world of paved streets and tall buildings crowded one on top of another. He saw the growing frustration of the dark faces walking those streets, feet used to the uneven surface of plowed fields experiencing difficulty finding purchase on paved avenues. Here there were no plows, no shovels, no fruit trees to harvest, crops to plant or harvest, cows to milk, fences to erect, in short he could see no workers plying trades with which he was even remotely familiar.

He explored farther and came upon a crew laying cobblestones on a dirt road that made its way through newly erected row houses. In the distance, he could see a barn and thought he might walk there to see if he could hire on as a farm worker. But as he ambled past the crew, he saw that all the workers were black. Then a voice boomed out at him from the side of the road.

"You lookin' for work?"

Jim nodded.

"Ever lay stones?" the man said with a glance at the workers.

"No, but I got a strong back and an empty pocket."

The foreman smiled.

"That' ll do. The others will teach you how."

Benson walked ahead of Drummond to the ticket booth.

"Yessir," the agent said, "he bought a ticket to the city, and just like you told me, I called your man there."

Benson turned to Drummond.

"You coming along?"

"Of course. But aren't you concerned your package might elude you again?"

Benson shook his head.

"I've got one of my best men on him. He'll keep an eye on him. Detain him if necessary. Until I get there."

"I see that you take especial care of your packages."

"It's personal with me. I've got a long history in this business."

"As do I," Drummond said, "as do I."

Jim's back and shoulders ached and the abrasions from handling the cobblestones stung his hands. The pain felt good, a reminder of simpler times when all he had to do was work hard and the rest took care of itself.

"That's enough for the day, boys," the foreman said.

Jim straightened up, stretched, and walked over to the foreman.

"Doin' my job, boss," he said.

"Come back tomorrow, and if you put in another good day, you've got a job."

"Yessir," Jim said in the subservient tone that came unbidden from his memory.

As he trudged back to his room above the tavern, he sensed somebody following him. He stopped to light a cigarette, turning his back against the slight breeze and looking through the smoke rising in front of him. He saw only ordinary pedestrian traffic, women herding their children, working men, shoulders hunched from their labor, and sprinkled among them, the idlers, mostly young men whose eyes never seemed to focus on anything or anybody for more than a second. None of these seemed a threat, and yet Jim still sensed that he had missed something. Or somebody.

Maybe I worry too much, he thought, but my worry has always been right in the past.

He walked on, reached the door next to the tavern that led to the stairs and his room on the second floor. He took one more direct look behind him, thought he saw a figure duck into another doorway, and then climbed up the stairs.

He would show up for work again tomorrow. He needed traveling money and would leave as soon as he had it.

CHAPTER NINE

There was frost on the apple trees. Sam approached the tree at the beginning of the row, and for a moment he was back on his own farm on a crisp November day, his boots making a cracking sound against the thin ice covering the grass, his mind pleasantly empty of any troubling thoughts, focused only on the hours ahead of repetitious motions plucking fruit off branches, pausing every once in a while to bite into an apple to test its quality, to assure himself that this crop would, at least this time, relieve some of the usual financial pressure.

But this was not his orchard, nor his apples. They belonged to the state of Michigan for whom he was an unpaid laborer. Still the activity was welcomed. He had always been a physically active man, whether performing his farming chores, playing baseball, working a piece of wood on a lathe, or nailing boards together on a house he was building. He had a vital energy that demanded an outlet, sometimes in good ways, at others in a more destructive manner, a barroom brawl perhaps, or an ill advised dalliance.

Given this element in his nature, his prolonged solitary confinement had been particularly difficult for him to tolerate. The occasions when he was walked out to do his solitary labor were insufficient to counterbalance the hours spent pacing in his tiny cell or performing meaningless calisthenics, push-ups or sit-ups, an activity he abandoned not long after he was first imprisoned.

Now, he had regular activity laboring in the prison's orchards. He did not bother himself with contemplating how the state was profiting from his work. In fact, he sensed the other prisoners shared his lack of concern for any political or moral considerations. Just being outside doing something productive was salutary, so he and his fellow inmates were generally in good spirits as they hopped off the wagons that carted them to the trees, and trudged to the places of their appointed tasks.

Besides his innate need for physical activity, or perhaps in part because of it, Sam had always enjoyed the camaraderie of other men, and in turn, he was well respected and welcomed into the masculine community. Today as he walked along he looked for an opportunity to joke with the other laborers, as he always did, but now he had an even more important and deeper reason for sociability. He needed to keep his ears wide open as his mouth chatted superficialities. It had been a while since the warden had laid out how his future very much depended upon his being a conduit through which would flow the plans of the more incorrigible prisoners.

Up ahead, he recognized the stocky body of the catcher from the baseball game, the one who had explained that the pitch aimed at his head was a message from those who were not sure he could be trusted. He increased his gait just enough to close the ground between them without being obvious that he was trying to catch up. As the catcher reached the first tree, Sam took one last big step, bringing him within striking distance. He swung his right arm into an arc that brought his hand clapping against the man's shoulder.

"Hey, there," Sam said. "You remember me. The one who almost caught a high hard one with my head."

The man whirled around, his own arm drawn back as though about to launch a punch.

"Easy," Sam said. "Just introducing myself. Sam Logan."

The other grinned and relaxed his arm.

"Don't you think I know who you are, and what the message of that pitch was?" He held out his hand. "Mark Butera, but folks call me Chub."

"Well, Chub, let's go pick us some apples."

A ladder leaned against the tree. Sam looked up at the branches laden with red fruit.

"Delicious," he said.

"How'd you know?" Chub asked.

"What..." Sam began and then he understood.

"They probably are, but that's the name of the type of apple."

"I knew that," Chub replied.

Sam placed his basket on the ground, and put one hand on the ladder.

"I can take those up there," he said, pointing toward the upper branches.

"That's good with me," Chub replied. "I'm not too happy on ladders."

On this late fall morning with the sun rising and providing a little warmth against the chill announcing the slow but steady arrival of winter, Isaiah walked among others, some strolling, some hastening, from Front Street over the bridge that crossed the river toward the train depot. Somebody viewing him from a little distance would have taken note of how slowly he moved one foot in front of the other, each step, it seemed, requiring a great effort as though he were treading across a field of mud sucking him down. In fact, the sidewalk he trod was freshly laid cement, the street cobblestone. It was his feet that were leaden.

In his wallet, neatly folded was the letter whose contents provided him the opportunity to take this trip. That letter, to his surprise, had come in response to the one he had sent in which he asked for a dispensation he had no reason to believe would be granted. But it had. And now, having asked for and received a few days off from his on again and off again duties as chauffeur, and having with great reluctance explained to Eunice where he was going, but not quite why, he approached the ticket agent.

"Jackson," he said in a whisper.

"Pardon?" the agent asked and leaned toward him.

Isaiah took a breath and forced himself to increase the volume.

"Jackson," he said in a louder voice, "I need to go to Jackson." He took out the train schedule that he had cut out of the newspaper, and found the departure time he had circled. He looked at the grandfather clock ticking loudly in the corner of the ticket office. "There is a train to Jackson in half an hour, isn't there?"

"Yessir," the agent replied. "8:50 this morning. Should arrive..."

"Yes, I know. You don't need..." he began, then stopped himself. Hearing the arrival time was more than he wanted to deal with just now. It would be enough to will himself onto the train.

And the first step would be the purchase of the ticket. He slid a bill and several coins through the window . "Round trip," he said.

The agent counted the money and smiled.

"I'm sure you want a round trip. You wouldn't want to be staying there, would you?"

"No," Isaiah said, "no longer than I have to."

He sat with his face pressed against the window, staring at, without really seeing, the countryside as it slid by. The rocking of the railroad car, the rumble of the steel wheels over the tracks, the monotony of the pattern of woods interrupted by fields and the occasional farmhouse, settled his nerves.

When he had taken his seat, with a nod and a forced smile that denied the turmoil broiling within him, he had acknowledged his traveling companions sitting across from him, a stout businessman who returned the greeting and then unfolded his newspaper and lifted it in front of his face, and a young woman whose anxious expression mirrored his own troubled state of mind, and who could not quite force herself to acknowledge him, as though so to do would make her unfaithful to whoever was waiting for her at her destination. Fortunately, the train was lightly peopled so that the seat next to Isaiah was empty. He had worried that someone would start a traveler's conversation with him, and that if that had happened he would have been utterly unable to answer any question more demanding than a how do you like this weather kind of opener. Had someone asked him his destination, he did not know if he would have been able to stutter out the name of the town printed on his ticket. It took all of his inner reserves to still his shaking hand when he offered his ticket to the conductor.

After that, he turned his face to the window and kept it there. He heard the rustle of the businessman's paper for a while, then a quiet snore. He sneaked a glance out of the side of his eye at the young woman and saw that her eyes were closed and a smile had formed on her lips. No doubt the purpose of her journey was a pleasant one, perhaps even one that would culminate in a reunion with a lover.

Under other circumstances that thought would have brought a sympathetic smile to his own face, for he was an empathetic person who delighted in others' good fortunes as much as he commiserated with their difficulties. But at this moment, he preferred the boring presence of the businessman. It raised no responsive thoughts in him, leaving him free to wrestle with his own demons. The young woman's almost beatific smile, on the other hand, reminded him of his own lost love, and the nerve of that memory, usually encased in a sturdy wall of emotional scar tissue, began to ache, and he pressed his face even harder against the glass until the pain in his nose and forehead acted as a counterbalance to the throbbing of that nerve.

At the next stop, he stood up, took his satchel and walked to the rear of the car where he had noticed an empty set of seats. The businessman roused himself from his nap, glanced in his direction, and then picked up his newspaper to resume reading. The young woman's eyes remained closed.

He found a seat by himself, and as the train lurched into motion, he settled back, closed his eyes, and tried to think of nothing but the rocking of the train and rhythmic rumbling of its wheels over the tracks as it carried him to a confrontation he had spent so many years avoiding.

Sam enjoyed the pressure of the ladder rounds reaching through his thin prison shoes to the soles of his feet. The activities that brought him back to familiar sensations had at first served to remind him of the dismal fact that he would never again experience them outside the walls of this prison. But now when the warden seemed to have held out the promise, however remote, that he might once again be a free man, anything that reminded him of what awaited him should that happen gave him a moment of bittersweet pleasure. As much as he had chafed as a free man at the burdens of farming the prospect of doing that again, even on somebody's else's land as a hired hand, was a ray of light through the everyday gloom of his imprisonment.

For a moment, the contrast between where he had been, where he now was, and where he hoped once again to be froze him as he stood on top of the ladder. It was like he was on a mental carousel, sometimes spinning fast, sometimes slowing almost to a halt, and passing before his eyes as he traversed the circular path were images of both worlds, that of a free man walking with concentrated energy over his own land following his own responsibilities or impulses, whether toward a chore, or a woman's bed, the sun always shining bright above, alternating with the dark walls of the prison constraining his every movement, whether to eat or to work or marching back to his cell, the sky always gray verging on black.

He must make a grab for that gold ring as he whirled by it each time, whether fast or slow, securing it in his hand, as Chub's voice floated up toward him announcing the arrival of the guard who would check their progress. He would hold that ring firm in his grasp to open the door to the return to his free state, whatever the risk, therefore, snatch and hold it he must, for if he didn't, the damned carousel might stop, leaving the key to his freedom forever beyond his reach.

He stretched for an apple on the very topmost branch. The ladder swayed under his shifting weight against the limb that was holding it up. He felt a rush of excitement at the sudden danger. Damn, he thought, what a long time it has been since I felt fear, and how refreshing it is, what a break from the crushing boredom.

The ladder steadied and he grasped the fruit. He started to put it into the basket he had hauled up the ladder with him, but instead looked down to where Chub was, without any great enthusiasm, plucking apples off the lower branches. Standing next to him, clipboard in hand, sun rays seeming to bounce off his bald pate, was the guard.

He could pluck some apples for his basket to assure a proper mark next to his name on that clipboard.

Or he could choose to act on another idea that was forcing itself into his consciousness.

"Hey, " he called out, and as Chub shaded his eyes against the sun and nodded, he dropped the apple he had just picked. The fruit changed direction as it glanced off a branch. Chub lunged to align himself with its new path and held out his own basket.

But his reach was a little short, and the apple plopped onto the ground at the feet of the guard. The guard bent down, picked up the apple, wiped it off on his shirt, and took a bite, looked up at Sam and nodded a sarcastic thank you, then with his handkerchief swiped the beads of sweat off his bald head. Still holding the apple in his left hand, the guard brought his closed right fist down hard on the back of Chub's head. Chub staggered forward, spun, his own fists clenched, but then thought better of it.

"That's right," the guard said. "Hey, Logan," he called out, "come on down. Let's have a little talk."

Sam reached up and plucked another apple from a branch a little lower than the previous one. He dropped it and watched it bounce off the outstretched hand of the guard and plop onto the ground.

"Logan," the guard yelled.

Sam reached for another apple. Then he felt the ladder begin to move. Looking down, he saw the guard with both his hands on the sides of the ladder.

"Down!" the guard demanded.

"Coming boss," Sam replied and took a step down. The ladder kept moving as one rung at a time, he made his way toward the ground.

He stood facing the guard, offering his basket for inspection. In it were two apples. The guard took the basket and put it on the ground next to Chub's, which was half filled. He pointed to that one, smiled and said, "Good boy." With the smile still on his face, he glanced at Sam's basket and shook his head.

Sam knew what to expect, and braced himself. He must accept the blow that he knew was coming, fight off the impulse to block it and then answer it with one of his own. That would not do at all, that would remove that gold ring beyond his grasp.

He saw the fist coming toward him, felt it, experienced his head snapping back. His own right hand insisted on responding but he willed it still. Another blow followed, then another.

Now on the ground, he did not feel the guard's boot as it with slow deliberate, and well practiced accuracy dug into his exposed ribs.

Isaiah felt a strong hand on his arm followed by a gentle voice.

"This way. I'll take you where you need to go."

Isaiah shook his arm free, turned around, and against the background of gray steam rising up from beneath the now motionless locomotive, he saw a young man of about his own age.

"I've come, the warden..." Isaiah began, his hand reaching into his jacket pocket to retrieve the letter.

"I know," the young man said. "He sent me to fetch you."

"But I thought I was to see, to speak with..."

"Perhaps afterwards," the young man said. "But for now, you must come with me."

Isaiah followed the young man who walked toward a Model T.

"That your Ford?" Isaiah asked.

"Not exactly 'mine,' but yes it is going to take us to the prison. You know your cars."

"I do," Isaiah replied.

"For your job?" the young man asked.

"How did you know what I do?"

"We've done our research. This whole thing is very important to us. Not just the warden. But higher up."

"How high?"

"High enough to get something done."

"We know how anxious you are to see your father after all this time," the man who had been introduced to him as Warden Higgins said. "But I need to talk with you first. To see if we can clear up some things. And that young man who brought you here is Larry Morgan from the governor's office."

Isaiah sat back in his chair. Sunlight coming through the office window glinted off the warden's glasses. A spent cigar sat in a large ceramic ashtray on the corner of his desk. Papers on the desk were in neat stacks. The expression on the warden's face was hard to read. It was neither particularly friendly nor hostile. Rather there was something in it that said that this was a careful man who did not make mistakes, and one who was not easily moved to do something that was not in his own best interest.

For a moment, Isaiah was again sitting in a chair across from Sheriff Billingham whose fleshy face offered an expression of feigned benevolence. Isaiah knew then not to trust that expression, and he had squirmed around, as best he could, the sheriff's questions. He did not want to lie, but nor did he want to provide ammunition for the prosecution's case against his father. As he did that day, he felt a trickle of perspiration creeping down his spine and incipient dizziness in his head.

He now knew what was coming.

Again he would be quizzed, where was he on that day, where was his father, what time was it when they worked on the road, from what direction did his father come. He must give the same responses, he was plowing in the morning, came to work on the road some time in the afternoon, he had no watch, did not know exactly the time, but the sun was pretty much straight overhead, and his father arrived to meet him coming from the west.

When he was questioned by the sheriff, he had felt his body shrink to the size of a child, and try as he might, he could not inflate himself back up to his near adult size. Now, however, in spite of the similarities in the situation, confronting again an authority figure with the power to do great harm to his father, placing him in a position to defend what he felt to be indefensible, this time he experienced no shrinkage. Rather, he was an adult and would present himself as such.

He took out the warden's letter.

"You said if I came to Jackson, I would be able to talk to my father."

"I did," the warden replied.

Isaiah scanned the carefully worded letter.

"I don't see anything here about having to clear up anything."

"No, it doesn't. And I will personally guarantee that if you answer a few questions, I will authorize exactly what the letter does say."

Isaiah let his head drop onto his chest, then shook it back and forth.

"Look," the warden said, "this situation has gotten a lot bigger since you wrote to me. I had to promise what I did to get you here. You can understand I had no legal way to force you to come here." He shrugged. "I do what I have to do. As honorably as possible."

"As honorably as possible," Isaiah repeated. He took a deep breath. I've come too damn far, he thought, too damned far to go home empty.

"Go ahead, then," he said. "Ask what you have to."

The warden leaned back, staring at the ceiling as though the questions he might ask were inscribed there. He closed his eyes, then snapped them open.

"Just one question. That is all I need from you. But on the answer hangs everything. For you. For me. For your father."

"And..." Isaiah began.

"Yes, and those others who are behind all of this."

"Ask it, then," Isaiah said.

And he did.

Sam woke up on a bed in a small room. It was not his cell, he could see that much. He looked around for the source of light illuminating the space around his bed, and found a small window behind his bed. As he stretched his neck to get a better look, his body reminded him of the beating he had taken.

He took an inventory of his injuries. His right eye was swollen shut, his lips were puffy, and a finger pressed against his lower front teeth indicated they were loose. He was pretty sure that nothing was broken, but his ribs ached with every breath. I must look a good mess, he thought and smiled. This should convince them that I can be trusted. He remembered being wheeled into this room on a gurney, but he had no idea where he was.

As if in answer to that question, the door swung open. Two men walked in. He recognized the one in the white coat as the prison doctor he had encountered the last time he had taken a beating. The other individual wore a suit and projected an air of bureaucratic authority.

"So you are now awake," that individual said.

Sam nodded.

"Nothing too serious," the individual said to the doctor.

The doctor ran his hands over Sam's body, pausing here and there, observing the places that caused Sam to react.

"Ribs are probably bruised, not broken. Everything else is cosmetic. He'll heal in a week or so."

"Well, it's too bad, he won't be looking better for his visitor."

"Visitor?" Sam asked.

"Yes," the man in the suit said. "The warden has sent me to see if you were in a fit condition to receive a visit." He paused, seeming to enjoy the suspense he was creating. "Yes, a visit from your son."

"Son?"

"Isaiah is here to see you."

On the other side of the door, Isaiah waited, his sweaty hands shoved hard into his trouser pockets, his stomach threatening to demand immediate attention, and his mind struggling to control the sense of dizziness that caused him to shut his eyes tight so that the narrow corridor that led to this place would stop spinning.

His tongue felt as though it would not obey his commands to move in the proper direction to enable him to speak. And just what would he say when after all these years he would stand in front of the man who both gave him life and then ruined it in ways that neither of them had fully appreciated? A simple hello seemed woefully inadequate. But anything more, quite literally, unspeakable.

He had demanded this meeting, written to the governor, insisting that his own thorough review of his father's case warranted a review. In doing this, he was in part honoring the commitment he had made to his grandmother whose unwavering support of her son was something Isaiah did not, could not, share, for did he not have knowledge of that accursed note?

But what of that note? In and of itself it proved nothing. It did not, at least so he had argued with himself hundreds of times, establish anything. She had wanted to meet her lover. She was found at a spot that may, or may not, have been their accustomed trysting place. Sure, his father might well have met her there. Even conceding that possibility, he found it near to impossible to accept that his father, a man of many faults short of violence necessary to commit murder, could have, as the prosecutor at the trial insisted, placed his powerful hands around that fragile neck and squeezed the life out of a woman for whom he, no doubt in his careless, unthinking way, felt a genuine affection. And if his father did not commit this act, who could have? That the woman was distraught and stubborn to the point of lunacy in pursuing what she should have known she could never have, that being, a wedded life with the man she loved with whom, together, in some fairytale way she would raise their child, Isaiah's own brother, about this characterization Isaiah was well aware.

He had rehearsed these same arguments with himself so many sleepless nights always to the same unsettled place. He simply did not have an answer. He could not believe his father's guilt. Nor could he come up with any alternative that made sense.

Thus these same thoughts whirled through his mind as he stood on the other side of the door from the one person who could, should he choose to do so, provide an answer. And now, as he strained to hear the muffled words that did not quite make their way through the wood of the closed door with sufficient clarity for him to decipher what was being said, he steeled himself for the confrontation he had so devoutly pushed to arrange, not just to do his grandmother's bidding, for that would not have been sufficient motivation to place himself where he now stood, but to measure whether he had the strength to put his long nightmare to sleep in the only way that could be accomplished.

The murmuring from the other side of the door stopped. He thought he heard the scraping of a chair as it was being moved, or perhaps it was the shuffling of shoes against the floor.

And as the door began to swing open, Isaiah stepped back and peered into the room.

Sam had been staring hard at the door. Neither the emissary from the warden nor the doctor was either able or willing to offer any explanation as to why the young man, whom he had last seen as a teenager at the conclusion of his trial, was now on the other side of that door. All he was told was that this visit had been arranged, and that it was considered by those in the most important decision making positions as crucial to his possible parole. Having told him that much, his visitors asked him if he needed a few moments to prepare himself.

"I don't know if a few moments will be nearly enough," he said, "but I'll take what you can give me."

As his visitors nodded and took up positions near the door, turning their backs to offer him a semblance of privacy, he tried to come to some kind of guess as to what was involved in this most unusual circumstance so that, as he had done his whole life, he could try to play it in a way that would work to his advantage. And while he was probing for a strategy to serve his self-interest, unbidden came washing upon him a complicated emotion, part warmth at the opportunity now offered him to see the son he was sure he had lost, and part a profound regret that this reunion was to be conjoined to the consequences of the events responsible for that loss.

And with brutal force came the thought that in his effort to save his own life that fateful day he had ruined that of his son who waited on the other side of the door. For what? Recrimination after all these years? Empathy at their mutual loss? None of this made any sense.

The representative of the warden turned to him, and Sam nodded. He watched the door open. Then he lifted himself from his bed, and beckoned Isaiah in. The door shut behind him, and he stood a foot or two into the room. Sam motioned him forward. He hesitated, unsure as to how to respond to the injured man in the bed. But then Sam shrugged and smiled, and the smile so familiar in Isaiah's memory, part knowing, and part self-deprecating steeled the young man's nerves and he approached. He leaned over his father holding his hand above the injured face as though to ever so gently touch the swollen places, but stopping an inch or two above the bruised flesh.

"It's nothing," Sam said. "Just a little disagreement. Between me and a guard. He didn't like how I picked apples."

Isaiah dropped his hand back to his side.

"I can only guess why you are here," Sam said.

"Because..." Isaiah began but Sam shook his head.

"Not yet. First let me say how glad I am you came, for whatever reason."

"My reason, and the reason I have been given this opportunity, I just don't know if they are exactly the same."

"Probably not," Sam said, his voice now authoritative, father talking to son. "I don't care what they want from you." He struggled to rise in the bed, ignoring the pain in his ribs. He reached his hands out and took Isaiah's. His eyes glistened.

"I need to tell you something."

"And I you," Isaiah said.

"I know, after all these years, it's so late, I want you to understand that I am so very sorry for ..."

"Don't," Isaiah said. Sam settled himself back in the bed, shook his head from side to side, then fixed his glance on his son.

"I was there. Where she was found. But I didn't, I never would have hurt her. I can't really explain what happened."

"I never could believe you would have. Hurt her, I mean."

"They want you to tell them..."

"That I told the truth at the trial."

Sam nodded.

"They asked me the question just that way," Isaiah said. "And I gave them what they wanted."

Sam placed his two strong hands on Isaiah's biceps.

"You said you had to tell me something." He squeezed hard. "Don't. Whatever it is, I don't want to hear it. Just as long as you know I would not hurt her. Or you. Do you understand?"

"Yes," Isaiah said.

As he was led away, Isaiah's head whirled with conflicting emotions. On the one hand, he realized he still carried the burden of the note. Perhaps his father guessed at some such thing, and spared him the telling of it. On the other hand, he felt relief that he had not been compelled to reveal the secret of the note, for so doing would most certainly have spoiled the reconciliation he had just experienced after all these years. What mattered, he concluded as he walked with the guard, was that he and his father had come to some sort of an understanding, as incomplete on both sides as it might have been. The revelation of the note would have spoiled that delicate balance.

And what would have been accomplished after all? His father had acknowledged that he had been there where she was found, implicitly also confessing that he must have been there when she died. Isaiah told himself he did not really need to know the details of what transpired between them leading to her death. He could even forgive his father's efforts later on at self-preservation. And his telling his father that he already knew he was there at the scene would not have accomplished anything positive at this point.

Thus, with an internal sigh he let the guard lead him away. They made a turn that did not register in his memory as leading back the way they had come. He stopped.

"We're going somewhere else first," the guard said.

"Yes, governor," the warden said into the phone. "We have interviewed the young man. As you requested, we did not push him hard. He is now talking to his father, as he had requested, and as you indicated you wanted us to make possible. We will check in with him on the way out."

CHAPTER TEN

Edward blinked against the morning sun coming through the window of his room. He heard the familiar noises rising up from the street, announcing yet another parade. And that large woman, no doubt, would be at the front of it.

The noise got louder, cheers from the onlookers on one side of the street, jeers from those on the other. Above the heads of people on both sides of the street were signs. Those from the cheerers declared their allegiance to the striking Western Federated Miners, demanded negotiation toward a fair wage, while those of the jeerers insisted that the outside socialist agitators go home, there would be no red star floating above their town. Edward struggled to read these signs, and then leaned back in his chair, his head beginning to ache from the effort to sort out the contesting views. He had to confess that both sides seemed to have a point. But then, as he usually did in situations where the evidence confused him, he gave up the effort to come to his own conclusion. He would await being told which side had the better of the argument, and then he would act as though that answer was self-evident.

He resumed looking out the window. Now he could see her, as before, in the front carrying that huge flag, and behind her a child beating on a drum. But then a different noise came from the opposite direction. He turned toward it and saw a cloud of dust accompanied by the familiar sound of horses' hooves. The sunlight glinted off something. After a few moments, he could see that the something was a sword in the upraised hand of a soldier in a blue uniform. He was followed by six or eight other mounted soldiers. They had been approaching at a gallop, but now they slowed first to a trot, and then a walk.

They stopped when they were within fifteen or twenty yards of the oncoming parade. The officer with the sword prodded his horse forward. Big Annie kept moving but those behind her hesitated, and then stopped. The drummer ceased his playing. She turned to the marchers and said something to them that Edward could not make out. They responded with a cheer and closed ranks behind her. The child resumed drumming, even louder than before. The officer moved slowly toward the marchers. His troop followed.

The officer stopped his horse immediately in the path of Annie. He leaned over his horse's head and said something to her. She shook her head with a violent side to side motion. He rose up in his saddle and motioned for his troop to come forward. They did. The officer swept his arm first to the left, and then to the right, and his troop formed a line on each side of him, so that the whole street was effectively blocked. Annie walked toward him until she was face to face with his snorting horse. He again spoke, and she again shook her head, and this time raised her huge flag as high as she could.

The office swung his sword in front of him. As though to block the weapon's path, the woman tilted the flag toward the officer. Steel met cloth, riping the flag almost in two.

The woman seized the flapping end of the flag and then furled the banner around its pole. The street had become silent, all eyes fixed on the two protagonists. They stood glaring at each other for several moments, and then the woman began to walk forward. The officer held his sword stretched out in front of him. She continued until the sword point pressed against her breast.

From the corner of his eye, Edward detected a movement, which against his will, so engrossed was he in this confrontation, caused him to look in that direction. There he saw a man holding something and pointing it toward the woman and the soldier. At first, Edward thought it must be a gun, but even at this distance he could see that it was in the shape of a box, with nothing like a barrel protruding from the end.

"Do you want to slice me too?" the woman said in a voice loud enough to be heard by everyone. "If not, stand aside and let us continue."

Watching from his window, Edward forgot the man with

the box like contrivance, and tried to understand the woman's actions. He could not imagine challenging authority in such a manner. Did she not know that the soldier must be obeyed? That he held a weapon while she held a flag, which was no more than a piece of cloth on a wooden pole? Foolish woman, he thought, you will get yourself killed, and you will have no one to blame but yourself. He was about to give voice to that thought when to his stunned amazement, the officer lowered his sword, turned sideways, and with a sweeping gesture of his unarmed hand beckoned her to continue. As she took a step, he motioned for his troop to clear a path for her. They did, and now in silence, the marchers continued on their way while the onlookers just stood looking at them.

Edward, too, watched the departure until he heard a shout. He turned in the direction from which it came just in time to see the man with box like apparatus start to run, pursued by two other men. He lost sight of them as they disappeared down an alley between two buildings farther up the street.

As he was the first time Edward witnessed the march of the striking miners, Jablonski was waiting for Edward to emerge from the boarding house.

"What'd you think?" he asked.

That was the kind of question Edward always had difficulty answering. He never knew what he was supposed to think. His thoughts resided at the lower end of the cognition scale, concentrated on what he needed or what he wanted. If his stomach told him it was empty, he thought about what he might eat, or whether he had the money to buy food. If his eyes lit on an attractive woman, his thoughts would be a bit more complicated. On the most basic level, his brain told him that he wanted that woman. But then if he tried to figure a way to satisfy that carnal appetite, he had to deal with a range of more complicated thoughts, how he might meet her, what he would do if he were successful doing that, but also the societal and religious barriers between one such as he and the woman, unless she happened to be of his status, or better yet, lower. As for political situations, such as the one that was the context for the scene he had just witnessed, he had not a clue as to what he should think. To be sure, he thought the woman was putting her life in danger by offering her unprotected breast to the hard steel of the officer's sword. Why she would do that, what motive she might possibly have, was beyond his experience as well as his imagination. Even more startling to him was the officer's yielding the road to her when he so clearly had not only the authority of the government on his side and the ability to prevent her from moving forward, and yet had stepped aside as though she were a lady of superior rank.

As Jablonski waited with an expectant look on his face, Edward struggled to find a thought he could send from his brain to his tongue to answer the question, just what did he think?

"The woman was very foolish," he said. "I thought the soldier would use his weapon on her."

"I see," Jablonski said. "And the soldier, why do you think he did not?"

The answer sprang unbidden to Edward's lips.

"Because she was a woman. If she was a man, maybe he would have."

"You might be right. What would you have done, if you were that soldier?"

"I don't know," Edward confessed, for he could not see himself running a sword through the exposed breast of a woman.

"Do you know how dangerous that woman is?" Jablonski now asked, his tone harder. "How she should mind her business, be with her children, her husband is already in jail, and no doubt, she will join him as soon as it is safe to arrest her. She and those she is leading are socialist agitators. We cannot tolerate them here, they are closing down the mines, and that is not doing anybody any good, not them, not the townspeople, and certainly not us. Do you understand?"

Edward moved his head with an uncertain nod.

"Did you see the man with the camera?" Jablonski asked. "The one being chased after the strikers moved on?"

"A camera?" Edward muttered. "That's what it was."

"Yes. And I know that man. If he is not caught by my associates, if he can develop the picture he has taken, that picture will appear in a newspaper. He is more dangerous than the woman herself. If you ever see that man, I want you to bring him to me."

"I will," Edward smiled, content that although he did not fully understand the significance of the man and his camera, he was happy to be given a simple, unambiguous task to do. "I will snatch him up if ever I see him," he continued, "and bring him right to you."

A thousand miles away, that morning Jim paused as he was about to open the door leading onto the street. The feeling that the net was closing around him had intensified during the night. He put his hands in his pockets in the hope that somehow he had more money than he remembered counting the day before. His fingers scrounged around searching for metal and came up with a few coins. He looked at them. Confirmation that he had two choices. He could try to travel without money, by sneaking onto boxcars, walking, or begging rides. Or he could work for a few days or a week or two, just enough to fill his pockets so that he could leave this city, get someplace where again he could stop and find work, he could always do that, land some kind of menial task, his back was still strong and he knew how to play the role of the servile black man, then with money again in his pocket move on once more.

To where, he did not know. Just someplace beyond the reach of the approaching net. If that net gathered him in, and he was again asked to tell what he saw that day, he would have to figure out what the person asking wanted him to say, and then determine if it was in his own best interest to provide the desired answer.

All he wanted to do was live in peace. Why couldn't those white folks do what they want to do without involving him?

He peered up and down the street as he emerged into the morning sun. People were hurrying along, no doubt on their way to their jobs, jobs they could keep as long as they wanted to and not be looking over their shoulders, as he was, with every troubled breath he took. There were young men, perhaps apprentices, and tired looking women carrying baskets on their way to the market, some of them with small children in tow. Scattered among them was the occasional well-dressed white man, some carrying briefcases, although what they were doing in this run-down neighborhood was a bit of a mystery to him.

Nowhere did he see anyone who aroused his suspicions as did the man who seemed to be following him last night, and he relaxed for a moment. Maybe he was, after all, just imagining that he was in danger, that he would not be snatched up and dragged back into that dead woman's case, as he had been that time in Cadillac, when one white man was trying to give him the means to go far away while the other, apparently with greater power, insisted that he come back with him and testify.

With the happy thought that he might be imagining a non-existent threat, after all the man he helped convict was still locked up as he had been for years, he began walking, enjoying the sun against the chill of the late fall day that suggested winter would not be long in arriving. For the moment, he let himself think that he was like all those others among whom he was walking, and that like them at the end of the day, weary from his labor, he would be able to have a simple meal at the restaurant near his room, and then retire for the night.

When he arrived at his work site, however, those pleasant thoughts dissipated against the reality he saw waiting for him. There talking to the foreman who had hired him was the thick bodied man he remembered, the one who had been offering money so that he could travel on from Cadillac, away from the court where Sam Logan's fate was to be determined. That man was the one who had been out-muscled by the local sheriff in Cadillac, with the result that he had found himself on a train heading north to the courthouse in Traverse City.

Even though the man talking to his foreman had at that long ago time tried to help him move beyond the reach of the law, seeing him now caused his pulse to quicken. His presence could not augur well, Jim calculated, it did not matter whose side the man was on, whether Logan's as he was then, or the law, as he might be now, whichever it was, he represented precisely what Jim had been trying to avoid since the moment he walked out of the courthouse after giving the testimony that sent Sam Logan into a lifetime imprisonment.

He stopped walking. Maybe he could just turn around, return to his room, pick up his few belongings, blend into the multitudes the city offered, wait for night, and in the darkness, find a way to escape this dreaded entanglement one more time.

The foreman's glance turned toward him. The two men had stopped talking. Still, he could probably outrun either one of them. He spun around, his eyes darting for an alley into which he could duck and then disappear. But there in front of him stood another man. His shape looked familiar. He realized that this man was, in fact, the same one he believed had been trailing him last night. So, he was not imagining the threat after all. He should have believed his well-developed instincts for survival. He had permitted himself the folly of ignoring those instincts, walking among others who did not share his problem, believing he could be just like one of them, and failing to take the simple precaution that had served him so well for so long, of making sure he was not being followed as he strolled toward work, immersed in the fantasy of being a free man, able to go where he wanted. Clearly, he had been tailed this morning, and the man standing not ten feet away from him was one end of a vice, the burly man the other, and he was about, once again, to be squeezed until he acceded to whatever demands they would now place upon him.

His blood rose in anger against the injustice. What had he ever done to deserve to be placed in this predicament? All he ever wanted was to be allowed to earn his daily bread, and otherwise to be left alone. The ancient scars on his back should have reminded him that was not to be his fate. Mr. Lincoln's emancipation did not free him from the whip held in the hand of a white man who felt the need to remind Jim that though the chains of his servitude had been lifted, those invisible ones based on the immutable color of his skin remained. True, he had glanced at the man's pretty daughter. The color of his skin did not change the fact that he was a healthy young male himself. And yes, he had averted his eyes as soon as he realized what he was doing, but it was not fast enough. The scourge of the whip told him that he had to be even more careful, to train himself to deny the most natural of feelings.

That is how he felt looking at the lovesick mistress of Sam Logan. She lived on another planet, as did Sam. That fool, Edward, protected by his white skin, could stare at her if he wanted, talk to her as he chose, so long as he did not cross the line established, not by his color, but by his status as a worker on the young woman's father's farm. Edward managed, just barely, to stay on the right side of that line, but where he stood was miles beyond where Jim could imagine being.

He saw an alley some fifty yards away on the right hand side of the street. He took a step in that direction. The man in front of him stepped sideways to remain in his path. The man shook his head from side to side ever so slowly. Then, a voice called out to him.

"Now, Jim, I just want to talk with you. I'm getting too old to run after people, that's why my friend there is helping me."

Jim turned back.

"What you want with me, mister, I'm through with all that trouble."

"Mister Benson, Wendell Benson," the man said. "And I'm afraid trouble has a way of dogging your steps."

The foreman of the street gang walked over to them.

"This boy in some kind of trouble?" he asked.

"Not at all, leastwise nothing serious, nothing to concern you," Benson said.

"He's not getting paid to talk with you."

"He just quit," Benson said.

The foreman shrugged, and walked back to the job site.

"I needed that job," Jim said.

"Don't worry. I'll make it up to you. I just need you to answer a couple of questions."

"What about?"

"You know what about," Benson said with a half smile. "Don't play dumb nigger with me."

"Ain't playin'. And if it's about all that, I got nothing new to say."

"Maybe so. But we want to hear it again. Maybe you'll now

recall a detail or two that you didn't last time when you testified."

"And if I give you what you want?" Jim asked.

"Now you seem to understand. Then, we'll see what we can do
for you."

They began walking, Jim flanked by Benson and the other
man who had blocked his retreat. After a few steps, they were
approached by yet another white man, this one also not young,
with a thick white mustache and a smile on his face although
his labored breathing indicated he had not been able to keep up
with the others.

"We're both getting too old for this game," Benson said to
Drummond."

"Right you are," Drummond replied.

"Any more of you white folks gonna join this party?" Jim asked.
"I don't see no tree anywhere nearby."

"Just a few questions," Benson said. "And my friend, here, is
also most interested in your answers."

"Do you want me to get somebody to translate?" Fred McGinnis
asked.

On Governor Woodhouse's desk was the front page of a Finnish language newspaper. The governor looked up from the page
at his assistant.

"I can read the God damned pictures, Fred. I don't need the
words."

"Maybe context..." McGinnis began, surprised at his boss's
unusually angry tone and even rarer resorting to any kind of
profanity. The governor, after all, had a well-deserved reputation for a cool head and a church going man's reluctance to take
the Lord's name in vain.

"Sorry, Fred, you'll have to excuse me. But these pictures, I
was the one who sent the troops in at the bequest of the local
authorities who told me serious civil unrest was threatening the
peace of their community, that this strike was becoming violent,
and maybe some of that was true, but I can't help feel I was
being played to take their side in this dispute, which was never

my intention, as you well know, I can see both sides, the mines need to make money, and the miners need to have fair compensation for their very dangerous work, but now, one of the men I sent there to preserve the peace is shown here," he slapped his hand down hard on the newspaper, "shown here with his sword slicing through the American flag being held by a woman, not a striking miner, but a woman, who stands there for all the world to see. And then, if that isn't enough, another picture, of the officer's sword against the woman's breast. My possible opponents are smiling, and others are reconsidering whether they should join in the contest."

"Yes, I understand all that," Fred said. "But the context I was talking about would not excuse that officer's behavior, but I just think we ought to see how the incident is described, after all this newspaper is being read by those miners you are talking about."

Woodhouse reached underneath the newspaper and pulled out another.

Fred picked up the paper and read the headline, "Should Woodhouse Get Another Term?"

"I've seen that one," Fred said.

"Just a reminder," the governor said.

"Have you decided to run?"

Woodhouse shook his head.

"Not yet," he said. "But I can tell you this, I don't want to leave office with this strike the last thing people remember about my administration."

"Do you want me to..."

"Yes. Get up there. See what we are dealing with."

"And that other matter?"

"Mr. Logan?"

"Yes."

"We'll talk about him when you get back."

Woodhouse sat at his desk after Fred left. The two situations, up to this point discrete issues, were beginning to move toward each other in ways that he could not fully understand, and yet he felt the movement as though he were standing at a point where two streams converged, their combined waters now beginning to rise up his body.

Would he be able to float above or would he be driven against waiting rocks?

Edward was not sure he could handle his new assignment. It was one thing to eavesdrop on a conversation at a bar, which he had only managed to do with the assistance of the barman, and even then he did not understand what value there might be in the nugget of information he dutifully carried back to Jablon-ski, who seemed more than a little interested to hear about the plans for a holiday party, why, Edward thought, would he be so interested in something like that which seemed to have little to do with the woman offering her breast to the sword of the cal-vary officer, but yet there was something there, for wasn't it the very same woman in both situations, the one at the table in the tavern, and the one holding the flag at the front of the parade.

Such analysis made his head hurt, and so, as was usual with him, he simply stopped trying to figure things out. Better to just do what he was told to do. That is why he found himself trying to blend into the crowd of striking miners entering a meeting hall some blocks from the tavern, there to just listen, Jablonski said, listen to what the men giving speeches said, and just as import-ant, try to get a sense of how the audience responded. When he asked how he was to do that, Jablonski, with irritated patience, said, why do they applaud, stand up and cheer, or seem to be sitting on their hands?

As he entered the building, out of the corner of his eyes he saw Willie Forsch talking to several other men. As if remembering Willie's hard fists digging into his sides, his ribs ached as he took a deep breath. He turned aside and pushed his way through the oncoming crowd so that he would no longer be visible to Willie or his companions. Their conversation seemed animated, and so he was fairly certain they hadn't seen him. For a second, he contem-plated sidling up closer to them so he could hear what they were talking about. No doubt Jablonski would want to know. But the pseudo pain in his ribs intervened and blocked the thought, after all in any event, his assigned task was to gauge the crowd's reaction to the speakers, not just a few men talking to each other. No sense, he thought, going beyond what he had been told to do.

With that sensible thought fixed in his mind, he sought a seat that would give him a sufficient vantage point to be able to bring back the information Jablonski wanted. He figured it could not be in the front because then he would have to make himself conspicuous by turning around with his back to the speaker as he looked at the crowd. Sitting all the way in the rear seemed to offer a different problem, he would not be conspicuous, but he would not be able to see faces of the men in the audience.

He stood perplexed for a few moments until his brain seized upon the answer. He would go to the side, either extreme left or right, somewhere about halfway back from the speaker's place on the platform, from which he could in profile gaze at the audience, and even sneak a look toward the back.

He made his way through the crowd until he saw just such a seat on the left side of the auditorium. He worked his way down the row toward the seat, stepping carefully past the feet of those already sitting. Just as he was about to sit down himself, another man came toward him from the aisle. Edward froze. He wanted that seat, but he did not want to call attention to himself. To his profound relief, the man waved to somebody back in the center of the row and kept walking, edging with a nod past Edward. Edward hastened to sit down, and turned his attention to the front of the auditorium where a man dressed in a suit and tie ambled up onto the platform. Up to that moment, the hall had been alive with dozens of small conversations, a sea of words butting into each other, floating above the heads of the speakers and arriving in Edward's ears as incoherent linguistic fragments. He strained to separate out the strands to connect the disparate words into meaningful utterances, but to no effect, managing only to pick out from among all the words a name, first just Joe, and then Joe Michaels. Now, however, the hall was silent. He saw that all eyes turned toward the speaker. So complete was the silence, it was almost as though all there had ceased even breathing.

Edward turned his attention back to the podium. He now

saw that the man standing there was tall and wide shouldered with a jowly face and a strong jaw, altogether the kind of man, thought Edward, used as he was to making such calculations, that you would not want to get into a brawl with. The speaker raised both his arms, hands clasped above his head in a greeting to the crowd, and the silence was broken first by an occasional sound of clapping hands, followed by a low murmur, and then an explosion of cheers, as the audience rose. Edward, too, stood, and aware of the need to be inconspicuous, added his voice to the cheer, although he was not quite certain what words to say, contenting himself with a version of Hurrah, Hurrah.

Michaels unclasped his hands and extended them toward the audience palms down, and then lowered them. The crowd quieted and sat back down. Edward followed suit.

"Thank you, thank you," Michaels said. "I am not going to bore you by telling you what you already know. I have come here to tell you that the national fully supports you and with that support you will win."

The cheering began again, and once more Michaels gestured for quiet. As he cleared his throat to continue, a woman's voice familiar to Edward called out, "Does your support, Mr. Michaels, include the hard cash we have been promised?"

All eyes, Edward's included, turned toward the source of the voice. There in the rear of the hall stood Annie.

"Why, Miss Annie, how good of you to raise that most important question."

"Sweet talk don't put food on my child's plate," Annie said.

A murmur arose in the audience. Although Edward knew he had no business having an opinion on the matter, he felt himself siding with the tall, ungainly woman, who had so freely offered herself to the sword of the officer.

"No it don't," Michaels said, and the murmuring quieted. "If we only count dollars, the fight is uneven. The company has the money. But we have something else," he raised his voice, "don't we?" He waited, then again, louder, his voice now turning hoarse. "Don't we?"

"Yes," came from one in the audience, then another, tentative at first, but growing in strength.

"And what is that we have?" Michaels demanded. "I'll tell you. We have each other, and that comes down to one word, don't it?"

This time the response was quicker.

"Union," came from scattered voices.

"Right," Michaels said. "That word is Union. Let's hear it.'"

"Union," the crowd now answered, voices now together as one.

Edward was impressed. Listening to Michaels brought him back to those few occasions when his mother took him to church and made him sit still while the minister preached. But that was long ago, and Michaels was certainly preaching a different message. Here there was no talk of God, or sin, or redemption. There was a kind of amen in that one word, union, and in its way it seemed far more powerful than the murmured amen he dimly recalled hearing from the congregation in that church so many years ago.

In a far corner of the auditorium sat Fred McGinnis. The first time he came up here, he tried to do so, as instructed by the governor, with an open mind. He struggled to do what the governor had asked him to do, namely to leave his politics at home so as to enable him to bring back an objective view of the strike.

Easier said than done, he realized at that time. His politics had a nasty habit of first intruding and then shaping what he witnessed. In moments of honesty, he admitted to himself that his politics were also informed by his self-interest. As the governor's career would go, so, at least for the immediate future, would his. If the governor weathered this crisis and went on to a second term, well, then, Fred McGinnis would be with him to share the ride. That would be the best outcome, the one Fred assured his wife would be theirs to enjoy.

But now this damned strike could ruin everything. It could seriously diminish the governor's re-election effort. When the governor tried to put his finger on the pulse of public opinion, Fred knew, the reading he received was not nearly as accurate as Fred's. For the governor's fine sense of decency, justice, fair play, all those nice abstract concepts, interfered with what the public pulse reading told him. It wasn't that Governor Woodhouse wasn't smart enough to perceive the attitudes of the ordinary citizens, those whose vote would determine his political future. Rather those perceptions sometimes lost the argument with the governor's deeply held principles.

That was where the governor had come to rely on Fred's hard-headed political realism. Yet this time, the governor had instructed him to leave his politics at home. But somehow they had sneaked into his luggage, or perhaps hitched a ride in his wallet, however they had managed it, they had come with him, so that now as he sat in this hall, listening to the union leader, he could not help trying to consider how that ordinary citizen would react. He imagined, first, his wife, the daughter of a businessman, and brought up with the simple idea that the boss made decisions in the best interest of the company, and here was the important part, that the company's success or failure directly determined the well-being of its employees. For after all, if the company failed, there would be no money to fund the workers' paychecks. Wasn't it that simple?

Moving on from what he imagined with some confidence would be his wife's disapproval of the strike because it threatened the success of the mining companies, his mind moved on to their neighbors in the solidly middle-class enclave of Lansing where they were raising their two daughters. Would they not agree? And then factor in the stories of occasional violence that filtered down to them from up here and place those stories against the high value placed on order in the civil society, and he could not think his neighbors would be any more sympathetic to the miners than was his wife.

But then into his calculations came that photo of the large woman confronting the bare sword of the cavalry officer, and added to that remembered image was the woman herself, now challenging the union leader to make good on his promise to enable the striking miners to continue living without their paychecks. He also had enough experience dealing with corporate executives to realize that they would not, as these striking miners no doubt were, be facing an empty larder with not only themselves but hungry children to care about.

He turned his attention back to the speaker who had been droning on about union solidarity because now he was speaking about something very specific. Was it not important, the speaker now demanded, to convince the bosses how unsafe the new one-man drilling machines were? We all know, he continued, how dangerous our jobs as miners are, how many of us are injured, maimed, killed, how important it is when an accident happens that there is somebody there to call for help, but the bosses,what do they care about that, all they worry about is saving the cost of labor, our labor, so if one man can do the job of two or three, why let the one man do it with this wonderful new machine, and what if the man running that machine by himself gets hurt, who's gonna be there for him?

The words rolled, now, and the audience responded to each of his rhetorical questions. Fred felt himself being carried along, how could he not, and for the moment his usual hard edged cynicism while not quite disappearing, softened. When Michaels first used the plural pronoun, we know this, we need this, that cynicism protested that this man, this speaker probably had not been in a mine in years. But there was a sincerity and passion there that was hard to dismiss and so Fred let himself ride along with it, making sure to take note of the audience's response.

For his part, Edward felt the pull of camaraderie with the miners, but it was only a gentle tug that stirred a new thought in his mind. In truth, he had never thought of himself as a victim of corporate greed or indifference. He had simply accepted the lot into which he had been born. He had not placed a value on it, did not aspire to rise above it. It simply was what it was. That was as far as his thinking went in that direction if it went there at all. He could understand the danger of the one-man drill, as the speaker described it, but his emotions were not engaged. Just as he had been struck by wonder at seeing the woman confront the soldier with the sword, he was not moved to enlist in the struggle of labor against the bosses. A boss did what bosses do, and workers accommodated themselves to the demands placed upon them.

But still, he recalled, Jablonski would want his impressions, and so he sought words to capture what he had witnessed. The one word that did come to mind, and the one he repeated silently to himself so as to store it into his often porous memory, was fight, these men seemed ready to fight for what they thought they deserved.

Back in his room, Jim stretched on the bed. He had some money in his pocket, enough to pay his rent and feed his belly for a while. All he had to do was stay put until the transcript of his testimony proved to be satisfactory. When it did, Benson said, he would send him on his way to a place where he could start a new life. In the meantime, he knew, the same sturdy fellow who had blocked his retreat in the street would be keeping an eye on him. Should he choose to take off again, he'd have to get past that fellow. And if he succeeded, Benson had assured him, it would not take long for him to be tracked down again, and this time their reunion, Benson said with a wide smile, would not be nearly so cordial as the one just concluded.

Things surely could be worse, Jim figured. His testimony was only slightly different from what he had offered at trial, not that he would be too troubled by any changes he might now make to accommodate the obvious preferences of Benson and whoever it was who had sent Benson after him. He just didn't give a damn about Sam Logan one way or another, he could rot in jail or do a dance at his homecoming as a free man. All Jim cared about was that once and for all he could leave this tangled matter behind him. In any case, the change he willingly made seemed to have given Benson what he wanted.

Drummond found Benson on a stool working on a boilermaker at McSorley's on 7th Street. He sat down next to him, and motioned to the bartender. "Bourbon," he said, "neat."

"I expected you might turn up," Benson said.

"An old reporter always wants to get the whole story. Finding you here was just a good guess."

"I've sent the package on his way."

"Where to?"

"That you'll have to find out for yourself."

"Oh, I will. You are not the only one with sources."

"To what purpose?'"

"Like I said. All good stories have an end."

"And no doubt an audience," Benson said.

The barkeep placed Drummod's drink in front of him. He picked it up and took a good sized sip, and nodded.

"That there is, that there is."

CHAPTER ELEVEN

"Just needed to check in with you before you leave," the warden said.

"What passed between me and my father is private, isn't it?" Isaiah demanded.

"Yes and no. Yes if you want it to be. No if you want your conversation with him to perhaps be of some use to him."

"I really just wanted the chance to speak with him. It was long past time."

"I can understand. But I have to tell you that I'm getting a lot of pressure. To get a sworn statement from you. To see if releasing him is a viable choice."

"Viable?"

"Politically?"

Isaiah felt the anger rise in him. His father's fate, a political question? Outrageous. His face reddened and the pulse in his neck quivered.

"The real world, son," the warden said.

"I'm not your son," Isaiah snapped.

"No. And I can't imagine what you are thinking, or what I would have my son do in your situation. So why don't you take your time before you decide what you want to do."

"I was going to catch a late train back home," Isaiah said.

"There's a decent hotel near the station. If you need...."

"Thanks, but I can pay my own way. And make my own decisions."

"Good."

"I'll let you know tomorrow."

But Isaiah did not go to the hotel to contemplate his answer to the warden. Instead, as the sun began to set and the air to cool, he stood outside the walls of the prison. Then he walked around the huge facility, always in sight of its tall gray exterior walls. And as he walked, he tried to imagine where his father was inside, and what he might be doing at that moment, and further, what his life day to day would be like, this last, of course, impossible for one such as he to conceive.

Then, much to his surprise he realized that equally difficult for him to imagine was his father a free man. He had long ago accepted that he would grow into old age without ever again having his father in his life. That reality was, he now understood, a hidden motivation for his determination to visit with Sam inside those grim gray walls that would forever form an impenetrable barrier between them. He needed to confront his father in person, to clear the air between them, that air thick with unstated, and therefore inarticulate, incriminations on both sides of their tragic history.

Of course, there was that other motive behind his visit, the one that helped guide his pen as he wrote his letter requesting permission to visit a man whose sentence had been for solitary confinement, and though that severity had been lifted, routine visitation was certainly not available. However haltingly, he was attempting to fulfill the mission his grandmother had burdened him with.

To free her son. His father.

Those were reasons enough, he thought, to want to be in the same room with his father. But once he actually was, when the idea of Sam that had occupied his mind for all those many years, was, perforce, replaced by the actual man lying in that bed, uncalled for, and to some extent, unwanted, emotions had flooded over him with a physical force that left his knees weak and his heart beating as though it would break out of his chest.

Those emotions were complex enough to cause his eyes to lose focus as he stood outside the prison, so much so, that he felt the need to lean against the hard walls, their indifferent coldness providing a degree of stability to the whirl that was spinning in his brain.

There he stood shivering in the advancing cold until in the darkness he pushed himself away from the prison walls and made his way toward the hotel. As he walked, he reached into his pocket to assure himself that he had enough money, as he told the warden, to pay his own way. That was important. His fingers told him that there were enough coins to pay for his dinner and his bed for the night. In his coat pocket as well he found the return ticket that would take him home. All that he now had to do was hold firm to the decision that settled into his mind as he leaned against the wall. In a situation where there was no absolutely right course, he felt comfortable that he had landed on the best one.

For him.

And for his father.

Sam dipped his tin spoon into the tin plate containing the slop that passed for beef stew. It was no better than luke warm after having sat untouched for half an hour since it had been brought into him. Still, his stomach demanded, and he lifted the spoon to his mouth and ate. He repeated the motions until the plate was empty and he set it on the floor next to his bed.

The repetitive motions performed to fulfill the necessary function of providing himself with sustenance had allowed his mind to go blank. He needed time to settle his thoughts down. Seeing Isaiah, talking to him, coming to some sort of an understanding had left him drained. But now that his stomach had been somewhat satisfied he lay back and allowed his brain to recall the details of his interaction with his son.

Remembering the Biblical verse from long ago, he for a moment thought of Isaiah as the prodigal son returning. But of course that was false for so many reasons. After all, not only was he himself the one who left, albeit not of his own volition, but in a deeper sense he knew that it was he who abandoned Isaiah when Margaret entered their lives. At that time, much to his shock and chagrin, he found himself in competition with his son for the affection of a young woman who for her own reasons preferred the older man in this unspeakable triangle.

Now years later as he lay in bed bruised from the fists and feet of a guard, with no more warning than a whispered "there's someone here to see you," and before he could even begin to wonder who that might be, in walks Isaiah. He remembers searching for something to say and, finding nothing, could only hold out his arms into which, to his surprise, Isaiah walked, stopping from entering a full embrace only because of concern raised by the obvious bruises on the face of his father. Sam, though, pulled Isaiah to him, enjoying the sharp shock that ran through his body as though confirmation of their reunion as well as a reminder of the shared pain of their history.

It was fortunate, he now thought, that he had not had more time to prepare for this visit. The awkwardness between them was far better than any prepared strategy he might have dreamed up. At last, they confronted the issue that had haunted them both. He had been able to confess that he had, in fact, been with her when she died. As he gave halting voice to that confession, he felt as though a huge weight of which he had been only dimly aware lifted from him. Isaiah, too, seemed relieved to have that bare fact placed between them where they could both view it. And it had, it seemed for both of them, become incarnate, almost as though they could reach out and touch it.

On some level, Sam knew that Isaiah held his fate in his hands. As a man who his whole life had figured odds, read human nature, and when able to control his impulses, charted the best route among the various choices life offered, Sam calculated that he was not far from securing his freedom. He knew that his mother had been unrelenting in her support of him, but he figured that now there was pressure coming from far more compelling sources, who that might be, he could only guess, but whatever the source of that pressure, it had its hand on the knob of the door that would open to the outside.

It must be, he concluded, that the door's lock must also be opened, and that Isaiah, somehow, could be the key. That key could only be his support for his alibi. As Lowe had underscored so many years ago, an alibi is the best of all defenses. It is simply impossible to be in two places at the same time. Isaiah's declaring at trial that he met his father coming back from a direction opposite from that at which her body had been found was powerful support for that alibi.

Yet, Sam recognized then, and reminded himself as he lay

in his prison hospital bed, Isaiah's testimony had not been full throated. His son had walked a very careful line out of respect for what, for the truth, and so he must have had his own doubts, maybe even something stronger. He must have been torn between his suspicions and his desire, in spite of all that had transpired between them in their competition for Margaret's love, in spite of all that, there must have remained a solid nugget of filial feeling, and so he had trod that very fine line.

Because of that careful support from Isaiah, the testimony of that black hand, which otherwise would not have prevailed in competition with that of an obviously upright white young man, Sam was realist enough to understand the racial attitudes then, and still, prevalent. In spite of those attitudes, his hand's opposing testimony was enough to provide a jury set on convicting him a basis so to do.

At the time, he admitted to himself that he felt betrayed by his son. After a while, though, he acknowledged that the boy had done as well as anyone under the circumstances could have done.

But now, Isaiah must be confronted with the very same situation. The meeting was authorized by the authorities, the warden, and perhaps someone even higher up. It was a favor granted to Isaiah.

Would Isaiah grab the opportunity?

Isaiah was up before the sun. All night after he thought he had reached a firm decision as to what he would tell the warden, and as he attempted without success to nail that decision down in his mind by going to sleep so that it would still be there when he woke up, for all of that fruitless effort, doubts ate away at his resolution. At one point, he rolled out of bed and paced back and forth trying to tire his body out. If he couldn't shut down his mind, perhaps he could reach a state of exhaustion compelling enough to bring on sleep.

Finally, though, he was able to wrestle his doubts into a corner and to restore his confidence in the rightness of his decision.

Now, looking out the window and seeing the first rays of the sun creep over the building across from him, he got up, put on his shoes and then sat back down on the bed realizing that although he was up, those he had to talk to would not yet be available.

"Since you are here," the warden said, "can I assume you are ready to answer our questions in a written statement?"

"I am."

The warden got up from behind his desk and walked to the door of his office. In a moment, he returned followed by a young woman with a pad. She took a seat in a chair next to the warden's desk.

"Miss Olsen will take down what we say, word for word, my questions, your answers in shorthand. Then she will prepare a typed version on her machine, which we will go over for accuracy, and then she will witness your signing it."

"And that will be it?" Isaiah asked.

"If you mean will anything further be required of you, the answer should be 'no'."

"Should be?"

"Yes, should be," the warden said.

Isaiah looked from Miss Olsen to the warden.

"Let's begin," he said.

"At the beginning, then," the warden replied. He turned to Miss Olsen. "Ready?"

She looked up from her pad, her pencil poised over it.

"Yes," she said.

The warden looked down at a pile of papers on his desk. Shuffled through them, found what he was looking for, and ran his hand over the page.

"The trial transcript," he said. "Let us begin, by identifying you for the record. You are Isaiah Logan, son of Sam Logan, presently incarecerated in this facility, Jackson State Prison, for the murder of Margaret Cutter on Old Mission Peninsula."

"Yes," Isaiah replied.

"And you are here of your own volition, with no expectation of anything promised to you on behalf of your father or yourself, but here only to tell the unvarnished truth as best as you can now recall it?"

Isaiah heard Miss Olsen's pencil scratch out these words, took them in, no expectation, unvarnished truth, as best...laid them on the table of his mind for seconds after the pencil scratching stopped. Could he really swear to all of that?

"Mr. Logan," the warden said.

The unvarnished truth as best he could remember.

The sun was shining down hard on that day, perspiration running down his back, into his eyes, his arms and legs tired from the plowing he had just finished, his mind whirling with a mixture of hope and fear, now there was expectation, what would he find when he reached the place where he and his father were clearing brush on that road, would his father be there, as he should, or would he be with her, as her note indicated he would, that he would be even at that moment lying next to, maybe on top of her, that disturbing image returned to him as out of the corner of his eyes he saw Miss Olsen's pencil twitching as though impatient to resume, and with a quick sidewise movement of his head, he saw the warden's lips begin to tighten.

"Mr. Logan," the warden said again. "Can you not begin?"

"I had been plowing that morning," he managed to say.

Miss Olsen's pencil scratched across her paper. The warden ran his forefinger down the page in front of him on the desk, then turned the page over and repeated the motion on the next page until his finger stopped, and he looked up at Isaiah.

"Continue," he said.

Isaiah glanced at the papers containing the transcript. Just the unvarnished facts, Isaiah told himself. With no expectations. As he could remember them.

"I hurried back to the road we were clearing of brush, the new road for the resort on the shore of the west bay."

"Yes," the warden seemed to make a check mark on the transcript. "Go on."

His father was walking toward him, his face red and covered in sweat. Had he been working? Or rushing back?

"I saw my father," Isaiah said. He paused. The air in the room seem suddenly to be heavy with anticipation. Silent. As though all three had stopped breathing. This was the critical point.

"Go on," the warden said, looking up from the transcript, "you saw your father."

Isaiah took a breath.

Was it possible that they knew about the note? The warden sitting so calmly behind his desk, pencil in hand, suspended over the transcript, waiting to spring a trap that would ruin everything.

"Coming toward me. From the west," he said. And waited. He heard Miss Olsen's pencil, saw out of the corner of his eye that the warden again checked off something in the transcript.

"And you took that to mean what?" the warden asked.

No, he did not have knowledge of the note.

"Just that he had been working on the road. And because I was probably a little late, he was walking toward me. He knew what direction I would be coming from after finishing plowing."

"Knew what direction," the warden repeated. Miss Olsen's pencil scratched. "Why would you tell us that?"

"Because," Isaiah said, "because what you and I know, that his direction, coming from the west, is the most important thing I could say."

"Indeed," the warden said. He put his pencil down, folded his hands over the transcript, then pushed it aside as though it were no longer relevant. "And do you now, knowing that you will be swearing to whatever you say, do you now repeat that your father met you coming from the west?"

"I do," Isaiah said.

The warden pulled the transcript back in front of him. Isaiah noticed now that protruding from it was a thin strip of paper marking a place farther on. The warden lifted the transcript up and away from that place, looked down, and then at Isaiah.

"You say that even though later on your testimony is directly contradicted by another witness?"

"I know what Jim, the hired hand, said."

"And?"

"I can only tell you what I saw, what I remembered then, and recall now."

"Which is?"

"What I just told you."

"Tell me again."

"You're trying to trip me up," Isaiah said.

"Just doing my job," the warden replied. "So once more. And we'll be done."

"He was coming from the west. When I met him. Then we worked on the road together."

Miss Olsen's pencil point snapped. She lifted up another pencil, scratched a few more words.

"We're done," the warden said. He turned to Miss Olsen. "Do you have it all?"

"Yes," she said.

"Have it typed up, three copies, as soon as you can, but do not hurry so as to make mistakes. I'm afraid we've worn out young Mr. Logan's patience, and he, no doubt, wants to be on his way."

"I do that," Isaiah replied.

Harvest season was over, and so Sam trudged with the others in a long line of prisoners heading toward the chair factory where he would now do his required work. Up ahead of him by about ten or twelve men was Pete. Behind him by the same distance was Chub. Got me covered, Sam thought, but what of it? As Pete reached the door he paused long enough to bend down and say something to the guard who was sitting there marking off each prisoner as he passed by. The rest of the line came to a halt until Pete straightened up after a few moments, and walked in to the factory.

Sam reached the door, and the guard, a plump, red faced man Sam had not seen before, looked up.

"Name?"

"Logan..."

"Yeah, Sam Logan," the guard said, "I got you." He looked down on his list, and put a check next to Sam's name. "You know how to work a lathe? If not, they'll show you what to do. It's pretty..."

"I don't think I'll need lessons," Sam said, and walked through the door.

The scent of wood shavings greeted Sam's nostrils, the rich aroma as welcome to him as the smell of freshly mown grass or the fragrance of the rose bushes outside his father's house, those flowers tended not by his mother as one would have expected, but by his father, that tough old man, who, Sam now thought, as his mind filled with the olfactory memory of that fragrance floating up to his childhood bedroom window, that old man cared more for those damned flowers or his trees than me. Sam allowed his thoughts to stay fixed on that angry recollection, then chided himself for being so childish now that he was a twice over grown man who had not done such a good job himself as a father.

But, nevertheless, here he stood on the floor of the prison factory in front of a lathe spinning in front of him as he held the sharp blade of his cutting instrument ever so gently against the rotating wood, pressing it here, letting it up there, to form the simple pattern of the spindles that would be glued into the chairs being manufactured by the prisoners on behalf of some company. Sam did not care to think about how his labor, along with the other prisoners working beside him, was being used. No, what mattered, was the rich odor of the wood shavings rising from the floor.

Next to him, working with considerably less speed, care, or apparent satisfaction, was Pete, no accident that, Sam realized, just another part of the warden's strategy to get a different kind of use out of Sam.

"Take it easy," Pete said, "you're making the rest of us look bad."

"You do that all by yourself," Sam replied.

A sharp rap on the floor with a baton announced the arrival of a guard.

"No talking, you two, you know the rule," he said. "You ain't getting paid to chat."

"We ain't getting paid at all," Pete said.

"Why, boys," the guard replied, "what about your room and board, three squares, and a roof over your head?"

"If you look at it that way," Pete said.

The guard rapped the floor one more time, and then moved on.

When he was well out of earshot, Pete leaned over his machine toward Sam.

"Later," he said in a harsh whisper, "we got something to talk about."

"Later," Sam said.

Back in their cell, Pete stood over Sam as he lay on his cot.

"They did a pretty good job on you," he said. "What were you thinking when you were up in that tree?"

"Problem is," Sam replied, "I wasn't thinking."

Pete leveled a gaze at Sam intended to make him flinch. Sam did not.

"'Tis the season," Pete then said, "and we got something planned to liven up the holiday. The boys want to know if you would be in with us."

"What is it?"

"That's not how it goes. You're in, or you're out. In, and I'll lay it out for you. Out, and you won't have anything to worry about. In, and something goes wrong...."

"You don't have to worry about that," Sam said.

"But I do. All the time. You in?"

"I'll let you know."

"Don't keep us waiting too long. What we got planned can't wait. Santa's coming. And so are we. Think about it. Until the morning."

Later against the rhythmic snoring coming from Pete's side of the cell, he had to analyze the situation he now found himself in. His unthinking provocation of the guard, resulting in the beating that put him in the bed where Isaiah found him, had bought him increased credibility with Pete and his followers, sufficient now to invite him to join them in their next mindless and futile act of rebellion against the prison authorities. He could well understand their frustration, their chafing under the restrictions placed on them, all designed to dehumanize them, to break their will to resist, which only served to strengthen their backbones, to convince them that actions that verified their sense of themselves as men were well worth taking, whatever the consequences, for what more could be done to them, their freedom had long ago been lost without any hope of being regained, as their past uprisings had reached the point of making any possibility of parole the other side of remote, these were, Sam recognized, desperate men who found the only reason to continue living, to be able to stare back with some sense of pride at their blurred reflections in the shaving mirrors they were privileged to visit in the shower room once every week where the very razors they used to scrape off their gray prison stubble were handed out to them by clean shaven guards to whom they must be returned, lest they be used on each other, or more likely, themselves as their final act of rejection.

All this Sam understood, for he shared much of the same feelings. He resisted falling fully into their mindset only by his stubborn conviction that he did not deserve to he imprisoned with them, and that one day, somehow, his belief would be justified.

He looked up through the barred window into the night sky. His line of vision enabled him to see part of the crescent shape of the bright yellow moon. Must be a clear, early winter night, he thought, his memory roaming all the way back to his childhood when he enjoyed gazing up at the starlit sky through his bedroom window, and for a moment the memory warmed the chill core that had formed around his heart through the long years of his imprisonment. But then, as memories are wont to do, it shifted gears and brought to him the recalled image of the night sky visible from his jail cell at the top of the courthouse in Traverse City on the night he was first incarcerated, the bright pinpoint of the north star mirrored in a perverse manner by the torches of his neighbors gathered below to witness his humiliation, one light promising to direct his steps away from where he stood, the others reminding him that he was not going anywhere.

He turned his thoughts back to his problem. Just like the horns of the crescent moon, Pete had placed him on the horns of a dilemma. Throw his lot in with Pete and his crew of hardened troublemakers and secure their good will and trust in him at the huge cost of threatening the efforts manifestly being waged on behalf of his liberation, or risk being ostracized from that group resulting in the enmity of his cell mate, a man whom you simply did not want to cross. And then there was the middle road between these extremes. Join the group only to secure the information that he would then pass on to the warden.

And hope he somehow would survive the fallout from that very dangerous decision.

The sun woke him. Opening his eyes, he saw Pete standing in the center of their cell staring at him.

"Rise and shine farmboy. I thought you guys got up with the sun."

"Used to," Sam replied.

"Well?"

"I'm in," Sam said.

Pete walked over to him and clapped him hard on his shoulder, the pain from the bruised bone radiating down through his body.

"Good," Pete said.

Sam grasped Pete's wrist in his own powerful hand and squeezed.

"Two can play that game," he said.

"Easy," Pete said.

"Easy it is," Sam replied. "Now tell me what you boys have planned.

CHAPTER TWELVE

I t was early morning in the logger's camp in the Upper Peninsula, about fifty or sixty miles from Calumet on the Keewenau Peninsula and the copper mining country. Jim, sitting among a group of grizzled men around an outdoor fire, held his tin cup of hot, black and bitter coffee. A light snow was falling, and he shivered.

"Don't worry," the man next to him said, "as soon as we start working you'll be warm enough."

"Not worrying," Jim said, "I been cold before, hungry before, and just plain down before. I'm good now."

For emphasis, he gulped his coffee and then sprinkled the last of it onto the fire. He looked at the faces of the other men in the six man crew. For all he knew, one of them might be working for Benson. After having been tracked down to that potato farm on eastern Long Island in New York, he had no reason to doubt Benson's reach. But he did not care. He was a long way from that conversation with Benson back in New York. If Benson's man had followed him the thousand miles to the middle of this wilderness, the more power to him.

"They seemed ready to fight," Edward said.

He and Jablonski were walking together away from the building where the meeting had been held. Jablonski put his heavy hand on Edward's shoulder, forcing him to stop.

"Explain," Jablonski said.

"At first, they were just kind of sitting there and talking to each other, not much happening."

"But...?"

"Then this fellow began to speak, and after a while they were all cheering and standing up."

"What was he saying?"

"Why how the companies were trying to break them..."

"Break them?"

Edward searched his memory for the words.

"The strike, the companies were going to break the strike. And then he asked them if that was going to happen, and they all yelled back, No, it wouldn't."

"What did you think?" Jablonski asked.

"Think? I was just trying to listen and remember as best I could so I could tell you like I am doing now."

"I see. Would you say that the men in the audience were ready to follow that man speaking wherever he took them?"

Edward shook his head up and down with some vigor.

"Over a cliff, I'd say."

Jablonski stared hard at Edward.

"Then, he's our problem, isn't he?"

At first, Edward did not understand how the man was *his* problem. But then he did.

"What are we going to do about him?"

"Good. We have plans for Mr. Michaels. And we're going to want you to help us take care of him."

Edward smiled. Being given direct instructions always made him feel useful without the burden of making decisions on his own.

Jablonski reached into his coat pocket, took something out.

"Hold out your hand," he said.

Edward did, and into it he felt something hard and cold.

"Keep it out of sight," Jablonski said.

Edward slipped the gun into his pocket.

"Now, let me tell you what we want you to do."

Edward leaned forward while Jablonski whispered in his ear.

"Now, Fred, tell me what you saw and heard. You can tell me what you think about all of this later."

"Well, Governor, our problem is not going away any time too soon."

"What you saw and heard, Fred," Woodhouse demanded.

"A meeting of the striking miners. Listening to Michaels, he's the UMF leader, promising support, he was well received."

"Well received?"

"Yeah, applause, verbal responses, are we going to win, yes, we're going to win, that kind of thing."

"Everyone?"

"Pretty much. There was a moment, when this large woman, that Big Annie I think, got up, the same one that was in the newspaper picture, she wanted to know when there would be some tangible support behind his nice words."

"How was she received?"

"With respect. But the men were buying into what Michaels was selling."

"Anything specific you can tell me about the union's plans?"

"No more than what I just said, cheerleading, and promise of support from the national organization."

Woodhouse looked hard at his assistant.

"Now, Fred, your view of the situation, and its political ramifications."

"Neither side is going to give in any time soon. The companies have the money, and the thugs making life difficult for the strikers, there is a trickle of scabs but not enough to get the mines fully operational, for the most part the local politicians and legal officials are supportive of the companies. There's a new wrinkle, some kind of organization called the Citizens Alliance, clearly the creation of the mining companies. The local press divides. Finnish language newspapers, according to a young man I met who, for a couple of dollars, translated for me, support the miners. The English language papers in the area are either on the fence or pro company."

"Good," the governor said. "And the politics."

"Difficult," Fred replied, "very difficult."

"Explain."

"As I said locally, more pro company than pro striker. But, of course, you are running in a state wide election. I think your sending in the military is generally viewed as a positive step toward establishing the natural order of things, which is the bosses run the show and the workers do what they are told. But that sentiment is not as universal as once it was. As the story gets out, as it will, of the suffering of the strikers, and, most important, the wealth of the companies, as we have seen in other places that sentiment might shift some to the strikers' side. As it..."

"Yes," the governor interrupted, "as it did in New York."

"The shirtwaist factory. A do-gooder, like Ann Morgan, JP's daughter might pop up, or this Big Annie woman might get a following."

"Or there might be..."

"Yeah, something like the fire with women and girls jumping out of the window. Not likely in a mine."

"Don't," the governor snapped, "ever make light of that tragedy. And yes, if not a fire, something else, maybe not so spectacular could occur. There have already been some shootings, people killed. The winter is coming."

"Sorry," Fred said, "didn't mean to be disresepectful. About the fire. And, agreed, there is serious hardship brewing once the snows come up there."

"Your political assessment. Adding up the pluses and minuses. At this point."

"Probably a draw. If you can manage to get a settlement. A big plus for you. If you don't, but it lingers on, hard to say, but probably not much influence one way or another. If something bad happens, then a definite negative for you."

"Thank you very much, Fred, as usual," the governor said. "We're done now. I need to digest all of this."

"He's in Room 205," Jack said. The foreman, along with Mike Norris, was standing in front of a two story wood frame hotel. Mike was staring at a row of windows on the second floor. All but two were dark, then the light in one of those went out.

"His is still on," Mike said. "When it goes out..."

"We snatch him, right?' Edward asked.

"Well, it's not likely he'll just come along with us, if we ask him nicely," Mike said.

Edward, remembering the size and menacing shape of Joe Michaels, reached into his pocket for the hard steel of the gun.

"I guess we'll have to persuade him, then," he said.

Jack's eyes focused on Edward's hand in the pocket with the gun.

"Learn how to use that thing yet?" he asked.

Before Edward could answer, Mike pointed up at the windows on the second floor.

"It's out," he said.

The desk clerk, a fuzzy faced young man, looked up from a book he was reading as they walked through the lobby toward the stairs.

"Can I help you gentlemen?" the clerk asked.

"No, sonny," Jack replied. "We're just here to visit Mr. Michaels, he's a friend of ours."

"It's hotel policy..." the clerk began.

"He's expecting us," Jack said and started up the stairs. Mike followed with a nod toward the clerk. Edward glanced at the clerk, whose hand hovered above a bell on his counter. Edward walked over to him, making his hand on his gun conspicuous by pushing it out against the fabric of his jacket. He stood in front of the clerk, and just shook his head slowly and meaningfully from side to side. The clerk nodded, and withdrew his hand from its position above the bell.

"Is that a good book?" Edward asked.

"Yessir," the clerk replied. "Very good."

"I don't read much," Edward said.

Jack and Mike were waiting on the landing where the stairs turned to complete the rise up to the second floor. Jack motioned for Edward to come on up.

"He was going to ring the bell," Edward said as he joined them. "I didn't think we'd want that."

"We wouldn't," Jack said.

The corridor was dimly lit by gas fixtures in sconces along the wall. The room numbers were in brass on each wooden door. Mike pointed to one about half way down the hall.

"Probably that one," he said.

Jim had open calluses on both hands, and his shoulder and back muscles ached from the labor of manning the big two- man cross-cut saw. As he walked back to the bunkhouse for the evening meal, his thigh muscles did not want to bend, and his calves complained. As a result his walk was more like a shuffling gait than a comfortable stride at the end of a day's labor.

Holding his tin plate, at the end of the line, he made his way to the cook who held a large ladle over a steaming pot.

"First day?" the cook, a middle-aged black man asked as he held the ladle over Jim's plate.

"Yeah. Ain't as young as I used to be when I was cutting cotton."

"I hear you," the cook said, as he plopped a ladle full of steaming stew onto the plate. "Well, Jim, my name's Henry, and I need to talk to you. Finish up what's on your plate, eat slow, come back for a bit more when they all have left. They won't pay you no mind, seeing as you're the new man. And we're both..."

"Yeah," Jim said, "we must be brothers."

"In a way," the cook replied, "in a very special way."

"Oh, I think I see," Jim murmured, "Benson. Here?"

"You just do as I say," Henry replied. "Got to pass some information on to you. I guess you didn't wonder how you got the tip about this job."

"Thought my luck was turning," Jim replied.

"Well, nigger, you should've known better."

The stew was not bad, Jim thought, so this Henry must really be a cook besides working for Benson, who seemed to have eyes and ears everywhere. One by one, or occasionally in pairs, the others left to find their bunks in the adjoining room at the back of the building. Jim took his time moving his spoon into stew, letting it scrape along the tin surface of the plate ever so slowly before lifting it to his mouth. When there was no more stew on his plate, he mopped up the liquid remains with the piece of bread that came along with the dinner. Then he got up, walked over to the cook who was cleaning his large pot with a rag. Jim held out his plate.

"Sorry, you're too late," Henry said.

Jim shrugged.

"I'm not hungry."

Henry glanced over his shoulder toward the door that led to the sleeping quarters from which the sounds of sleeping men, snores, occasional grunts, floated toward them.

"You got something to tell me," Jim said, "I'm pretty damned tired."

"Just this. An old friend of yours from way back when, you know, that time you trying to forget…"

"That time like a ball and chain on my leg, no matter where I go, it follow me, so why am I not surprised, but which old friend you talking about?"

"Fellow you used to work with back then."

"Worked with a lot of men back then."

Henry put his rag down and took Jim's hard, callused hand in his own, which was surprisingly soft and warm.

"Look, I know you don't want to hear what I've got to say, so here it is, straight and simple, the man I'm talking about goes by the name of Edward, a white boy, none too bright."

"Why, what the hell, what is he doing, and where is he doing it?"

"Not more than fifty or sixty miles from here, up on the Keweenaw, copper mining country."

"He's mining?"

"Not exactly."

"Got himself in trouble?"

"Somewhat."

"What that go to do with me?"

"Nothing much," Henry replied. "Just your shared history. The man thought you ought to know."

"Well," Jim said, "from me, just thank the man. "For nothing.""

With Mike and Edward standing behind him, Jack knocked on the door that Mike had indicated.

A voice came from within the room.

"Who's there?"

"That's him," Edward said. "I know that voice."

"Mr. Michaels," Jack said, "we're here from the *Mining News,* the paper in town that's been covering the strike. We heard your speech last night, and we'd like to follow it up with a couple of questions, and get a picture, if that's alright."

"You fellows know how late it is?" Michael's voice shot back.

"Yessir. But you know we have a deadline, and we want to beat the other papers."

"Well," Michaels' voice softened.

"He's taking the bait," Mike whispered.

Edward listened to all of this with a kind of stunned attention. He could not recall ever hearing such falsehoods so smoothly offered. Nor could he imagine coming up with anything like this on his own. He, once again, sought the comfort of the hard steel of the gun in his pocket. It was all the persuasion he would ever think of using. He struggled for a moment to remember, then reached into his pocket and pulled the hammer back into the cocked position. Michaels was a big man. He might need the extra persuasion the gun could offer.

"We'll only take a minute of your time," Jack said.

Michaels did not answer, but the noise of creaking floorboards under his substantial weight came through the closed door, followed by the click of the door knob as it began to turn. Then the door started to slide open.

"Come on in boys," Michaels' voice said.

Jack stepped in, followed by Mike. Edward, as was his wont, held back. The door slammed shut in his face, and then there was the thuds of fists against flesh, bodies crashing into the walls and the door, grunts of expelled breath, a body hitting the floor. Edward pushed the door open.

Mike was on the floor rubbing his jaw. Michaels had his hands around Jack's neck, his fist raised about to deliver another blow. He turned to Edward.

"Come on in, and join the party with your pals," he said. "You boys must think I am something of a fool to fall for that old gambit."

Later, Edward could not explain what happened. What he remembered was the loud explosive sound, the large man dropping his raised fist, his body recoiling, the red blood appearing on the white shoulder of his undershirt, the look of stunned amazement on his face, and then the burning sensation on Edward's own side, his own blood dripping down his flesh, and finally the realization that as if operating under its own impulse the gun in his pocket had fired hitting Michaels.

He could recall vividly what followed, how Jack taking full advantage, pounded Michaels about the head as the big man grabbed at his wound, unable to protect himself from the blows that rained down on him, those soon joined by more from Mike, now on his feet, until finally he put up his good arm to shield his face and staggered back onto the bed from which he had risen with such confidence in his ability to take care of these pests, so many little bugs to be swatted away now swarming all over him.

And all the while, Edward stood and watched. Finally, he lifted his hand holding the now warm revolver out of his pocket. He shifted it to his other hand so he could reach to feel the ragged flesh at his side where the bullet had swiped by on its way to Michaels' shoulder.

"Thanks," Jack said.

Edward nodded, then leaned over clutching his side.

"We'll have to take care of that," Jack said. "After we take care of him." He pointed to Michaels lying on the bed, a soft moan escaping from between his clenched lips, his eyes darting around the room, stopping on each one of his assailants. He tried to sit up, but then fell back down.

"I'm sure you would like to, if you could," Jack said. "Mike take a peek out of the door."

Mike slid their door open, poked his head out into the corridor.

"All quiet," he said.

"Heavy sleepers," Jack said. "Just as well."

"Chicago, you say?" the governor asked.

"Yes," Fred answered.

"On a train. By himself. In Chicago."

"Yessir. Alone when he was found. Seems a witness reported

that a couple of men were with him when the train pulled into the station, at least they were sitting near him, but they got off, leaving him there, so maybe they had nothing to do with it."

"Sitting near a man with a gunshot wound, and just getting up and leaving. Don't think so, do you?"

"No."

The governor sat staring out of his window while tapping his desk with a pencil. Fred looked toward the door, unsure whether their conversation had ended. The door swung open just wide enough for the angular and lined face of Miss Hooper, the governor's secretary, to peer in.

"Mr. Lowe is here to see you, governor," she said.

"Tell him to wait while we finish up," Woodhouse replied. He watched the secretary's face back away and for the door to close. "What do we tell him?"

"He no doubt has read the papers. He's from Chicago after all. He's going to suggest you're drowning, and..."

"Offer me a life line."

"The question is," Fred said, "whether you'll take it."

"I just don't know," the governor replied.

Edward met with Jablonski in the same office where he first found him after getting off the train carrying the piece of the circular announcing the availability of work in the mines. At that time, Edward knew nothing about copper mining, and perhaps even less about a labor dispute during which men who could work and earn their daily keep chose not to. Now, albeit somewhat dimly, he understood the latter while still having learned virtually nothing about the former.

"Get patched up?" Jablonski asked.

"Wasn't much," Edward replied.

"The gun?"

Edward knew this request was coming. He reached into the intact packet where he now carried the gun and pulled it out. He extended it toward Jablonski, who took it by the butt between his thumb and forefinger and slid it into an open desk drawer. He took a small key out of his vest pocket and locked the drawer.

"There it will stay. As long as you continue to do as you are told."

"Am I in trouble? I didn't mean..."

"Doesn't matter what you meant. Your gun shot that man, and that proved more than a little inconvenient for us. We are still dealing with that. As for you, well, the sheriff has already made inquiries. The desk clerk gave, well let's say, we had a talk with him, so he didn't provide a description of you three, said you must have come when he was answering a call of nature."

"A call of nature," Edward said, "more like..."

"He's a young man with a wife, and he knows what's best for him. Just like I expect you do. Am I right?"

"Yessir," Edward said. "Just tell me what I'm to do."

"Lay low for the while. We'll be back in touch when this whole affair settles down."

"Saw the morning paper," Lowe said, skipping the formalities of greeting the governor and asking how he was doing, how was the family, no, his courtroom experience for which he was justifiably famous, instructed him that in this particular case he should go right for the jugular.

"Saw that picture, as I said, and I got on the first train up here. Then, you know, when I reached the station, I picked up your city's paper, and, if anything, the picture and the headline were even bigger than in the ones in my home town..."

"And, Mr. Lowe, how are you?" the governor asked and shared a knowing smile with Fred. Both of them were well aware of Lowe's flair for the dramatic.

Lowe settled into the chair that Fred offered him.

"You can guess why I am here, we have, after all, been corresponding on behalf of my client, or more precisely, his mother."

Fred glanced at the governor, who nodded.

"Well, sir," Fred said. "Let's not guess. You see some connection between Mr. Logan and the strike in copper mining country."

"A labor leader bleeding from a gunshot wound," Lowe said, "does put the spotlight on that dispute. Not to mention that other incident, the soldier and..."

"And Mr. Logan?" the governor interrupted, his voice usually so well modulated and controlled now showing his growing impatience with being played like a fish on Lowe's line.

"Come, now," Lowe said, "you have an election coming up, and this business is not doing you any good."

"And Mr. Logan?" the governor repeated.

"Can provide you the opportunity to finally right a tragic wrong that has cost an innocent man nearly half his adult life..."

"You exaggerate," Fred interrupted.

"This is not a question of arithmetic," Lowe snapped. "Anyway, in short, you need me as my client needs you."

"Maybe," the governor said. "Why don't you lay it out for me."

"Good," Lowe said. "Let me do just that."

"That's it, gentlemen," Lowe said.

"Interesting," the governor said. "But..."

"You are not yet persuaded," Lowe finished the thought. "I expected so. You are a prudent man. You see the possible advantage for you, as well, as, if I may say so, the duty to right a wrong, if it's in your power to do so."

"That is the nub, isn't it, whether there was a wrong. You were not able to convince a jury of his peers of that."

"Sadly so," Lowe replied. "But juries are not infallible in their judgments, and in this case, well, the facts were not so important as was the attitude of those fine men on the jury toward my admittedly imperfect client, who, though, for whatever his warts, is not, was not, a murderer."

"We'll take your suggestion under advisement," the governor said. "Good day, Mr. Lowe."

Lowe stood up and extended his hand.

"As I expected. "Just don't wait too long."

"Is there an offer on the table you might remove?" Fred asked.

"No, not at all," Lowe replied. "Events, young man, events have a way of steering the ship. This bloody incident may only be a prelude."

"You didn't tell him that you had heard from the warden," Fred said.

"I may not be the practiced politician you are, nor the slick attorney that Mr. Lowe is, I know how people see me, a solid man with perhaps some good ideas, but not overly smart."

"But..."

"But I've played a fair amount of poker in my life, believe it or not, even and including small wagers on the outcome, and I did learn some things that apply to other situations, and one of those things is not to reveal your hole card until you have to. I'm quite sure Mr. Lowe has some cards up his sleeve as well, not to suggest that he is cheating, just another poker metaphor, he's got his card, or cards for that matter, and I've got mine."

"Are you persuaded, then, by the young man's affirmation of his trial testimony, that supports his father's alibi?" Fred asked.

"Not fully, he is still the man's son, after all, but I am leaning in that direction."

The governor tapped his finger on his desk, nudged some papers aside, and picked up a small sheaf of papers.

"My card," he said, "to be played when the time is right."

Lowe looked through his window at the sun's rays falling on the water, sending a streak of red across the dark blue surface. His phone rang.

"I've been waiting," he said, "and not all that patiently."

"I have the package," the voice on the other end of the line said.

"Good man, Benson. Is the package what we had hoped?"

"It is."

"And the man himself?"

"Learning to be a lumberman. In the company of one my operatives."

"Excellent!" Lowe said. "Let's just keep an eye on him in case we need him. But for now, you bring me his statement just as soon as you can get on a train to Chicago."

I was watching you closely, Mr. Governor, Lowe thought, and I think you were holding something back, but then why should you not, since I am as well. But, we both must understand, we are talking about a man's life. Make that two men. We cannot forget the young man, ah the young man, so you have been in contact with him, no doubt, I should think you would have, just as I have been looking for his adversaries, the one now cutting the timber, the other recently located in the middle of that strike, a peculiar joke of fate to place those two so close to each other at just the time when they are again of so much immediate interest.

"Will there be anything else before I leave for the day?" asked the secretary, who had been standing at the doorway as Lowe, with eyes closed, sorted through his conversation with Governor Woodhouse. He now looked up at her, and then toward the encrimsoned waters of the great lake.

"No, thank you." He pointed out his window. "Grand isn't it?" he asked.

"Yes, it is," she replied.

CHAPTER THIRTEEN

A s the same declining rays of the setting sun forced their
way through the dust encrusted window in the train
car, Isaiah sat staring at the passing landscape. Before
long, he would be back in Traverse. Eunice, no doubt,
would be waiting to hear about his trip. He had not told her
where he was going, or why, but he was fairly certain she had
figured it out.

Somehow until this moment, she had not been in his thoughts.
But now he realized that she would be affected by his father's
release as much as anyone else, perhaps even more. After all,
she had testified at his trial, their dissolving marriage having
been, Isaiah realized now more than at the time, as much of a
factor in setting the jurors' minds against Sam as the actual evidence of Margaret's death. And now she was living in the town,
raising the convicted murderer's son.

How would she deal with her ex-husband's return? What would
Sam, himself, expect of her, if anything? Would he want to claim
a relationship with the son he barely knew, who he perhaps had
seen once, as Isaiah had, at the trial sitting next to Eunice?

These questions, Isaiah realized, as the train slowed down
entering the outskirts of Traverse City, served to distract him
from his own feelings concerning the stepmother and step-
brother, he had only recently begun to know. As a child, he witnessed the increasingly antagonistic relationship between his
father and the woman who had replaced his own mother. He
now could understand that as that distraught young child, still
aching from the day his mother packed her suitcase, hugged him,
walked out the door, and essentially disappeared from his life,
that he must have experienced confused emotions concerning
Eunice, but among those feelings was very probably an expectation that she would fill the void left by his departing mother.

Of course, Eunice could not. She was young, naïve, very much
in love with the man she imagined Sam was, but increasingly

185

unhappy with the man he turned out to be. In her unhappiness, her efforts at raising her stepson were at first indifferent, and then hostile as Isaiah naturally gravitated to the one adult who had been a constant in his life, and whose adult foibles were of no matter to him.

After the divorce, Isaiah fell into a more or less comfortable life with his father, who was, if truth be told, a doting father when he remembered that he had a son solely in his care. For solely, it was, because not only Eunice, but Isaiah's own biological mother played no part in his life. His mother, he learned when he was old enough to absorb such information, now lived in a house in town, but she had so fully immersed herself in her life away from Sam that her only presence in Isaiah's life was a yearly birthday greeting in which she expressed her continuing love for him.

Those greetings came in envelopes addressed to him in a delicate, careful hand, clearly that of a woman. There was nothing on the envelope to identify either the sender or the sender's address, other than the stamp from the post office in Traverse City. The first of these arrived when he was old enough to read his name. It was also his first piece of mail. He showed it to Sam, who looked at it with a bemused expression on his face. Later, after Isaiah opened the envelope and read the few simple words, appropriate to his age, which he was able to sound out to understand that the message was a wish for him to have a happy birthday, coming from a woman whose pretty face still remained, albeit somewhat blurred, in his memory, he puzzled over that look on his father's face. It was not angry, Isaiah decided, nor happy, somewhere in between as though Sam himself could not decide how he felt about Isaiah's mother's intrusion into the life he was creating for himself and his son.

Each year thereafter, a greeting came. Isaiah chose never to ask Sam if he knew where his mother was living. It was as though a tacit agreement had taken shape between them that placed any conversation concerning her out of bounds. For his part, Isaiah took the lack of any identifying location as his mother's way of insisting that their communication remain a one way street.

As he grew older, he increasingly became aware of his father's wandering among available women, culminating with his attachment to Margaret at the same time Isaiah himself felt drawn to her with the intensity of a first love.

Up to that time, and gradually, he came to see the yearly greetings from his mother as a thin thread connecting him to the woman who had given him life, and year by year the thread grew thinner and thinner, though the wishes for his happiness contained in the greetings remained the same, until that gossamer thread had virtually disappeared at the time of the trial. He never knew if subsequent greetings had been sent to him thereafter when he had already left, stopping first in Chicago and then onto the lakes as a seaman.

These thoughts roiled in his head as he disembarked from the train and began in the early winter dusk to walk toward his room above the leather shop. Without conscious thought, he slowed his pace. As he did so, he glanced at the large clock on a pole outside of the jewelry store on Front Street to see its hands indicated a few minutes past five, and he became aware that he was adjusting his gait so that Eunice would most likely be gone by the time he arrived at the store.

She was standing in the doorway, envelope in hand, as he approached. Jonathan was peeking out at him from around his mother's legs.

"This came for you a little after you left."

He took the envelope. Jonathan stepped around Eunice.

"Glad you are back," she said.

"So am I," Isaiah replied. He glanced down at the envelope, saw that it came from a prestigious law firm in town, guessed at its contents, but did not want to deal with them just now.

"Thanks," he said to Eunice. "I'm tired from the trip."

The opportunity Sam was waiting for came unexpectedly one morning as he worked on his lathe. Out of the corner of his eye, he saw one of the guards who acted as factory foremen making his way down the row of machines toward him. As the man, casually swinging a truncheon at his side, approached, Sam began to press especially hard on the blade of his cutting instrument at the same easing up on the foot pedal. The machine groaned as the blade gouged the piece of wood that was intended to become a spindle in a chair back. Sam muttered a curse and leaned over his machine. As he expected, he felt the whack of the truncheon across the back of his calves. He did not stand up right away, and the truncheon came down again, this time a little harder.

"Logan," the guard said. "Are you sleeping?"

Sam turned around, his fist ready, his arm back. The guard shook his head ever so slowly from side to side.

"Now, why would you want to do something as stupid as that?" he asked.

As if there had been a silent command, quiet descended over the factory floor, and eyes lifted from their work to stare at Sam and the guard. Sam lowered his arm, but kept his fist balled. The guard stepped closer to Sam's lathe, leaned over and examined the ruined piece of work.

"Tsk, tsk, this won't do," the guard muttered. "And I heard you used to be a master carpenter, real good with this kind of work."

"Maybe I was," Sam muttered, "when I was working for myself. But come a little closer, I want to show you something." He relaxed his hand and pointed to the foot pedal. The guard bent down.

"I don't see anything," he said.

"Keep looking," Sam whispered without moving his lips. "I got something I gotta tell the warden. So, when you straighten up, I'm gonna take a swing at you, and you catch it, and walk me out of here. Got it?"

The guard nodded, and lifted his head up. Sam swung. The guard caught the blow, and then brought his truncheon down hard on Sam's side.

"That's just in case you're fooling with me, trying to get out of work."

"Take me to the warden, you son of a bitch," Sam muttered. "If you don't you'll have hell to pay."

"As you say," the guard replied.

As they started to walk down the aisle of machines, out of the corner of his eyes Sam saw Pete staring at him.

"Hit me again," he muttered to the guard.

"Glad to oblige," the guard replied.

The truncheon thunked against Sam's back, and then again. He staggered to his knees.

"Just one for luck," the guard said.

Isaiah sat on the one chair in his room staring out of the window as the early evening strollers on Front Street down below went about their business. Most businesses were shut for the day, but the tavern up the block was open as was the restaurant where he usually took his meals.

On the little desk on the wall next to the window sat the envelope Eunice had handed him. He reached over to pick it up, felt the heft of its quality bond paper, squeezed it to assess the thickness of its contents, guessed no more than one sheet of similarly thick paper, imagined whether its text had been inscribed by machine or ink pen, put it back down on the desk.

He had taken note of the law firm's name, Mullen and Smith, knew from some long ago memory that it had represented his mother in the divorce from his father, remembered hearing Sam mutter about the money his soon to be ex-wife's family was willing to spend to free her from him while his own father, predictably, sought a less expensive alternative for Sam's representation, saying that no doubt Sam was primarily to blame for the failure of the marriage, all of this coming back now to Isaiah, fragments of muttered comments over the years, most when he was too young to understand their significance, a few more meaningful when Sam would wax philosophical about the institution of marriage, and how it just did not seem to fit his needs for more than a short period of time. Through all of this, Isaiah recalled, his father had not given himself over to bitterness, a kind of tacit acceptance of old man Logan's judgment.

Isaiah again lifted the envelope up from the desk. This time he ran the nail of his index finger along its seal and very neatly lifted up the flap without tearing the thick paper. As he suspected, there was only one sheet of paper inside. He lifted it out between his thumb and index finger as though it might be, in some mysterious way, dangerous to his flesh. He laid the paper on the surface of the desk, unfolded it and smoothed it with several motions of the palm of his hand.

Its typed text informed him that at the bequest specifically written in his mother's will, he had been bequeathed her house on Washington Street. He now surmised that it was from that house, his mother had mailed her yearly good wishes on his birthday, but never expressed any interest in seeing him in person, nor had he, for his part, any desire to spend time with the woman who had deserted him so many years ago.

For that desertion, he had been unable to forgive her. As an adult, he realized that he was perhaps being unreasonable, that, at the least, he could imagine she might well have her own reasons for keeping her distance. Still, the warmth of the birthday greetings seemed to cool in their trip to his hands. Each time one came, he read it, thought briefly about reciprocating, considering that the greetings were perhaps his mother's invitation to bridge the gap between them, and then he would light a match and watch the paper burn.

Washington Street.

That only added to his confusion. He would have to talk to Eunice in the morning.

He folded the letter and started to place it back into its envelope when he felt the outline of an object. His fingers probed inside the envelope and withdrew the object.

The key to his new home, should he choose to live there.

He got up early enough to wait for her to come to the store and open it for business.

"Why didn't you tell me?" he asked.

"I wasn't sure I should. It wasn't my place."

"Your place?" he said with a trace of anger. "To tell me that my mother was your neighbor."

"Neighbors, no," Eunice said, her voice rising a little to match his. "I only knew she lived nearby. And after all what would we have said to each other? Exchanged stories about the man to whom we were both unhappily married?"

"I suppose not," Isaiah replied.

Eunice put her hand on his arm and gave it a gentle squeeze. "And then, the last time I saw her she was not well. I saw that she hunched over in a coughing fit...."

"Yes, it was lung disease," Isaiah replied. "That is all that I know about it."

For a moment, that statement struck a dissonant chord in Isaiah's mind. All he knew about his mother's death was that she had lung disease. Nothing else. Birthday cards once a year sent from a house he now owned, which happens to be not far from the one where Eunice and Jonathan live, but about his mother he knew only how she died.

"Yes, you were not back yet. Still on the lakes, I think, and when you did come back for that girl's father's funeral, well, your mother had died, and I didn't see any purpose in bringing her proximity to me up."

"Did you learn anything about her?" he asked.

"My mother knew her a little," Eunice replied. "She, I mean my mother, was always something of a gossip. After, you know, after, she went back to her maiden name, and taught piano for a while."

"That's it?"

"Yes."

Sam and the truncheon swinging guard emerged from the tunnel that led from the chair factory to the administration building. They climbed the stairs to reach the second floor. There sitting in front of the warden's office was the red faced, plump guard, his stomach pushing against the front of his uniform. He looked up at Sam with a knowing glance.

"In trouble again, Logan," he said.

Sam shrugged. He leaned down and read the guard's name on his badge.

"O'Brien, it finds me," he said. "You Irish should understand that."

"Ah, we do," O'Brien replied.

"Tell me, O'Brien," Sam said, "do you ever get on your feet to earn your pay?"

Sam sensed the motion before he felt the truncheon on the back of his knees.

"We didn't come here to talk with the likes of him," the other guard said. He knocked on the door.

As they entered the office, the warden, who had been sitting in his chair looking out over the grounds between the prison walls, turned.

"Have you got something for me, Logan?" he asked.

"Yes," Sam replied.

The warden motioned for the guard to leave.

"Talk to me," the warden said.

Isaiah walked along Washington Street, reading the descending house numbers as he went. And as the numbers went down, the sizes of the houses became smaller. He paused before the one where he had picked up Jonathan to attend the baseball game. Its number, he now remembered was 231.

His new possession was number 97. It was a neat little house, suitable for a single woman who sometimes gave piano lessons. He imagined that the instrument itself might still be in the front parlor. He turned around and gazed back in the direction from which he came, envisioning how Eunice might have encountered her when his mother, as he now understood, was dying from the same devastating lung disease that had afflicted Daniel, his one, good friend and keeper of his terrible secret.

He couldn't put a name to the feeling he now had concerning the indiscriminate hand of tuberculosis that in some perverse way tied together the two most significant incidents of his life, the departure of his mother when he was so young, and the happenstance that had placed in his friend's hands culpatory evidence that his father was a murderer.

Looking at this quiet, now empty house, where the remains of a once carefully tended flower garden could still be seen in the front yard, and where the brown stalks of some long dead flowers hung sadly from the box beneath the window next to the front door, he permitted himself to wonder about his mother, something he had conditioned himself long ago not to do, for so to do was like picking over the scab of an ancient wound that had never fully healed. How had she dealt with the proximity to the woman who had become her husband's second wife, or how did she feel upon learning that Sam had cheated on Eunice as he once had done to herself. Surely, living so close by, she must have been aware of the child, of Jonathan, who would have been not much older than Isaiah was when she left. Did seeing Jonathan in any way remind her of her lost relationship with her own son?

He stepped onto the brick path leading to the front door. That path and everything he could observe about the house indicated that it had been well cared for, that his mother had been, a careful, perhaps overly so, woman, and the thought then struck him at how ill-matched she must have been in her marriage to the tempestuous Sam, a man in whom seemed to be the embodiment of the life force itself. Eunice seemed a little bit stronger, perhaps a better match, but still not enough to hold onto, or be held, by Sam, he was not sure which characterization of a failed marriage struck closest to the truth.

He took the iron key out of his pocket and inserted it into the lock on the front door. He gave it a twist, and it turned smoothly and the lock clicked open. In the front parlor, a scent rose up to his nostrils. He knew he had smelled it somewhere, but his nose still accustomed to its long familiarity with the odors rising up from the waters of the great lakes or from the cargo laded onto the ships on which he served, struggled to place it. He looked around at the bare floor of the parlor and thought he saw slight indentations in the corner where a small piano, perhaps a spinet, might have sat.

Then his brain pulled up the memory of the scent in the room. It was the same as in the parlor of his grandmother's house. Lilac, he thought, she must have liked lilacs, just as his grandmother did. Through the front window the view was of a quiet street across from which stood two substantial bare leafed maples and beyond just a glimpse of the dark winter blue of the river. It was a place of peace and serenity, it seemed to Isaiah, fitting for a woman who had decided that life should be calm, that it should not be disturbed by unpleasant reminders of the turmoil that preceded her residence here, an explanation, perhaps, of why she did not permit herself to get any closer to the child of her womb than a yearly birthday greeting, capped off now by the gift of her safe haven, her house.

Lying on the cot in his dark cell, an hour or so before the early winter sun would illuminate it, Sam thought about the card he had played the previous day. He had, in fact, been a good poker player, a consistent winner, rarely taking big chances, preferring instead to bet when the odds were very much in his favor. He would pass up the opportunity to win a big pot if something warned him that his hand would not be good enough, that something might be a tell that he had picked up from his opponent, or it might be more intuitive, just a certain feeling arriving from some place he could not identify. More than once, he had folded only to see another's hand rake in the pot. He didn't care. He still had his money and he would live to play another hand when he was more confident.

His card playing strategy was, in fact, in contrast to the way he lived the rest of his life when his desires led him to take risks that were foolhardy. He just loved the rewards of those acts too much, and the hell with the possibility of bad results down the road. Thus two failed marriages before, in the baseball analogy that came readily to mind, the third strike in his ill-advised relationship with Margaret.

In his conversation with the warden, he figured he could not afford to be as careful as he would be in a hand of poker, nor as rash as in his love life. This situation fell maddeningly between those two contrasting extremes. Two men seemed to control his immediate life. The warden promised the possibility of freedom if he cooperated. Pete, now snoring across the few feet that separated them in their cell, posed a violent response should he violate a trust he never asked for and would have refused had it been in his power so to do.

Before the sun made its appearance, the dark quiet of the cell was rudely shattered by the sound of truncheons rattling against the steel bars along the corridor. The sound increased as it approached where Sam, now fully awake, eyes peering at Pete waiting to see how long it would be before he stirred himself awake. He did just as the guard's truncheon beat its staccato rhythm against their cell's bars.

"What the..." Pete muttered.

"Mornng," Sam said. "You know I was just thinking..."

"Thinking what?"

"That it is always foolish to draw to an inside straight."

"So?"

"Just that is what I find myself thinking about," Sam said.

In the back of the house were two bedrooms. The one on the left, although devoid of furniture still had a wallpaper of delicate pink flowers. This must have been hers, he concluded. It too offered the faint aroma of lilacs, and when he looked through the window that gave on to the rear of the house he saw lilac shrubs of some ten or fifteen feet. So, she liked the real thing as well as what came in a bottle.

He opened the door to the bedroom on the right. Unlike the adjoining bedroom there was no light. He peered into the darkness and could sense that this room was a bit smaller. A thin line of light seemed to outline a window on the rear wall. That window would look out at the same lilacs as the room that had been hers. He took a step, then another toward that window. A jolt of pain ran up his right shin, which had banged into something hard. He reached down and felt something wooden. He edged around the object and made his way again toward the window. As he got closer, he could see that two curtain panels covered the glass. He parted them, and the mid morning sun poured in illuminating the room.

Unlike the other rooms in the house this one was fully furnished.

He saw that the object his shin had struck was a small chest in front of a child sized bed. On one wall was a little bookcase, on its shelves the spines of dust covered books. He picked out one of the books at random and saw that it was a leather bound, illustrated copy of *Tom Sawyer*. As he scanned the other titles the recognition began to form in his mind. The titles were of books that a young boy might be expected to be in interested in reading.

The bed was fully made up with a pillow and blanket. The pillow case and the blanket were blue. The parlor walls were white. One bedroom where she slept had wallpaper with a pink theme while the one in which he was standing was painted blue.

Pink for the woman of the house.

Blue for the boy of the house.

Who never lived there.

CHAPTER FOURTEEN

Edward listened to the other boarders, who having gotten up from the breakfast table, stood by the front window muttering about the weather. He got up and joined them peering out the window. All he could see was white.

"It is December," one of them said.

After breakfast, he waited for the others to leave. They all seemed to have regular jobs or tasks assigned to them. But since the night he shot that big union leader, and Jablonski had told him to lay low, and had taken, once again, his gun from him, he had had nothing to do. He knew Jablonski would find him sooner or later, and then tell him what to do next.

For want of something better, he spent a lot of time in the tavern, sometimes being the lone patron, at others finding a few men as idle as he. He figured some of them were striking miners, but he wasn't sure. Nor was he sure what he thought about them. He admitted to himself that some of the things that Michaels said that night at that union rally had made some sense to him, had caused him to understand that he, too, had always been powerless to create his own destiny, impotent to secure his day to day existence without the constant threat of having the basis of his life pulled out from beneath him. He had always accepted that condition as his lot, indeed found a little level of comfort in not have to figure things out for himself, yet, and for all that, the energy in the room that night as the collective voices of the audience rose to support the leader's call for continuing the fight to get what was rightfuly theirs, that energy had found a resonance within him.

On the days when he did not feel like nursing a beer by himself in the tavern, and in respect of the dwindling stock of coins in his pocket, he walked about town. On these walks, he ventured farther and farther from the town center until one afternoon he found himself within sight of the same railroad tracks that had carried him here so many weeks before. He found a stump on which to sit while he gazed down the tracks in both directions, both those that had taken him here and those that led away. As he sat, an idea began to form in his head.

That idea took the shape of a suspicion that Jablonski might not have his best interest in mind after all, and if that were the case, maybe he should pay more attention to these tracks, begin to find out when a train might be coming by, one that he could get on and leave this place behind.

The falling snow thickened. Edward just sat. He was unused to being as unsure as he now felt, unable to make up his mind. The sure anchor of authoritarian guidance now seemed to be lifting out of sand rather than something firm enough to hold it in place. He closed his eyes against the falling flakes. Opening them, he struggled for a moment to locate himself. All was white. He stood up feeling dizzy as the cold snow coated his face. His hands were numb and he shoved them into his pocket.

As suddenly as the snow intensified, it now let up. He was able to see the direction that would take him back toward the tavern. He began to walk. With each step he seemed more confident that things would work out for him, as they always did as long as he did not think too much. Yes, he had been told many times by many other men that his one problem was that he thought too much. That memory caused a smile to form on his face and added a little spring to his step.

He did not see the man who was following him, who had, in fact, been on his trail from the moment he had begun his walk, and who had withdrawn far enough away to be invisible against the blanket of falling snow, and who now trod the tracks that Edward left behind him.

He sat on his usual stool in the bar. He pulled his snow covered coat tight around him. Sheriff Cooper, with a loud sigh, settled his bulk down next to him.

"Been out walking in this weather?" Cooper asked.

Edward began to answer but could not stop his teeth from chattering. He clenched his mouth tight shut and nodded.

"What ever for?" the sheriff asked.

Edward shrugged.

"Give the man a cup of hot coffee," the sheriff said to the bar-keep. "He can't stop shivering."

The barkeep poured out a cup of steaming hot coffee and slid it to Edward.

"Thanks," Edward managed to murmur. He picked up the cup and held its warmth in his hands for a several moments before lifting it to his mouth and sipping the hot liquid.

"Take your time, warm up your innards," Cooper said. "Then we'll have a little chat about this walk you just had."

Edward drank slowly. When he finished the cup, he loosened his coat a little.

"Why were you walking out by the tracks?" the sheriff asked.

"I wasn't..." Edward began.

"Yes, you were. My man was following you. On my orders. In case, you had any ideas in your head about hopping a train and leaving the same way you came to town."

"I just had nothing to do," Edward said. "And so I walked."

"And just happened to find yourself out by the railroad line?"

"Yes."

"Just an accident?"

"Yes."

The sheriff clapped his big hand onto Edward's shoulder.

"Good. Because Mr. Jablonski says he's gonna need you, and he asked me to make sure you would be available. You will be, won't you?"

"Yes."

The sheriff heaved himself off of his stool. He pointed up toward the ceiling.

"You know what's up there?"

"A big room. Meetings sometimes in there."

"Well, you take a look at how you get up there. Find the stairs. Mr. Jablonski wants you to check them out."

"Is that where I gotta do something?"

"You just do what I told you. Find those stairs. Walk up and down them a couple of times. Get the feel of them. At the top of them, there's a door. You make sure you know where that is, how it opens."

Edward held out his hand.

"Gun? My gun?"

Cooper guffawed.

"Nah, you won't need a gun this time, All you need is what the good Lord gave you."

Edward stood and looked down at his toes and then up his legs and torso.

"Just what you was born with," the sheriff said.

And then he left.

Jim looked up at the towering white pine. Its trunk was mostly devoid of branches all the way up until just below the top where green branches remained forming a triangle with an apex at the very top. They were in a section of the woods where a number of trees were in the same condition.

The foreman came over to him and stood by his side, following his gaze up to the top of the tree.

"Some kind of rot," he said, "in case you're wondering."

"I wasn't," Jim replied.

"Well, today, I need you to get your black ass up there and cut off that top. When it comes down, it'll make a nice Christmas tree for you boys to set up in your quarters. Or maybe we'll put it with the others that we are planning to sell. Waste not, want not," he said and then strolled over to talk Henry, who was serving coffee.

Jim had seen others do what he was now being asked to do, but had hoped that given his inexperience he would be left to do those activities that kept his feet firmly on the ground. He had spent his whole life, after all, working the soil, digging holes in it for fence posts, plowing furrows in it for seeds, driving animals over it in and out of barns, to and from meadows, always his feet whether bare or shod never more than a second or a few inches removed from the earth.

Henry came over to him with a cup of steaming hot coffee.

"Today the day?" he asked.

Jim nodded.

"A couple of the white boys are sick."

"Thought so," Henry replied. "Boss told me to put a little something extra in your coffee. Just enough to take the edge off, but not to..."

"Got you," Jim said, and took the coffee. He took a sip and his tongue told him that there was a hint of raw whiskey.

"Thanks," he said.

"Just go slow," Henry said. "And you'll be fine."

"Never been higher than a four foot stone wall."

The foreman walked over.

"Finish your java," he said. "Then, we'll get started."

Jim took one big gulp from his tin mug, and then emptied the rest onto the ground. He stared at the black liquid for a few moments as though communing with the ground he would soon be leaving.

"When you get to the top, make the piece you take down to be no more than eight or nine feet. Good length for a Christmas tree. Got it?"

Jim nodded, picked up the one-man saw, looked down at the spiked shoes now on his feet, and stood next to the trunk of the pine while the foreman fastened the rope around him, snug enough so that he would be able to embrace the tree as he climbed, just like you're dancing, the foreman said. That description struck Jim as almost comical, dancing, when was the last time he had been dancing, or even touched a woman, not since when he was barely an adult, still a slave, when the white owner tacitly encouraged sexual relationships as long as they didn't interfere with regular work, and as long as there was a possibility of reproduction, because what was better than getting a new slave for nothing rather than paying good coin at the market.

As he was about to start his climb, the foreman's hand pressed down on his shoulders.

"Remember, don't look down, at least not until you really know what you're doing. We want the top to come down, not you."

The trip up was not as difficult as he thought it would be. The few remaining branches were brittle and came off easily. When he approached the top, he felt strangely liberated as he pushed himself back against the restraining rope, his knees still firm against the bark of the tree, above him the bright blue sky and white clouds between which, just visible, a hawk swooped in a graceful arc toward him. He stared at the hawk as it neared, steeling himself against a possible attack as though the bird could confuse him with its usual prey, but then it reached the bottom of its arc and with a gentle flap of its wings climbed up again and disappeared behind a low lying cloud.

As instructed, he had not looked down as he worked himself up to where he now was positioned some eight or ten feet below the very top of the tree. The branches right above him spread out about six or seven feet and then tapered to less than a foot just below the very top where the tree came to a green point. He could see that if he cut right above where he was, the result would be a nicely shaped Christmas tree. With that in mind, he edged himself up until his chest was where he wanted to cut. He lifted his saw, leaned back hard against the restraining rope, squeezed the tree with his knees like it was the hips of a lover, and drew the blade across the trunk on his right side. The saw, which he had sharpened that morning, bit easily into the soft wood. Then, lining up his blade to meet that initial cut at an angle,as he had been instructed to do, he began sawing toward it from his left. It did not take many strokes before the top began to topple. He kept sawing, being careful not to put too much pressure into each stroke. It would not do for the saw to come clear with his weight behind it. One more stroke, and his blade met that first cut and the top fell.

Still, he did not look down. He heard the thud as it hit the crowd. A cheer went up from those below, and he permitted himself a smile.

He took a deep gulp of the cold, clear air, saw again the hawk circling above, looked down at the ground, at the men gathered around the tree top, then stared up again , seeing the bird's dark spread wings in sharp contrast to the brilliant blue sky and puffy white clouds. Turning his gaze again to the ground, he felt a sickness in the pit of his stomach. On the ground, he thought, that was where all my troubles have been my whole life, what will it profit me to plant my sorry feet on that earth again, nothing but trouble, if only like the bird I could soar up and far away from here, land somewhere else, leaving my difficulties behind me, no more white men on my tail.

But if I can't fly like that bird, maybe I should come down in a way to end my troubles.

He reached for the knife in the sheaf attached to his belt. Withdrawing it, he tested its keen blade with his thumb and then pressed it on the rope that was holding him against the trunk of the tree.

Among those watching now was the white mustached man.

"Well, you're Thomas Drummond, aren't you?" the foreman asked. "Henry said you might come by to check on things."

"It is, and I am," Drummond said.

They both looked up.

"What is that fool still doing up there?" the foreman said.

Henry came over.

"He's got his knife out," he said.

Drummond shielded his eyes from the sun.

"So he does."

"Damn fool," the foreman said. "We're already short on the crew."

"You gonna sit there all day, or do what you was told to do?" the barman asked.

Edward stared up over the beer, which had replaced the coffee he had been drinking. He was now more than warm, the snow had melted off him and his outer garments, although his sox inside his shoes were cold and soggy.

"What was that?" he asked.

"Why, check out the stairs to the upper level." He pointed to doors at the side wall of the tavern. "Over there. Start over there."

Edward nodded and strolled over to the doors. He realized that he had never noticed them before. He would come in to the tavern through the front door, make his way to his stool, drink while facing the bottles lined up across from him, and when he was done, he would retrace his steps, and out the same door through which he had entered.

Now, he was looking at a non-descript door, barely visible against the background of the surrounding walls, door and walls of the same dark stained wood. He found the knob, turned and pushed the door open. He was on a small landing. To his left and down a couple of steps was another door. To his right was another door. He tried the door on his left and found that it gave onto the street. He closed that door and walked to the other. He pulled it, but it did not move. He pushed against it, and when it opened he saw that behind it was a steep staircase leading to the upper level.

At the tops of these stairs was another landing. To his right, were two doors. He stood there for a few moments, listening. He thought he heard some noises that might indicate the presence of one or more individuals. He tried the knob on the right hand side of the double doors. It turned, and he pulled the door open just wide enough for him to look into the hall. He expected to see rows of seats as had been the case in the meeting he attended. But here the floor was unencumbered by chairs, almost as though it were being prepared for a dance. Across it, he did see a raised platform in front of the wall on the left.

He pulled the door open and took a step in. For the most part, the hall was dark except for the glow of a lantern on the platform. The noise he had heard was coming from that direction. He peered into the darkness, and listened. Footsteps came through the still air of the hall from the side of the platform, followed by a large figure carrying something. Now, he could see that next to the lantern was an object, wider at the bottom, narrower at the top.

A tree. He understood. A Christmas tree.

And the figure was that same large woman he had seen before, at the meeting demanding money for food for the families of the striking miners, and more dramatically etched into his memory, at the front of the marching strikers, carrying that huge flag, confronting the officer with the sword.

This time there was no officer, no flag, but in her hands some sort of string that she now began to wrap around the tree, starting at the top and working her way toward its base. Something fell off the string and echoed off the wooden floor. It was followed by another, and then another.

Pine cones.

She was stringing pine cone decorations around a Christmas tree. She stopped what she was doing to pick up the cones that had fallen, and then lifted her eyes in his direction. He stood as still as he could, tried not to breathe, until she turned back to her task, and he was able, ever so gently, to close the door, and make his way back down the narrow stairs to the lower landing. When he got to the bottom of the steps, he first pushed the door, forgetting that he must pull it toward him. On the landing, he thought about resuming his seat at the bar for another beer. But perhaps he hadn't fully done what he had been ordered to do, to check out the stairs. He should be careful to complete his assignment, so he started down the few steps to the door that led outside. He opened it and walked out into the chill December air.

Jim took one more intense look up at the sky. The clouds continued to drift by, but as long as he held his gaze upward he could not find the bird. It had gone off to find some place more to its liking. Lowering his eyes, he saw the foreman wave up to him with a violent motion, lifting his right arm high above his head and then bringing it down toward the ground with enough vehemence to dislocate his shoulder. Jim permitted himself a wry smile. He made a sawing motion with his knife blade against the rope, but without exerting sufficient pressure to do it any harm. He saw the foreman's motions become even more frenetic, and he heard sounds rising up from below. Apparently, to supplement his arm motions the foreman was shouting his command to come down, but his words were swallowed by the breeze blowing across the tops of the forests' trees.

Jim nodded although he was not at all sure those below him could see the gesture. He lifted his knife from the rope, held it above his head for a few moments, and then very slowly slid it back into its sheath. He began his descent half sliding, half digging his spiked shoes into the tree's trunk. When next he looked down, he was close enough to the ground to make out the other figures gathered around the foreman. Among then he spied the man with thick white mustache.

"Well, I'll be a son of a bitch," he mumbled to himself. "Maybe I should have cut through that rope. That would give him something to talk about or tell whoever it was he reported to."

He slid the last five or six feet to the ground.

"Good job," the foreman said when his feet hit the ground.

"We were worried about you," Drummond said.

Jim placed his hand on the hilt of his knife, ever so slowly lifted it up until the bright blade glinted in the sun, then let it slide back into its sheaf. He walked over to the tree top, examined it for a few moments, and then strode away.

"The sheriff told me you took quite a walk for yourself," Jablonski said as he sat down next to Edward at the bar.

"I had nothing much to do," Edward replied. "Been waiting for you to tell me."

"That time is coming."

"Now?"

"Not yet," Jablonski said and motioned to the barman, who poured whiskey into a shot glass. Jablonski swallowed it down. "Don't want you to have to hold your instructions too long in your head. You might lose them, and that would not do at all. But be patient."

"Just taking a walk," Edward mumbled in the voice of a child being scolded without knowing why.

"To the railroad tracks," Jablonski said.

"Didn't know that," Edward replied.

Jablonski stood up.

"You know," he said, "I believe you didn't."

Edward suddenly remembered.

"I did do what you told me to do. After my walk." He looked toward the door at on the side wall of the tavern. "Went through there and up to the next floor. Looked into the hall."

"Where you saw something, didn't you?"

"Sure. That big woman stringing pine cones on a Christmas tree."

"Right!" Jabonski exclaimed with a slap on Edward's back. "You just remember that, and all will be well."

After dinner, Jim lingered at his place at the communal table, absent mindedly drumming his fork on his tin plate, working it into some rhythm that asserted itself from deep in his memory. For a while, he couldn't place where he must have heard it before. Music had never occupied much of a place in his life, at least not since he became a fully grown man. But as he drummed, he remembered.

The white folks were having a big holiday celebration, attended by all the planters in the area. The regular house staff was going to be overwhelmed by the flood of guests so field hands such as Jim were called in to help. Of course, they were not tasked with anything that required domestic skills, but they could lug things around, fetch more wine from the cellar, guide horses to the stables, or even perhaps take a lady's wrap or a gentleman's coat to be hung up.

That latter was Jim's job. He was ten or twelve, he could not remember which, and once everybody had arrived, all their outer garments attended to, he was told to wait around to be called upon if necessary, until the party was over and he would now help the departing guests back into those garments. Having nothing particular to do, he knew he should be close by but not visible, so he found a spot near the ballroom, and it was from there that he had heard the dance music, whose rhythms he was now tapping onto his tin plate, as if to remind him in this indirect way that the rest of the world was celebrating the holiday season.

Henry, who had finished his after meal chores, walked over.

"What were you thinking?" he asked.

Jim looked up.

"Wasn't thinking."

"That's a fact," Henry smiled. "Do you have any plans?"

"For?"

"Christmas?

"Hadn't thought about it."

"Everybody will be on their own," Henry said. "I've got a little cabin not too far. If you care to join me."

"Maybe I will do just that," Jim said.

Henry's cabin was a small, well constructed one room log house. A large cast iron stove dominated the room, along with a plank table of maple wood, and nestled in one corner was a small bed. Up above, reached by a ladder, was a loft.

"There's another bed up there," Henry said. "Sometimes my son come to visit me. He lives with his momma. I don't know where. But sometimes he just shows up and seems to know when I'll be here. Door's never locked, who's gonna come here to rob me, so if I ain't home, he just makes himself comfortable and waits for me. If I don't, he'll leave me a note."

"Don't have a family," Jim said. "Had a woman once, way back when."

"Too bad," Henry replied.

"Is it? Nobody to worry about 'ceptin' myself."

"That's what I want to talk to you about," Henry said.

CHAPTER FIFTEEN

Governor Woodhouse ignored the ringing phone on his desk for a few moments, leaning back in his chair, eyes closed.

"Get it Larry," he said to his assistant who was waiting for the governor to decide if he would be needed any more this day. Christmas was only a few days away, and Larry still hadn't bought Janet anything. If he could be relieved of his responsibilities, he would have time to stop at that jewelery store where he had seen a little cameo he thought he could just afford. Things were getting serious, and he wanted to make sure he could buy his girl a gift she would like. After that, well, after that, he would just see how things developed.

"It's the warden," Larry said, with his hand covering the mouthpiece. "He says he needs to talk to you."

Woodhouse held out his hand, and took the phone. With his other hand, he motioned Larry to retreat to his desk in the outer office. Sitting at his desk, with growing impatience, Larry heard snatches of the governor's side of the conversation, but not enough to piece together what the business was that the warden felt had to be discussed right then, even though Larry's pocket watch told him that it was almost five-thirty. That jewelry shop closed at six.

"Larry," the governor called. "Come on in." He reached into his pocket and took out a heavy silver coin. "Take this," he said, "and get something nice for that girl of yours."

"When do you think you will move?" Eunice asked.

On his walk back from the house he now owned, Isaiah pondered that very same question. The immediate answer was really quite easy and popped into his head as soon as he closed the door of that modest home on Washington Street behind him. Of course, he could not contemplate a move while in the middle of the drama to free his father which seemed very clearly to be moving into its final act. He had played his role in that play as best he could. There was no audience whose reactions could tell him whether his performance had been good enough for its purpose. He had no ambition to star in this play, that role had been thrust upon him by circumstances, and he would have been most happy to have joined that hypothetical audience waiting for the final curtain, and for the performers to take their bows. His audience, though, had been the hard, unrevealing face of Warden Higgins, and the pleasant, but uninvolved countenance of the young lady, whose name he could no longer remember, who took down his lines in shorthand, whose pencil scratchings, and occasional erasures, emulated backstage movements that barely register in the minds of the actors reciting their lines, and who not very long after he exited the stage brought, not a review from the press, but a typescript copy of what he had offered in response to the warden's careful questions.

Whether those questions were leading or not, he could not judge, which is to say, he had been unable to determine whether or not the warden had an interest in how this situation was going to play out. What was clear, though, was that the warden was operating under the orders of somebody, very likely the governor himself, who had a serious interest in whether or not Sam Logan would walk out of Jackson State Prison, or whether he would die there, which, of course, had been the State's original intention.

So, as Eunice stood in front of him outside the leather shop where he had encountered her just at closing time, he could only offer the most superficial and obvious answer to her question, an answer which they both knew did not begin to touch upon the deeper issues that his inheritance lay before them.

"I don't know," he replied. "Not until..." he paused realizing that he had not taken her into his confidence as he left for Jackson.

"Not until," she finished the thought for him, "you know whether your trip will have had a positive outcome."

"I didn't tell you," he replied, feeling his face unexpectedly redden, for really, did he owe her an apology? "I didn't tell you because I suppose I didn't know how you would react to what

I was doing. It would have," he realized as he mouthed these words, "some significance for you. And for Jonathan. The outcome, I mean."

"Yes, it would," she replied. She shook her head. "In all honesty, I do not know how I will feel, should your father one day come back to this town. And as for Jonathan, well, I can't even begin to go there."

"It's a nice little house," Isaiah said. He thought for a moment that he would tell her about the two rooms, the one clearly his mother's, the other painted blue with books intended for him.

"I think I know which it is," she said. "When that letter came, I took a walk in the direction from which I saw your mother walking that time, and came upon a house which quite clearly was not being lived in then."

"I'm glad you did," Isaiah said, recognizing that he was, in fact, happy to have someone with whom he could share this experience, if only at the periphery for now.

She seemed to read that thought, for she offered a warm smile.

"Jonathan has been asking about you," she said.

"About another baseball game? The season…"

"About Christmas," she replied.

"Christmas?" He looked up and down the busy commercial street he had walked across, seeing now what he had not noticed, that there was a different feel emanating from the passersby, some were carrying packages wrapped in gift paper, others were looking into shop windows, here and there hung a wreath on a door.

"Oh," she said. "I guess you were not thinking about the season."

"No. Not at all. You were saying something about Christmas."

"Yes. Whether you might join us. Maybe for dinner or to dress our tree. We could use the help, and, well, Jonathan has been asking."

"Your mother, I don't think she would approve."

"No, she wouldn't."

"Well, maybe for the tree," he said.

"We'll be doing it on Christmas Eve. Think about it."

"I will."

Isaiah could not easily remember more than a handful of times his celebrations of Christmas approximated the joyousness associated with the holiday. If he let himself dig deep into his memory he could pull up one time when as a toddler at his mother's knee he listened to her read from a lushly illustrated little book that tale of the jolly elf and his reindeer. He could even recall the stocking hung by the fireplace just like in the story, looking at it as his mother's soft voice recited the words of the poem. As hard as he tried, though, he could not bring an image of his father sharing that moment. He could now imagine the tension that must have informed their household at that time, the holiday insisting on the family gathered in the harmonious warmth of the holiday. True, they had gone together to the Christmas church service, sitting with his grandparents in that same church in which he had so recently watched the funeral service of Margaret's father. But the chill of marital discord had followed them into the building.

It was not long after that reading of the Christmas tale that his mother left. Thereafter, as he grew up living with his father, their holiday celebrations were, if anything, dutiful. Sam would dutifully take them to church, dutifully attend Christmas dinner with the grandparents, dutifully erect and, with Isaiah's help, decorate a tree, under which he would dutifully place a clumsily wrapped gift for Isaiah to open on Christmas morning. Perhaps, Isaiah now guessed, the holiday had lost any positive glow for his father because of what was going on between him and his mother that last time together when she recited the story. He could even imagine Sam stonily sitting across the room, but that was a thought, not a remembered fact. It was even possible that Sam had left the house before the reading.

For a brief period when he and his father were living in their new household with Eunice, the holiday regained a little of its glow. Eunice tried for a year or two, serving a fine goose or turkey dinner, having Sam, again, take care of putting up the tree, and then all three of them adding decorations to it. But as that marriage began to disintegrate so did the glow diminish. He could not now remember whether the holiday was celebrated the year of Eunice's pregnancy with Jonathan.

"You know," Pete said, as he and Sam walked into the dining area for their evening meal, "on Christmas eve we each get a slice of pie. Usually apple. Made from our very own orchards. Thin slices, though, with a crust that loosens your teeth."

"Christmas eve, isn't that..."

"It is."

They approached the door where, as usual, O'Brien sat, smoking a cigarette. He took a deep drag as with a nod Pete walked past him, and as Sam reached him, he exhaled. The tobacco smoke tickled Sam's nose.

"Ah," he said, "nice. But I always preferred a good cigar when I could get one."

With the present nicely wrapped in his pocket, Larry left the jewelry store. The little extra money the governor had given him enabled him to purchase a nicer cameo, a bit bigger and of a nicer design. He was sure Janet's eyes would light up when she saw it, and it would be evidence that he was, as he had been telling her, a young man with solid prospects, working as he was in the governor's office.

His mind turned to the telephone conversation the governor had with the warden. He only could catch a word here and there but what he did hear was the rising and falling of the governor's voice. He had now worked with Woodhouse long enough to conclude that those changes in pitch and volume, muted as they were coming through the heavy oak door, were atypical. The governor was man who seemed always to have his emotions under control. The few words he did hear with some clarity were "You don't say. On Christmas eve. Well, I'll be..." Something important was no doubt going on, and he would be glad to be part of it, whatever it was.

But not as glad as he was at the moment with Janet's present in his hand.

That night Sam lay on his cot staring through the darkness toward the ceiling he could not see. Somehow Pete's telling him about the slice of apple pie on Christmas Eve struck him with unexpected force. He had not thought about the holiday in years. Of what possible importance could it have for him during his solitary confinement?

Now memories of Christmas past in his life as a free man came, uninvited, into his mind, beginning first as a fleeting image or auditory fragment, but soon growing into a flood of scenes that try as he might he could not shut down. So in the darkness of his present he relived these moments from his past.

The images flashed in a dizzying round of ups and downs, a chronological jumble ranging from his own childhood when his austere father did not have much use for the holiday but grumpily permitted his more warm hearted wife to provide some measure of cheer, a tree, some presents, all concentrated on the day itself while the day after was a working day just like any other on the year's calendar, and moving in irregular fashion through his own ambivalent celebrations in his own households, more fully upbeat in the beginning of each of his marriages, descending into stony indifference, if not outright hostility as those marriages themselves disintegrated.

Out of this disordered montage, one scene emerged with startling clarity. Around a holiday dinner table featuring a plump goose, sat Eunice whose big belly prevented her from getting comfortably close enough to wield the carving knife, and Isaiah whose eyes shifted back and forth from his stepmother to an unseen individual, whose face eventually emerged and Sam found himself in his mind staring at himself, his face set in an insincere smile. And then he heard the slam of a door, and he was outside in a light snowfall trudging off.

The images dissolved, replaced by his recollection that he had returned to the table, sat down, and in silence ate the dinner plate she had left for him.

Christmas be damned he muttered, surprised at hearing his own voice.

He sensed Pete stirring in his cot and he held his breath while he ran through a number of ways he could explain why he had cursed the holiday. It wouldn't do at this late date to lose everything he had been working for. Nothing came to mind. He waited. And after a few moments, he heard Pete's body settle back onto his cot, and then a little later the usual snoring drifted into the dark, still air of their cell.

"Well," the governor said by way of greeting Larry the next morning, "did you make a good purchase?"

"Yessir, I did," Larry replied.

"Good. Now listen, this is what I want you to do." He pointed to a neat pile of papers on his desk. "Take those, study them over as if they were a case you were given to study in your law school. I'm going to want your legal opinion. Fred has been working on the political dimension of this situation. But he's not as well prepared as you are for the legal side. I'm not going to tell you anything more, I don't want to color your response to what you will be reading by guessing what I may, or may not, want you to determine once you have finished your analysis."

Larry began to take the papers, but the governor stayed his hand.

"You may have heard some comments about the matter in this case. I want you to clear your head of any thoughts you might have about what you might have heard. Is that clear?"

"Yessir. When do you need my opinion?"

"There is some urgency. But I don't want to ruin your holiday...."

Larry picked up the papers and held them suspended as though their weight could give him an idea as to how much time he would need."

"So, take as much time as you need, as long as you can report to me by the end of the day."

Larry had, in fact, heard snippets of comments about this fellow whose case he now began to study. The name had not been familiar to him, and so he had no idea as to why the governor was so interested in the matter. That was not, however, for him to worry about. He took out sheets of blank paper, picked up a sharpened pencil, and placed that paper next to the first page of the document and began to read.

Isaiah picked up the old baseball from its spot on his desk. He had not yet made up his mind as to whether he would join Eunice, her mother, and Jonathan for Christmas dinner, but he had pretty well convinced himself that he would help them decorate their tree. As to why he had come to that decision, he could not say, except that it had just felt right. Perhaps it was not so much Eunice, but Jonathan that pulled him in that direction. To his surprise, he realized he was beginning to feel attached to his brother.

And if he were going to help with their tree, he should put something under it. Thus, the old baseball. It was the baseball game, after all, that had brought him closer to Jonathan, had been the seed that seemed to be growing into a strong bond between them. But, he told himself, the matter was not that simple, it was not just a relationship between brothers, there was still a father, however remotely, in the picture, and a question as to just how would Sam fit in should he be freed, and no doubt Eunice might have some reservations as well about Isaiah's growing closer to Jonathan, never mind her mother who had already made up her mind that Isaiah's presence in their household was poisonous.

He tossed the ball up toward the ceiling, caught it, and repeated, with each repetition his mind argued with itself, yes he should, no he shouldn't. Finally, perhaps out of frustration, his toss was too strong, the ball hit the ceiling, came down at an unexpected angle, and bounced at his feet. He snared it, placed it back on the desk.

The answer to the question would have to wait. In the meantime, the ball wasn't going anywhere.

Larry sat back from his desk, rubbed his eyes, heard the grandfather clock in the governor's office chime four times. He had just finished the last page from the pile Woodhouse had given him, and had filled up the space on the last of the blank sheets on which he recorded his own observations as he went along.

He heard the governor talking on the phone. No doubt, he would be there when the clock chimed five. The end of the day. By which Woodhouse would want Larry's report. He turned his own handwritten pages over so that the first stared back at him. He would read through them, and then compose his opinion, the outlines of which were already firm in his mind. He just needed to fill in the details where they fit. Not miss anything. For certain, the governor would not.

As the fifth chime filled the two offices, Larry knocked, but without waiting for an answer, pushed open the door to the governor's office. A couple of barely discernible lines of tension furrowed the governor's brow.

"What do you have for me Larry?" he asked.

"It's complicated," Larry replied, "but I do think there's an argument to be made here, a pretty good one."

The lines on the governor's brow relaxed.

"Tell me about it, then," he said.

In his Chicago office, Lowe contemplated if, and when, he should play his next, and last, card on Sam's behalf.

It was time, he thought, past time, for me to sit down at the table again with the governor, and see just what he has, does his hand beat mine.

Or maybe, just maybe, we might be on the same side now.

The clock chimed the quarter hour after six.

"Very complete and detailed, as you would give to your law school professor," Woodhouse said. "What I need now is something a little more practical than that. Let's place that legal analysis into the real world of action."

"Or inaction," Larry said.

"Ah, so you do understand," the governor replied. "Very good."

"I think so," Larry said. "If we boil the case down to the alibi, we don't have any way of determining the truth. Motive is also not entirely clear, but even if it were, motive by itself is not probative. That goes back to opportunity, which goes back to alibi. Then you factor in the community's obvious hostility, and you could say the trial itself was less than fair."

"Yes, yes," Woodhouse said. "But I need to know whether I should intervene, as I have been importuned to do. And I do believe that Mr. Lowe, oh he's a clever one, is holding something back. I don't want to read about that surprise in the newspaper."

"My view, then," Larry said with the hesitation that comes with realizing how much his future might depend upon what he was about to say, "is that there are pluses and minuses to your intervention. But at the very least, you should be comfortable that what you do is based not only on your political interest, but also on what you think is right."

"And how can I be sure of that?"

Larry answered without calculation. Having gone through the case, he himself remained uncertain as to how he felt.

"I'd go speak to the man."

CHAPTER SIXTEEN

“**H**ey, Mister, are you going to the Christmas party tonight at the Itallian Hall?”

Edward looked down at the little boy, still clutching his mother’s hand. For a moment, he could make no sense of the question. For most of his life, the Christmas season was a matter of supreme indifference to him. He would be a hired hand on some farm, an observer of the farm family’s celebration. He would exchange holiday greetings, but when asked what he planned to do could only say he had no plans, an answer that would generate a sympathetic murmur but not an invitation to join the family at the holiday table. Sometimes a boss would give him a coin or two, which he would spend on an extra beer or some time in the bed of an accommodating woman.

“Now, George,” the little boy’s mother said, “don’t bother this man.”

“No bother,” Edward said. “Merry Christmas to you both.”

“But I wanted to know,” the boy insisted.

“Merry Christmas to you, as well,” the woman said, and tugged her son along as she walked away.

Edward watched them leave their footprints in the snow, and then resumed his own walk. Aware that he might still be followed, as he was the day he wandered out of town to the train tracks, and with nothing to do but wait for Jablonski to give him instructions that would somehow have to do with the large woman stringing pine cones on the tree in the meeting hall above the tavern, Edward walked up and down the main street in Calumet, always staying pretty much in sight of the building that housed the tavern and meeting hall. Since the onset of winter weather, the protest parades led by the large woman had stopped, and instead the street was filled with people, mostly women and children, going about their ordinary business.

But as immune as he customarily was to the energy of the Christmas season, he did sense something different in the demeanor of those individuals he now observed. Up until recently, the mood given off by those on the street was either one of anger or more recently, a gnawing pessimism. Both anger and pessimism remained, but they seemed to have been papered over by something more upbeat.

He had wondered at that change, but now the little boy's question, as innocent as it was, had given him the answer. Of course. There was going to be a party in that meeting hall where the large woman was decorating a tree. He should have thought of that at once, what else explained what she was doing that afternoon in the deserted hall? At the time, although the question formed in his mind as to her lone presence there, since no answer came to him, he did not bother to try to provide one.

But recognizing the obvious fact of the party was only the beginning of the answer. The rest remained in his as yet unstated role in the event. That he was to do something in that meeting hall was now very clear. What that something was he could not begin to imagine.

As if to answer that question, Jablonski's large figure now approached him.

The pungent smell of frying bacon wafted up to Jim in the loft. He sat up on the string bed, and peered down through the opening into the main floor of the cabin. Henry was lifting a sizzling pan off of the stove. He looked up.

"Didn't know when you were going to get up so I thought I'd start breakfast and see if that would rouse you."

Jim stood up and stretched. A day with no work to do. Bacon. Coffee. Maybe some eggs. Too good, too good by far.

"Why are you doing all this for me? Don't you work for that man been plaguing me?"

"I do," Henry said. "And that is why. Come on down. We'll eat, and we'll have that conversation I said we should have. But first eat. How do you like your eggs?"

"Cooked," Jim replied.

"Sunny side up, it is, then, because the sun gonna shine on your sorry life today."

"Do you understand?" Jablonski asked.

Edward nodded.

"You want me to wait until people stop going in, wait maybe another half hour to be sure. Then go up those stairs to the second floor, where the meeting hall is, where I saw that woman putting up that Christmas tree."

"Right," Jablonski replied. "The timing has to be right. And then...."

Edward reached into his pocket and pulled out the pin.

"I do what you told me to do. Put this on."

"Right. Not before. Just as you are about to open the door."

To his surprise, Edward felt a qualm, a sense that maybe this wasn't right, even though he knew he was just supposed to do what he was told, that was the way to keep out of trouble.

"And then with the pin on, you take a step into the hall..."

"And then I yell, just like you told me."

"Just once and then again, then turn and leave. Keep going, down the stairs, out the door."

"And find you. In your office. Where I first met you. And you'll tell me what I should do next."

"Right. One more thing. I don't want you to forget about eating." He pulled out some coins. "Get something when you feel hungry. We need you at your best."

Edward nodded, took the coins. It's going to be alright, he thought, just do what the man says.

"Now what I want to talk to you about," Henry said as he pushed himself back from the table, "is what you are going to do now. You've gotten paid. You don't have to sign up for the next job."

"Why woudn't I?" Jim asked.

"Because it's time for you to disappear."

"Tried that.

"Need to do it again. What you're involved in is going to end. One way or another. And whichever way it is you need to be gone."

"How am I going to manage that?"

"That son I told you about. He works for the railroad. He left me a note. Be here later today. For a Christmas visit."

"And?"

"And. He can be your ticket out of here to wherever you want to go."

"Wherever? Wherever I can disappear. Like you say."

Edward filled his stomach with a thick soup at a restaurant a short walk from his post outside the building he was to enter later that day. A light snow was falling as he emerged onto the street. He bunched his coat around him, made his way back to his position across from the building, lit a cigarette and waited.

Throughout the afternoon, people passing by him seemed to be moving faster than they usually did, but most of them, especially the women, paused to turn to him and wish him a Merry Christmas. Their faces wore a smile as they offered the greeting, and he found himself responding in turn. The children seemed infused with unusual energy, and looked toward the building on the other side of the street. Most of the men passing by did not offer a holiday greeting. Some just nodded at him, others looked at him with suspicion. A clergyman with collar stopped in front of him.

"Are you in need of something?" he asked.

Edward pondered the question. It had been a long time since he had interacted with a clergyman.

"No," he said.

"Do you have someplace to stay? If you don't, I can find somewhere for you. You needn't be standing out in the snow. Especially on this day."

"I stay at the boardinghouse, up that way," Edward replied raising his arm to point the direction.

"Oh, I see. Are you waiting, then, for somebody?"

"Yes," Edward replied. "I'm waiting."

The clergyman looked across the road at the building, then back at Edward.

"Perhaps I'll see you there later," he said.

Edward froze. How could he know? Maybe he was just being polite, like clergymen are. What to say. He took a deep drag on his cigarette.

"Just waiting for my friend," he said.

The clergyman put his hand on Edward's shoulder and gave a slight squeeze, then turned and walked across the road and into the building.

Edward waited and watched. As the sun started to set, his hands and feet began to feel numb from the cold. Now there was only the occasional passerby, and those that did hurry by seemed to be going somewhere else, as it had been some time since anybody had entered the building.

He lit one more cigarette. When he had smoked it down, it would be time for him to walk across the road. He murmured his instructions to himself. He was still a little troubled by what he was to do, but as he ground out his cigarette in the snow beneath his feet, he chastised himself.

Just do what you were told to do.

As Larry walked toward Janet's house where he was to give her present to her, he wondered whether the time was right to move their relationship a step closer to an engagement. Because the governor had entrusted him in such a consequential matter, he was feeling more confident that he could present himself as a young man on his way to a good position in life. But cautious by nature, he reined in that thought. True, the governor had sought his advice, and he had offered it. But what if he had missed something, if his advice turned out to be ill-advised, and he would have to then tell Janet, and indirectly her parents, for he was sure that she confided in them about him, tell her that his prospects did not look as good as he had thought them to be. Better, he concluded, to wait until he sees how things work out.

With the baseball in his pocket, Isaiah walked down Washington Street, returning holiday greetings to those he encountered, men and women hurrying on to their own Christmas Eve dinners, some carrying gifts needing to be wrapped, and then there were the children, enjoying the late afternoon in the dying sunlight building snowmen or tossing snowballs at each other.

Approaching Eunice's house, he crossed over to the other side of the street. He wasn't ready to make his entrance just yet. First, he wanted to continue on to the house he could now call *my house*, although that phrase did not yet sit comfortably in his mind much less on his tongue. He was not at all certain that he could ever settle into that house. When he undertook this mission to try to free his father, thrust upon him by his grandmother, he had done so as a matter of duty with the clear idea that once he was finished with it, whatever the outcome, he would again take himself onto the lakes, and therefore would have no need for a structure he could call *his* house. That urge to leave the land remained as strong as ever, but it was now part of an admixture of other emotions having to do with his father, with Eunice, and quite strongly with Jonathan. Perhaps that is why his hand had stayed wrapped around the baseball he would be giving to his brother.

He crossed back to the other side of the street and stood in front of the darkened shape of his house as it succumbed to the advancing shadows of the night. It is, after all, he told himself, just a house. It has no particular claim on me. I can do with it what I want. Sell it. Give it away.

But then he remembered the little bedroom painted blue with the bookcase filled with volumes suitable for a child. Well that does complicate matters, he thought.

Sam and Pete approached the chair factory. When they were within a few feet of the entrance, Pete stopped.

"Son of a bitch," he muttered. "Where is that fat pig?"

Sam looked past Pete to the guard at the door. It was one he had never seen before.

"Maybe he's on a break," Sam said.

"At this time. Today of all times. I don't think so."

The man in front of Pete had already been checked in. The new guard, a powerfully built young man, motioned Pete forward.

"Come on," the guard called out. "You're holding up the line. There's work to be done inside. You want your slice of pie, don't you?"

Pete moved forward slowly, his eyes darting from side to side. Just as he was within a few feet of the door, two other guards appeared at his side and took his arms. As he was being dragged away, he turned back to Sam.

"Logan," he called out, "you are a dead man."

Inside the meeting room on the second floor of the Italian Hall dozens of children stood in line waiting their turn to approach the Christmas tree, next to which stood Big Annie with a burlap sack at her side. As each child approached, she dipped her hand into the bag to find a small, nicely wrapped gift. Tearing off the paper, the boy or girl might find a piece of gum, or candy, or perhaps a tin soldier, or paper windmill. Eyes lit up. Comparisons were made. Trades offered. The little girl with the tin soldier exchanged it for a piece of candy, the windmill for the gum. Some of the bolder children got back on to the end of the line, hiding their gifts in their pockets. If Big Annie noticed, she did not care. It was Christmas after all, and these children had suffered deprivation during the long strike, they deserved a little joy, as did their parents who could not themselves provide them with even such small gifts as were now being handed out.

A pretty girl of nine or ten years, with long blond hair, stood on the line between two other girls, a little younger. Each of them held onto one hand of the older girl, whose eyes did not respond to motion, did not blink in the light.

"We're almost next," the younger girl in front of the trio said. "What do you think we'll get?"

"I'd like a piece of candy," said the other young girl.

"I wished for a little doll," the first young girl said.

"I will be happy with anything," the blind girl said.

Small smiles appeared on the faces of the adults as they watched the parade of children march up to receive their gifts, those smiles broadening as the squeals of delight reached them.

One grizzled miner walked up to Big Annie.

"Thank you," he said.

He was followed by a young woman holding the hand of a little boy who was clutching his tin soldier.

"Yes," she said. "We all thank you."

Edward lit another cigarette. He wanted to will his feet to cross the street and do what he was supposed to do, but something in his mind held him back. He was not certain what that something was. Never before could he recall a time when he found it difficult to follow clear and direct instructions, no matter what the task was.

Go on you fool, he muttered to himself, are you going to start thinking for yourself at this time in your life?

With those words uttered beneath his breath, his resistance faded and his feet now obeyed his command to carry him across the now deserted street. As he reached the door to the building, a voice floated out to him from the shadows.

"So glad you decided to join us," the clergyman said.

Edward froze. What to say? But the words came to him.

"My friend, I don't know what happened to him."

"I was just on my way home to a late dinner. I offered my blessing to the party upstairs. Then I saw you smoking a cigarette. Do you think I can have one?"

Edward reached into his pocket and took out his packet of cigarettes and handed it to the clergyman, who eased a cigarette out. From his pocket Edward felt for and removed a wooden match, which he lit with his thumb nail, and then held to the cigarette.

"Thank you. I just ran out," the clergyman said, holding out the packet for Edward to take. "And I like to smoke as I walk. Enjoy yourself, and good night."

Edward watched as beneath a barely visible cloud of smoke, he disappeared into the night. When he could no longer see the disappearing shape, he reached for the doorknob, pulled back his hand, then grasped it.

Inside, the stairway was at first empty. He did not want to forget his instructions, so he reached into his pocket, found the pin and attached it to his jacket. Then, as he began to climb he heard another door above him open. A figure appeared at the top of the stairs and started down. Edward tucked his head against his chest, sidled over to the wall and began his ascent, keeping his eyes on the steps immediately in front of him. Halfway up he sensed the presence of the other person.

"Happy... "a voice said, and then paused, "Christmas."

"Yes," Edward replied without looking up, "Happy Christmas."

Reaching the landing, he paused to catch his breath. Then he opened the door leading into the hall, poked his head into the room, surveyed the festivities, saw the large woman handing out gifts to the line of children, heard the high-pitched buzz of their excitement as well as the lower tones of the adults, snatches of words, some in English, others in a language he now understood to be Finnish, thought for a moment that he should have learned the Finnish version of the word that he was to shout into the room, shrugged, and then took a step into the hall and at the top of his voice delivered that word not once, but twice as he had been instructed.

He did not wait more than a second to observe the result, just long enough to see all movement stop, noise to disappear into a stunned silence. And then he turned, and as fast as he was able scurried back down the stairs, out the door and into the street, heading toward Jablonski's office.

Inside the hall, Big Annie looked around. Saw nothing. Raised her voice against the rising tide of panic, but was not heard. She placed herself in front of the gathering rush of children, but big as she was, she was not big enough to stop it. By her on both sides came children heading for the door and the stairway, adults, too, joined the movement, some of them carrying a child, the men on their shoulders, the women clutched to their chests.

"No, no," Big Annie cried out again and again.

No-one listened, except the blind girl, who steadfastly held the hands of her two companions.

"We must not go," she said, "until the adult tells us to."

Henry's son turned out to be a large young man with broad shoulders and a serious expression on his face.

"His name is Moses," Henry said. "Like in the Bible. Don't know why his mother give him that name, but she did."

"In the morning," Moses said, "we're going to leave. For your promised land. You be ready at first light. If we miss that train there won't be another for two days."

"You got to be out of here," Henry said.

"I be ready," Jim replied.

Larry paused at the door of Janet's house, hesitated, and then leaned forward. She raised her head to him and for the first time offered him her lips rather than just her cheek.

Isaiah placed the baseball under the tree.

"You must leave it there until morning," he said in the most serious tone he could muster. Out of the corner of his eye he could see Eunice smiling, her mother offering a grudging acceptance.

"As soon as the sun is up," Jonathan said, "I will pick it up."

"Maybe I'll stop by. In the morning," Isaiah said.

Jonathan beamed.

"You can have breakfast with us," Eunice said.

She walked Isaiah to the door.

"I have the feeling that you won't be around that much longer."

"Why?"

"I don't know. And I worry. About Jonathan. He's become attached to you."

"And me to him," Isaiah blurted.

"What the hell," Sam muttered. "I am back where I started."

He paced the small confines of his old solitary cell, found the cot whose mattress stank from mildew.

"It's for your own safety," the guard said before closing the door and shutting Sam, again, into darkness.

"I need to know if anyone saw you," Jablonski said. "I mean got a really good look at you."

"There was this priest or minister, I don't know which. He spoke to me and asked for a cigarette. Outside of the building. And then there was somebody on the stairs."

The realization began to form in Edward's mind.

"Did something bad happen?"

Jablonski nodded.

"Very bad."

"I didn't mean for anyone..." Edward began.

"Nor did I," Jablonski replied. "They'll be looking for you. So first thing in the morning you're going to get on a train."

"Going where?" Edward asked.

"Out of here," Jablonski said. "That's all that matters. When you leave my office, don't go near that building again."

Big Annie leaned against the wall next to the doorway through which the panicked throng had passed. She did not have to go out onto the landing to remember what had happened, how layers of bodies lay on top of each other, the muffled groans, the occasional movements here and there, and then the desperate lifting and hauling, the wails of those finding their loved ones dead, the rare, oh so very rare, cries of joy from those finding life in the mass of death, that scene, those sounds, would be etched in her memory for as long as she drew breath.

And along with it would be a rage that would not die for the man who caused it.

CHAPTER SEVENTEEN

A loud knocking came at the front door. Governor Woodhouse, still in his nightshirt, opened the wreath bedecked door and felt a cold morning breeze greet him. Standing there was a messenger holding a telegram.

"It is marked urgent, must be delivered," the messenger said.

"On Christmas morning?"

"Yes sir, came in just a little while ago, and I was sent right out with it."

With the telegraph spread out on his desk, Woodhouse spoke into his telephone.

"Larry, you need to come in right now. Forget about breakfast. We've got work to do. I've already called Alan."

First Alan, then Larry read the telegram while the governor studied their faces to gauge their reactions.

"More than sixty dead," Alan said.

"Mostly children," Larry added.

"Who would do such a thing?" Alan asked. "Or why?"

"The sheriff has started an investigation," Woodhouse said. "Talking to anyone who might have seen the fellow."

"Whoever it is, he should..." Larry began.

"Yes, he should," Alan replied. "But what we've got to think about is how we deal with it."

"Practical, as ever," the governor said. "But that is why you're here. Larry I want you to talk to the warden and set up that meeting we talked about."

"Oh," Alan said. "You're a step ahead of me on this one."

"The newspapers, when do you think the story will come out?" Woodhouse asked.

"Could be as early as afternoon editions, at least up there. By tomorrow. Everywhere. We're going to need to get out in front of this. I'll start drafting your statement."

"I've got a call into Drummond. He can help us. Still got friends in the press."

Edward shivered in the morning cold, his hands in his pockets. He knew he shouldn't be where he was not far from the building, but for once his curiosity, or perhaps his sense of dread, outweighed specific instructions. In his left pocket was the gun, and in the other a handful of coins Jablonski had given him. Among the coins was the pin. Jablonski hadn't told him what to do with it. So he just kept it in his pocket. He stared at the line of bodies lying in the snow. He was close enough to see that most of the forms in the snow were small. Standing over them were larger figures, their heads bowed. There was an eerie silence, hardly a sound rising above the crowd.

He felt a strong hand on his shoulder.

"I thought I told you to keep away from here."

"Mr. Jablonski. I just had to see what I done."

"You didn't do it. They did it to themselves."

"But why?"

"They weren't supposed to."

Jablonski's hands now turned Edward around.

"You do remember where you are supposed to go, don't you?"

"Yes."

"Then be on your way. There's nothing you can do for them now, nothing anyone could do. This damnable strike. That is what did it to them. Not me. Not you. The strike."

Edward took a couple of steps in the direction that led to the place where he had been instructed to wait. He paused to take one more look, Jablonski be damned, he knew that somehow he was responsible for that ghastly scene, bodies in the snow, mourners standing in a silent vigil. One figure in that morbid tableau stood out. It was the large woman. Holding her hand was one little girl, and that girl in turn held the hand of another smaller, and she a smaller one still.

"I told them," the blind girl said, "that we must wait."

"And thank God you did," Big Annie said.

She looked toward the snow. She knew that their parents lay there.

"It's coming," Moses said.

"Didn't hear nothing," Jim replied.

"I got a railroad man's ears," Moses replied. "When it gets here, you just wait for me to talk to the man. He'll open up a door on one of the cars, sorry, this ain't no passenger train, so you'll have to make do."

"Not the first time I rode like that."

"Good. My man will make sure you're not bothered."

"Which way is it heading?"

"West," Moses replied.

"West," Jim repeated. "I think I'll go that way just like that damned fool I used to work with want to do."

Drummond stroked his mustache.

"I've been watching you do that for years," Woodhouse said.

"Helps me think. Wired to my brain, I guess."

"What does your brain tell you? About Logan."

"Do you know if he's still alive?"

"The warden says he's got him stashed somewhere."

"Probably in the old solitary cells," Drummond replied. "Nobody get to him there. Hope he don't go crazy, though."

"He'll have to stay there for a while. I'm going to talk to him. About the plot, and why he gave it away, and, of course, why he's in prison in the first place. Mr. Lowe, it just so happens, is on my calendar."

"He have something to deal?"

"I hope so. But all of this..."

"Got to wait on that other. You thinking it can take some of the edge off the other?"

"I don't know," Woodhouse said with a shake of his head. "How can anything take the edge off, what's the latest count, some seventy dead children, clutching their little Christmas toys in their hands."

Sam heard the familiar sound of someone fumbling with the latch on the little door through which food would be passed to him. He watched the door slide open.

"Breakfast," the guard said and slid a tray through the opening.

"Not interested," Sam replied. "Want to speak to the warden."

"He put you in here."

Sam bit into the stale bread, one slow bite after another.

"The food hasn't gotten any better," he muttered. For a moment he stared across the empty space of his cell toward the other wall where Pete would be offering his own response to the meal.

But Pete was not there. He was again alone. Time on his hands, it seemed, to think about how he wound up where he was. To begin with, where the hell was Pete? Why wasn't he in one of these damned solitary cells, it was his idea, wasn't it? I was just the spy, like the one Moses sent into the promised land, like him I reported back to the one who sent me in except my promised land was a cell with Pete snoring on the other cot, and my Moses the warden, this reference buried in memory from some sermon heard decades ago when I sat with my mother and father in that little church.

As soon as we saw a different guard sitting outside that factory door, we both knew that the game was up, so Pete got dragged away, in full sight of all his pals, and that is why wherever he is now, I am not safe from them, it doesn't matter that they saw me get taken away as well, they never did trust me, and why should they?

It was a crazy idea, anyway, and for my own reasons, never

mind that I had no choice but to reveal it, but even if that were not so, I would not have been happy to put a match to that pile of wood shavings and see all that lovely wood burn, no, that would not have made a pretty sight for me, not at all.

He finished the last spoonful of gruel, thought about tossing the bowl and spoon across the cell, just to hear the sound it would make, but chose instead to lay it down on the musky floor next to his cot as gently as though it were a fragile piece of china, such as that on which his mother had meals served to them, placed ever so carefully on the large oak wood dining room table, too large, by far, for the three of them.

Alan shook the snow off his overcoat as he walked into the conference room off of the governor's office in which sat Woodhouse, Larry, and Drummond.

"It's out," he said, "as he held up the evening edition of the local Lansing newspaper, its front page dominated by one large image of the bodies in the snow, beneath a forty-eight point headline stating "Tragedy in Copper Country!"

"Have you read the text?" Woodhouse asked.

"Just scanned it. Very sensational."

"Any slant to it?" Drummond asked.

"Governor not looking too good. Strike went on too long, calling out guard promoted instead of tamping violence down, all of this, of course, opinions from unidentified sources, but we can guess where they came from."

"Any story can be retold," Drummond said. "I'll start working on it. Key will be tying the man who shouted into that hall to the mining company."

Woodhouse shook his head.

"I promised an honest governance," he said.

"Oh, we'll be honest," Drummond replied, "we'll just have different sources, legitimate ones."

"Are you going away?" Jonathan asked.

Isaiah glanced over the plates of eggs, bacon, and freshly baked muffins at Eunice.

"I thought I should start preparing him, just in case," she said.

Isaiah paused only for a second. He had decided that he must raise the issue for which he had been unable to figure out an answer.

"You know I've been working…"

"Yes," Eunice said. She turned to her mother.

"Could you take Jonathan out so he can play with his new sled?"

The old woman gave Isaiah a look that said I knew you were trouble, I tried to tell my daughter that. But she just nodded.

When the front door shut behind them, Eunice reached across the table and took Isaiah's hand.

"I think I know what you were about to say. And that must be between us. For now."

"My father," Isaiah said. "There's a chance he might be released. And if he is…."

"He'll come back here."

"I expect so."

"And you want to know how I feel about that."

"Yes."

"I don't know," Eunice said. "And you?"

"I don't know either. I just hadn't thought that far ahead. But I do know one thing for certain."

"The water," Eunice said.

"It calls to me," Isaiah replied. "Every day and every night."

In Calumet, the bodies were moved to the village hall, which served as a temporary mortuary. There were not enough coffins so manufacturers in neighboring communities provided the necessary number. Adults in black coffins, the children in white. The street that had been the scene of Big Annie's protest marches was now traversed by a line of horse drawn hearses heading to the cemetery where the striking miners had dug two mass graves in two lines facing each other, one for Catholic victims, one for Protestant victims.

Mourners lined the street as the funeral procession passed by, the sound of the horse's hooves muffled by the cushion of the newly fallen snow. Most of those watching the hearses pass by were adults, not sure which of the hearses carried the children they were related to.

In the first hearse sat Big Annie who was shepherding the blind girl and her two sisters to witness the burial of their parents.

At the cemetery there was not enough room to contain all the witnesses. A few of those who could not find a place to stand climbed the bare limbed trees to watch as one after another the caskets were lowered into the ground.

Miners well used to digging out the precious copper from hundreds of feet below the ground now pushed their exhausted muscles to layer dirt over the fresh graves. As the early winter dusk descended over the cemetery, the last dozen or so burials were lit by lanterns.

Then all went home to homes that would never be the same.

The guard serving Sam's supper had a message.

"Warden wants you to know you will have a visitor in a couple of days. A very special visitor."

"What?" Sam said. My son..."

"Not your son," the guard replied, and shut the door of the slot through which he had passed the meal.

At dinner in his home in Chicago, Lowe studied the photographs in the newspaper. He ran his finger over one that showed the bodies of the dead children their torsos covered by white cloth, their heads and legs clearly visible. He read the accompanying story, stopping when he came to the account given by some witnesses that a baby had survived because its mother held it above the crush in the stairwell while she and her husband expired.

"We'll have more to talk about, Governor," Lowe said. "I'm almost sorry to heap our business on top of this but my guess is your advisors have already talked to you about just such a possibility."

CHAPTER EIGHTEEN

"**I** guess you can say he did what he had to do," Warden Higgins said. "I wouldn't want to put too much weight on it as it being exculpatory. As to why he's in here."

"I'll be the judge of that," Woodhouse said. "I see he's been denied parole more than once."

"Not unusual," the warden replied. "Hardly anyone gets out of here the first, or even the second time. It's just the way the system is intended to work."

"To keep them locked up for as long as possible?"

"No," the warden replied. "To make sure we get it right."

Sam sat across from the governor in a room empty except for the chairs and the table between them. Woodhouse motioned to the guard.

"I'll be alright," he said.

"But," the guard said, "the warden gave me specific instructions."

"No doubt to report back to him. Just close the door behind you."

Sam kept his eyes on the man sitting across from him as he heard the quiet click of the closing door. He hadn't had time to plan his approach, hadn't in fact known who he was about to meet until he found himself being introduced to the governor.

"Sorry for the surprise," Woodhouse said. "My idea."

"I thought it might be my…"

"Son," Woodhouse completed the thought.

"You know about that?"

"Of course. But don't wonder about what else I might or might not know. Suffice to say I am now quite familiar with your case. Have been for some time, both because of Mr. Lowe's efforts, as well as direct correspondence from your mother who has been indefatigable in arguing for your release."

"My mother, of course," Sam said.

"Yes, mothers," Woodhouse replied. "We"ll get to your unfortunate history, but first I want you to tell me how you came to reveal the plot. Isn't it a rule that you don't, what do they say, rat on each other?"

"I am not one of them," Sam snapped. "Even though I've been living among them all these years. Well not exactly 'among them' as you also know."

"Yes, solitary, which was your original sentence, and which I worked for you as well as others to eliminate as a barbaric practice." He waved his hand in a dismissive gesture. "But I didn't come here to puff myself up. Please answer my question."

"I did so for two reasons. The first practical, as you well know. The warden made it clear that if ever I wanted to pass through the parole process I would have to cooperate. Well, cooperation under threat has usually made me do just the opposite. But not this time."

"And the other reason, you said there were two."

"It's simple, even if it seems silly to say. I have always loved wood."

"And you didn't want to see it burn?"

"Right," Sam replied.

"And if there weren't reason number one?"

"I just can't say. The warden put me in with a most dangerous man."

"Pete Morgan."

"Yes. Someone you don't want to get on the wrong side of. Maybe I would have gone along with him. I am no saint."

"No saint," Woodhouse repeated as though connecting that assessment with the man sitting across from him.

"But no murderer either," Sam replied.

Back in his cell, Sam reviewed their conversation. He had decided early on that he had to play this one straight. The man sitting opposite him was simply not one with whom to play his usual game of charming bad boy. That had worked well enough with women, perhaps including his mother, but not at all with his father, and if anything there seemed to be a lot of old man Logan in Governor Woodhouse.

And so he gave his version of the events leading up to Margaret's death in a narrative that neither avoided nor dwelt on his responsibility. As he talked, he kept his eyes steadily on the governor, searching for any sign to indicate how his story was being received by the man who, he now most clearly understood, held his fate in his hands. But to no avail. Woodhouse's expression did not change, not when Sam related the aborted effort to match Margaret with Isaiah, an idea that aroused scorn, if not contempt, in others who heard it, or when he described his own feelings when the prosecutor, may he be damned in hell, brought in the bottle containing the fetal remains pulled from Margaret's body, and most that steady gaze maintained when he described the final tryst.

"And then," Sam had said, "I positioned her arms over her chest in a peaceful way, it was I guess my way of burying her but instead of dirt I had leaves to serve my purpose of concealing the fact of her dead body."

"You just left at that point," Woodhouse commented.

"Left. In a hurry. I had to be able to meet my son coming back at him from the right direction."

"To set up your alibi."

"Yes, self-preservation, as I said before..."

"You're no saint," the governor said. "Nor a murderer. By your estimation."

As the guard arrived to take Sam back to his cell, the governor stood, and Sam thought he saw a glimmer of recognition in Woodhouse's eyes, maybe not empathy, but an understanding of the complexity of the situation.

"I'm afraid you'll have to go back into your cell for now."

For a second, Sam's old brash tongue awoke.

"Well, it's like a second home to me," he said.

"How'd it go?" the warden asked.

"He's an interesting man," Woodhouse said. "Most interesting."

"Whatever motivation," Higgins said, "he averted a major disaster that would have had the most serious repercussions. If that factory had gone up in flames, who knows what would have followed? Maybe an escape attempt, or another riot."

He shook his head, then glanced out of the window at the snow filled exercise yard.

"Your man was playing baseball out there. And I was watching from right here, as a buddy of Pete Morgan threw one at his head. Just to see how he would react. And to tell him that he was being watched."

"And how did he react?"

"Picked himself up and smacked the hell out of the next pitch. That told me something. That he had the spine to be useful for me. No matter what he had done to get in here."

"Seems to me like he's held up his end of the bargain. As far as you and he are concerned."

"He has."

"When is the next scheduled parole hearing?"

"For him. Why not for months."

"Move it up."

"Have you made up your mind?"

"Just move it up. We'll be in touch. In the meantime, keep him safe."

"Miss Hooper," Woodhouse said, "please bring in a pot of coffee for all of us. We're going to be in the conference room. Not to be interrupted."

Miss Hooper smiled.

"It's already there. And I'll have some sandwiches brought in later."

"Thank you."

"There's one more thing," she said. "Mr. Lowe is in town, and he called up, wants to see you at your earliest convenience, he said, earliest convenience, as if you had nothing else to do but see him."

Around the table in the conference room sat Drummond, Alan, and Larry. Woodhouse looked at Drummond.

"Anything new I should know about from the press coverage of," he paused, "of whatever word we've decided to use?"

"What we call it is of the most importance," Drummond said. "I've been going back and forth, between 'tragedy,' and 'incident.'"

"The first is judgmental, the second too neutral," Alan said.

"I agree," Drummond replied. He took a deep sip of his coffee and swiped at his mustache where the liquid had seeped onto it. "Definitely cannot call it an 'incident,' not in the face of all those dead children. So let's think about 'tragedy.' Judgmental, in a sense, yes, it connotes something really bad has happened, something that reasonable people will agree should most definitely not have happened. That conforms to the facts."

"But it doesn't attribute blame," Woodhouse said.

"No, it doesn't," Drummond replied. "It's what we associate with that word that can do that."

"There will be a coroner's inquest," Larry said.

"I don't think we can wait on that," Drummond said.

"Having been up there," Alan said, "we can be reasonably sure that somehow the miners themselves will be blamed. Both in the English language press and in any legal proceeding." He finished the coffee in his cup with one big gulp. "Finnish language newspaper claims a witness saw the fellow who yelled into the meeting hall was wearing a button that said Citizens Alliance."

"And this group, what do we know about it?" Woodhouse asked.

"Seems to be connected to the companies. According to the Finnish language papers."

"Only in the Finnish newspapers?" Woodhouse asked.

"At this point," Drummond said. "It'll only take one English paper to pick it up, though."

"Can you make certain that happens?" the governor asked. "To even the playing field? If we can't ascertain truth, at least let's have both sides represented."

"I can call in a favor or two," Drummond replied.

"What's clear," Alan replied, "is that there will not be an agreed upon consensus. Both sides will blame the other."

"And we can't be seen to be taking sides," Drummond added.

"Disagree," Alan said. "Most people in this state are on the side of the mining companies."

"But," Woodhouse said, bringing his coffee cup down hard enough to have it splash over onto the table, "this citizen of the state doesn't give a damn about the politics in this situation."

Silence fell around the table, as each sipped at his coffee as if the liquid in his cup would somehow provide the correct strategy, the one that did not do any violence to the truth, that did not diminish the feelings of outrage at the heaped bodies of dead children, that would preserve the governor's sense of priorities, and, for most of them, would not lose the governor the upcoming election.

Woodhouse stood up.

"Thank you. For your advice. For your political sense. You all have my political career in mind. But," he paused, "as for that, well, I don't."

He looked around at the table, at Alan his most perceptive political advisor, whose own career was so intimately tied to his own, at Drummond, his old friend going back to college, but a newspaper man at heart, always looking for the story and how it can be told for best effect, at Larry, eager young attorney, wanting to please, but with a solid core of competence that would enable him to move on no matter how this mess turned out. Each in his own way looked stunned.

No more than I myself, Woodhouse muttered as he finished his coffee and turned to leave the room, no more than I. That idea must have been brewing, so why did it come out now. Somehow the Logan affair, and Lowe's impending visit answered that question. But he was not sure how.

Lowe was waiting after Woodhouse adjourned his meeting.

"Will you need coffee?" Miss Hooper asked as she conducted Lowe into the governor's office.

"Not for me," Lowe said. "A glass of water will be fine." He sat down in the chair opposite the governor. "Shall we place our cards on the table?" he asked.

"Let's," Woodhouse replied. "It is past time."

"I've been reading about the tragedy up north, the Italian Hall," Lowe said.

"That needn't concern us," the governor replied.

For a moment, an expression of surprise passed across Lowe's face.

"I would have thought…" he began.

"So would I, a little while ago. But for my own reasons, not now. Let's talk about your Mr. Logan. Whom I have talked to very recently."

"Whoa," Lowe exclaimed. "I'm afraid you are well ahead of me."

"I imagine that is not a usual feeling for you," Woodhouse replied.

"No, it isn't. But not all that unpleasant, I must say."

"Let's leave that conversation until after we play our other respective cards. You first."

Lowe reached down for his portfolio and brought out a document, which he slid across the desk to the governor. Woodhouse picked it up, adjusted his spectacles, and read it, turned it over, then appeared to read it again. With a pencil, he underlined a couple of places."

"So a key witness for the prosecution has, well not exactly, but to a certain extent recanted his testimony."

"Let's say he now admits to being pressured both directly, but just as importantly, indirectly, a man of color, a dead white woman, suspicion predictably falling on him, a request, strongly urged, by the prosecutor to direct attention elsewhere, resulting in a questionable sighting being presented as hard fact."

Woodhouse glanced down at the document.

"And so it appears. And where is he now?"

Lowe shrugged.

"I'm afraid disappeared again. But as you can see this statement is signed and witnessed, and would stand up to challenge."

"Convenient," the governor said.

"Perhaps, but so it is. Now your turn."

"I have a couple of cards. The first has to do with the other witness."

Lowe stiffened.

"You spoke with the son?"

"No, not I. Rather a report of one who has."

"And?"

Woodhouse permitted himself a small smile.

"Unlike your witness he reiterated his testimony in a way that his interlocutor found, let's say, decently convincing."

Lowe relaxed.

"So my witness casts doubt on his previous testimony while yours confirms his, both then moving toward supporting Logan's alibi."

"Sounds good," Woodhouse agreed. "Except for one thing."

"Which is?"

"Mr. Logan himself."

Lowe sat back in his chair and shook his head from side to side. "You're kidding."

"No."

"He disowned his own alibi?"

"He did."

Lowe stood up, snapped his portfolio shut.

"I guess then there's nothing more I can do."

"You've done what you can," the governor said. "But I haven't yet."

"Do you mean you might still...."

Woodhouse extended his hand.

"Thank you for coming in, Mr. Lowe."

Miss Hooper poked her head into the governor's office.

"Is there anything else today?" she asked.

"No."

She began to turn to leave, but swiveled her head back around.

"I hope you don't mind my asking, it's not my place, but Mr. Lowe when he was leaving, well, I'd have to say he looked neither happy nor down, although perhaps a little more of the latter, but the best word would be, I think, perplexed."

"I'm not surprised. He received quite a shock."

"About Mr. Logan, can I ask have you reached a decision?"

"I have. But there is another piece to put in place, so I can't quite tell you just now. That piece is crucial."

"Is that why you asked me to set up a meeting with Mr. Drummond for dinner?"

"It is."

"Can we talk business now?" Drummond asked.

They had finished their meals at Clara's Station at the Union Depot. Woodhouse sipped his after dinner brandy while Drummond bit off the end of a cigar and lit it.

"I wanted to have a pleasant supper first," the governor replied. He drained his drink and eased the glass back down on the table. "I've come to a decision, a very difficult one, and your cooperation in implementing it is absolutely necessary to its success."

"You know I will do most anything you ask," Drummond said.

"It's the 'most' that I am concerned about. So here it is. I've decided to secure Logan's release."

"Not too surprising," Drummond said.

"And I don't want you to write a word about it."

Drummond sat back and puffed on his cigar.

"That's a big story you're asking me to bury."

"Yes. I know. But I want this done with as little notice as possible."

"But I, we all, thought, that if you went in that direction, you would want to do exactly the opposite."

"Yes. To counterbalance that terrible story of the dead children. Give the voting public something else to think about, how I got a wrongfully convicted man released."

"But?"

"But, here's why not. The most important idea is that we are dealing with two situations, one of which I could not control, and one of which I could. I could not stop the strike from starting, nor prevent it from turning as ugly as it did. I will redouble my efforts to get it settled, but my influence is limited. Some may argue that I took sides with the mining companies by agreeing to send in the National Guard. Maybe it looks that way, but I was just trying to maintain order, and was fed some information that turned out to be not very accurate as to the danger to that order provided by the strikers."

"And Logan?" Drummond prompted.

"There I can do something. And it is precisely because I don't want the juxtaposition that I ask you to do what you can to keep it quiet. You still have a lot of pull in the newspaper world so I am counting on your help. I am not doing this for political cover, and don't want even the slightest hint of that interpretation. I am doing it because I think it is the right thing to do. Oh, the case is muddy, and Logan certainly from what I have determined bears some responsibility but he said one thing that struck me, after all the investigation, to be the core of the issue. And I believed him."

Drummond leaned forward.

"And that is?"

"He said 'I am not a murderer.'"

"Well, many men in his situation would say exactly that.'"

"It's all that he admitted to before he said that."

Drummond shook his head.

"Are you sure you're not being taken in?"

Woodhouse nodded, waived at a waitress, who stopped by the table. He held out his glass.

"Another if you please." He looked across the table at Drummond. "For you?"

"Sure," Drummond replied. "I'd like to drink to your taking the story of my career away from me."

"Make that two," the governor said to the waitress. As she turned to leave, he reached over the table to take Drummond's hand.

"I know what I'm asking. Therefore, I will tell you what I probably won't tell anybody else. You make note of it. And if you ever write that novel you have been talking about since college, you may feel free to make use of it."

"That's a little better," Drummond said. "Go on."

"It's simply this. He admitted to everything, even to fabricating his alibi."

"But not to the act itself."

"Not to the act itself. But to every detail of their last encounter. He thinks, and he may be right, that she died from drinking too much laudanum."

"I've heard of such," Drummond nodded. "Young girls having a party. Dangerous. Maybe fatal."

The waitress returned with two snifters of brandy. Drummond held his hand half way across the table. Woodhouse smiled and clinked his glass against his friend's.

CHAPTER NINETEEN

Sam shuffled out of his cell, his legs at first refusing to obey his commands to move one foot in front of another. Since his return to the cramped dark environment of the old solitary confinement cell, he had uncharacteristically fallen into a black funk and spent his days lying on his cot looking up toward a ceiling he could barely see.

Then the guard had rapped against his door, opened it, and announced that he had been summoned.

"Where to?" he asked. "The warden?"

"Nope. The parole board."

As he walked next to the guard he told himself that he should not hope for a better outcome this time. Still, the fact that so soon after his last turndown, he was again being summoned before the parole board was simply a fact that could not be understood any other way.

"Move it along," the guard said. "They're waiting on you."

"Doing the best I can," Sam replied.

Isaiah spent his mornings in his house, eating breakfast and trying to imagine how he would live there. He decided the first thing would be to change the color scheme to eliminate the traces of the mother who had abandoned him, no more flowers, delicate touches of any kind but something, he didn't know what, that spoke to him of the vast power of the swelling waters of the lakes to which he yearned to return. Perhaps, he told himself, if he could make the house in some way stir memories of the water he might learn how to live there.

Whatever other changes he made, he had determined that he would leave the blue colored little boy's room just as it was. At first, that decision was motivated by a perverse desire to have it serve as a reminder of the childhood he had not experienced. It was like picking at a scab so that the wound would not heal. But after a while, another more positive thought occurred to him. Why could he not, after all, have his brother spend some time there, his house was a short walk away, Eunice should be comfortable with the idea, he concluded.

His time was mostly his own. The streets were too clogged with snow for Mr. Mueller to require Isaiah's services as chauffeur. He sometimes walked over to the river, which had not yet fully frozen over, and its black waters refreshed him. In the spring, he would, whatever the outcome was concerning his father, sign on to a ship.

He watched as Jonathan coming home from school walked along with his grandmother, and then broke into a staggering trot through the low drifts of snow on the walk leading to his house. Isaiah picked up a good handful of snow and worked it into a ball. As Jonathan neared, Isaiah tossed the snowball into the air.

"I've been waiting for you," he said.

"Throw it," Jonathan said.

Isaiah tossed it underhand, and Jonathan snagged it with one hand and threw it back.

"More mustard," Jonathan insisted.

Isaiah went into an elaborate windup and threw the snowball overhand with some velocity. Jonathan caught it with both hands and trotted up to his brother.

"Maybe in the spring..." he began.

"Yeah, maybe," Isaiah replied.

Jonathan ground the snowball between his hands and watched the pieces fall to the ground.

"My mother says you might be leaving us," he said.

"Maybe," Isaiah replied. "But not forever."

"Hey Buddy, do you know where we are?" Edward asked the man slumped against the wall of the freight car he had just hopped into. Next to the man was a bundle on a pole. A slouch hat was pulled down enough to cover his face. When he turned to Edward he pushed the hat back, revealing his face. Edward first took notice of the dark skin. Then, very slowly, something jarred his memory.

"You ain't..." he started.

Jim stood up.

"Yeah, I am. What the hell are you doing on this train?"

"Probably the same as you," Edward replied. "Do you want me to get into another car?"

"What for?"

"We never did get along so good," Edward said.

"That's so. But I think we're both leaving the same mess behind us."

Edward shook his head.

"Not exactly. I got into a different mess."

"I know. Up in the copper country."

"How'd you know that?"

Jim smiled.

"A little bird told me you were there. Don't know what the mess was, though."

"Got plenty of time to tell you if you want to hear," Edward said.

"Sure. Now, to answer your first question. I believe we're crossing into North Dakota."

"How far to California?" Edward asked.

"Mr. Logan, Sam Logan," the head of the parole board said, looking down at his papers, "here before us again."

Sam studied the face of the man, at his long sideburns, carefully trimmed, as was his mustache, the kind of man, he thought, who never got his hands dirty, the same man who had sat in the same place the previous two times. His face betrayed nothing, no clue as to why so unexpectedly this hearing had once again convened. The other two men were new. Was that significant? One was a young man, not much older than college age. The third was on the other end of the age spectrum, bald except for a fringe of white hair. Both of them had their eyes on the chairman.

"This is an expedited hearing, and it will be a short one," the chairman said, again looking down at the paper in front of him. "We are to ask only three questions, questions not of our own devising but of the individual who is responsible for this hearing. Do you understand, and agree to this unusual process?"

What do I have to lose, Sam thought to say, but instead, he offered a simple affirmative.

"Yes," he said.

"Good," the chairman said. "Here is the first question. We are to ask them in sequence, one leading into another. In fact, your answers will determine whether we proceed to each next question. So think about what you say."

"Ask what you must," Sam said.

The chairman seemed to stiffen his back in his chair.

"Were you with Margaret Cutter when she died?"

"So, no preliminaries," Sam said.

"Were you with Margaret Cutter when she died?" the chairman repeated. "Consider carefully your answer."

Oh, Sam thought, the governor, he has fed these questions to these examiners. What did he, does he, expect me to answer? What the hell, I have no choice but to roll the dice and hope I don't crap out, pull that card to the inside straight.

"Yes," he said.

The chairman's face revealed just a trace of a reaction. Sam could not tell if it was satisfaction or regret. The expressions of the other two showed more obvious surprise, and perhaps anticipation. The chairman put some kind of mark on his paper.

"You get the next question," the chairman said. "With that answer in mind, do you now state without reservation that your alibi was a fabrication?"

"I do," Sam replied.

All three now reacted, each in his own way, the chairman taking off his spectacles and bowing his head as if to assure himself that he had heard right, the older man leaning forward, the younger one's shoulders thrown back. Again, the chairman notated his paper.

The room was silent for several moments.

"Last question," the chairman said. "Did you kill Margaret

Cutter, who you now declare was in your presence when she died?"

"I did not," Sam said. "I believe..."

"We do not care what you believe," the chairman said, as he again, this time very carefully, brought his fountain pen down to the paper and put some kind of mark on it.

"But that is important, I want it on the record."

The chairman lifted his pen from the paper and capped it.

"It is not important to us. Nor to you if you knew what is good for you."

The phone on Lowe's desk rang. His secretary picked it up.

"The governor is on the line," she said.

"Is he?" Lowe asked, his eyes still staring out of the window toward the blue of the lake.

"Yes sir, it is," the secretary said. "Shall I say you are out?"

Lowe turned toward her and shook his head.

"No, I'll take the call." He took the phone from his secretary.

"Yes, governor," he said. "Oh, I see. I confess I'm not a little surprised. Yes, I'll see to it."

He hung up the phone.

"We need to get in touch with young Mr. Logan," he said.

The gate to the prison opened. Sam blinking in the sun bouncing off the white of the snow still on the ground this early spring day, walked out carrying a cardboard suitcase. At first, he did not see anything but the snow, but then his eyes adjusted to the brightness and there in front of him was Isaiah.

"I never thought I'd see you on this side of that wall," Isaiah said as he strode toward his father.

Sam held out his arms and waited for Isaiah to reach him.

"Nor did I," he said. "Nor did I."

"When Mr. Lowe sent me that telegram, telling me to be here at this time on this day, I could not, did not, believe him. I made him tell me at least three times."

For several moments they just stood there, unable either of them to continue the conversation. Finally, Isaiah looked at the cheap suitcase. Sam followed his gaze.

"The clothes I was wearing when they arrested me. I guess that besides the few dollars they gave me, which is probably just enough for a train ride to Traverse, besides that, what's in this suitcase is all that I now possess."

On the train ride down to Jackson, Isaiah had prepared himself for this moment.

"I have my own place now," he said.

"You do?"

"Yes, you can stay there. Until you get settled."

"Your own place?"

"It was my mother's," Isaiah said.

Sam closed his eyes, then snapped them open.

"Of course. On Washington Street. I remember now. I believe her father bought it for her."

"It has…" Isaiah began, "well, if you're interested, you'll see for yourself." He paused. "As soon as we are back in Traverse, I'll be signing on to the first ship that needs a crew. So…"

"Maybe," Sam said. "Until I get settled." His eyes brightened. "Do you know what I'd really like to do?"

"Build one?"

Sam clasped Isaiah's shoulders.

"You do know something about me after all. Damn right. I want to build a house. From the ground up. Like I used to do. Like I still can."

They began walking toward the station. Isaiah decided not to spoil the moment by telling his father about Eunice and Jonathan living up the block from his house.

That could wait. It was also too soon for him to digest the fact of his father being in his life again. That would have to work itself out.

But the bright sun melting the snow seemed to augur something good. He would leave it at that.

"You know that girl was crazy in love with him," Edward said.

"I guess I did know that," Jim replied. "But it wasn't then, and it ain't now any of my business."

The train rattled around a sharp bend, and Edward braced himself.

"I think they have different fruit trees in California. Like oranges. I think I could learn to like picking oranges."

"In California," Jim said.

AFTERWORD

Like *Murder On Old Mission,* this sequel creates a fictional narrative within a factual structure. In brief, that structure begins with the 1895 conviction in the courthouse in Traverse City, Michigan, of Woodruff Parmelee for the murder of Julia Curtis, his pregnant girlfriend. He was sentenced to life at hard labor and solitary confinement in Jackson State Prison. Twenty years later in 1915, after the direct intervention of then Governor Woodbridge N. Ferris, Parmelee was released from prison, apparently as a result of the commutation of his sentence. The record also suggests that after his release he was on parole for a year.

Those are the basic facts out of which I built the two novels. In my fictional versions, I changed the names of the historical characters to emphasize the idea that although my books are "based on a true story," as the movies like to say, they are not to be read as historical non-fiction. Consequently, Woodruff Parmelee becomes Sam Logan, and his son Louie is Isaiah. The other historical figures all were baptized with new names.

New names was the easy part. More important was finding the balance between the demands of faithfulness to the important facts of that true story while maintaining the freedom to construct a fictional narrative with its own focus and arc. To do that, I looked for something in the factual record to provide a basis for my story. For the first book, what struck me was the fact that Parmelee's young son Louie was put on the stand by the defense to verify his father's alibi. That in itself offered an opportunity for a strong emotional involvement with my Isaiah Logan, but I decided to intensify that possibility by having Isaiah a few years older than Louie actually was, old enough so that he could be a romantic rival with his father, Sam Logan. And to ratchet up the emotional difficulty a bit more for Isaiah, I gave him a very good reason to believe that his father's alibi was a lie, leading to the

257

possibility that Sam was actually guilty, a realization he could never fully accept.

That complicated father/son dynamic is the heart of *Murder On Old Mission*. For *Murder Undone*, I needed something as compelling. And here the facts gave me something quite obvious. Parmelee was convicted of a heinous crime and received the harshest punishment available in Michigan, which did not have the death penalty available for such a deserving individual. Yet, twenty years later, he was out of prison. Further research enabled me to track his return to Traverse City where he lived for another twenty-seven years, during which he sometimes resided with the same son who testified at his trial.

The stark contrast between his sentence and his relatively early release followed by what seems to have been a more or less normal life among the people of Traverse City, who had cheered for his conviction, was the start of my search for a focus. I early on decided that I would not deal with his post imprisonment life in Traverse although the facts of those years do provide some interesting possibilities, such as the presence in that small town of both of Parmelee's ex-wives, and another son besides Louie. It is possible, if not likely, to imagine these people bumping into each other.

But much more interesting to me than the possibilities of small town interactions between a convicted murderer and his community, including family members, was the striking fact of the governor's necessary intervention, for necessary it was, as Parmelee had been twice denied parole before Ferris chose to step in. Nothing in my research gave me any clue as to what motivated the governor. Jackson State Prison at that time housed several thousand prisoners. Why did Governor Ferris from among that number, and after twenty years, decide to intervene on Parmelee's behalf? The prison records indicate that the governor interviewed Parmelee, but not why. That question bedeviled me, but also provided me the chance to come up with my own fictional answer, one that would have both historical as well as novelistic credibility.

Not having yet answered that question, I began the book with Sam Logan being denied parole for the second time, and Isaiah, who had become a sailor on the Great Lakes (factually accurate), returning to Traverse for the funeral of the murdered woman's father. My plot was going to take us on a ride toward Logan's release with Isaiah still dealing with his conflicted emotions. So I would have scenes of Isaiah in town, meeting the brother he had never known whose mother was ex-wife number 2, alternating with scenes of Sam in prison. For the first plot line, I could make use of the historical fact that Louie had testified on his father's behalf in the divorce proceedings that ended Parmelee's marriage to his second wife, which occurred before the murder. Wife number 2 was pregnant with that brother when she left Parmelee, and so Louie would not have lived with him. That circumstance provides some of the tension in what we can call the Isaiah plot line, to which I added the fictional element of Isaiah's grandmother, whom I kept alive for this purpose, urging him to continue her long struggle to obtain Sam's freedom.

I researched conditions at the prison to find details I could use for the Sam plot line. A minor, but interesting, bit of information was provided by a picture I stumbled upon of prisoners playing baseball in the prison. That was serendipitous because in *Murder On Old Mission,* I have Sam as an accomplished baseball player. The historical record indicates that Michigan modified its solitary confinement sentencing practices, and so I have Sam released from solitary. I do not know whether, or when, that change would have affected Parmelee. The prison also operated a variety of contracted commercial activities so I have Sam planting fruit trees—Parmelee had been an orchardist—and in a chair factory—Parmelee has also been a carpenter.

I was left with the crucial question of the governor's intervention. Fortunately, the brutal copper mining strike on the Keweenaw Peninsula, culminating in the Italian Hall disaster, provided me with the beginning of an answer. That strike is not exactly coincidental with Parmelee's release, but it was close enough so that I felt comfortable in introducing it as a factor.

How I had it influence the governor was a problem I wrestled with until I came up with the solution that the book now offers.

All that remains to mention is that because this is a sequel, I brought along a couple of other important characters from the first book, namely farmhands Edward and Jim, both of whom played prominent fictional roles in the murder trial in *Murder On Old Mission*.

TWO DOCUMENTS

The Court then pronounced sentence:
After a fair and impartial trial, during which you were defended by able
counsel of your own selection, you have
been convicted of murder in the first
degree. The crime of which you stand
convicted has few parallels in criminal
annals. The logical conclusion to be
derived from the verdict of the jury is,
that Julia Curtis, in confidence and
in love, had given up to you the dear-
est and most sacred attribute of wom-
anhood; and in such confidence you had
become her betrayer; that to conceal a
guilty intimacy, and to protect you
from punishment, for days before the
fatal act, you had coolly, deliberately
and wickedly planned her destruction,
and on the fatal date, had enticed her
into the swamp, where you choked the
life out of her. The plan and its exe-
cution demonstrate a crime of the
greatest malignity, and for your rash
act the law has provided the extreme
penalty.
While I cannot but have compassion
for a human being placed in the de-
plorable condition where you now find
yourself, I cannot but remember the
circumstances of your guilt, and do approve the punishment provided by the
law.
It is the judgment of the law, and
the court now here pronounces the
judgment of the law, that you be punished by solitary confinement at hard
labor in the state prison, at Jackson,
in the state of Michigan, for and during your life.

Above is a newspaper clip reporting on the conclusion of Woodruff Parmelee's murder trial indicating in its conclusion in the
presiding judge's words of Parmelee's sentence of life at hard
labor in solitary confinement.

Below is a copy of the index card record from Jackson State Prison showing Governor Ferris's intervention on behalf of Woodruff Parmelee. Note the card says "Paroled by Gov. Ferris," but that is probably not exactly right. Legal experts I have consulted suggest that the governor commuted the sentence, and that act was followed by a period on parole.

A final note: Parmelee's name in the records is, as above, sometimes spelled Parmalee.

ABOUT THE AUTHOR

Born and raised in the Flatbush section of Brooklyn, Stephen Lewis holds a doctorate in American Literature from New York University, and he is Professor of English Emeritus at Suffolk Community College, on Long Island, New York. He now lives with his wife Carolyn, an award winning short story writer, on five acres in a restored farmhouse on Old Mission Peninsula in northern lower Michigan.

He has published eight previous novels including the Edgar nominated mystery Stone Cold Dead (2007), and Murder On Old Mission (2005), a finalist in the historical fiction category of ForeWord Magazine's book of the year awards. He continues working in various fiction genres and has also published six college textbooks, and numerous poems and articles.

A passionate sports fan, he claims to have had a near religious experience when the New York Rangers won the Stanley Cup in 1994 after 54 years of futility.

BOOKS BY STEPHEN LEWIS

Mystery Novels

The Monkey Rope And Baby Makes None
The Dumb Shall Sing
The Blind in Darkness
The Sea Hath Spoken
Stone Cold Dead
A Suspicion of Witchcraft
Murder on Old Mission
Murder Undone

Textbooks

Focus on the Written Word
The Student Critic
Writing through Reading
Discovering Process
Philosophy: An Introduction Through Literature
Templates: Models of Style and Usage for Writers